19th Century
French Mysteries

More Adaptations of French mysteries from Nina Cooper

Black Coat Press

Monsieur Lecoq, Emile Gaboriau, Volumes I and II

The Adventures of Miss Boston; The First Female Detective, Antonin Reschal

Thérèse Arnaud of the French Secret Service, Pierre Yrondy

Ethel King, The Female Nick Carter

The Casebook of Monsieur Lecoq

Le Cabinet Noir: Volume I, Charles Rabou

Brothers Of Death, (Volume II - Le Cabinet Noir), Charles Rabou

The Bloodied Girl (Volume III - Le Cabinet Noir), Charles Rabou

Le Marquis De Lupiano (Volume IV - Le Cabinet Noir). Charkes Rabou

La Louve (Volumes I and II). Paul Féval, Pending 2019

Distinction Press

File No. 113, Emile Gaboriau

The Ferry Mystery, Fortuné du Boisgobey

The Omnibus Crime, Fortuné du Boisgobey

19th Century French Mysteries

A collection of short stories

Adapted by Nina Cooper

Distinction Press
Waitsfield Vermont

Distinction Press, LLC
354 Hastings Rd
Waitsfield, Vermont 05673
www.distinctionpress.com

Cover design and layout by Kitty Werner

Cover images in the public domain.
> Map from the Library of Congress: lossy-page1-800px-Roussel,_Paris,_ses_faux-bourgs_et_ses_environs,_1731_-_Library_of_Congress.tiff

> Weapon from The Royal Armoury and Skokloster Castle with the Hallwyl Museum Foundation, Slottsbacken 3, Stockholm.

French author photo credits — from public domain
> Gaboriau: Bibliothèque nationale de France [Public domain]
> Julien Green: by photographer Carl_van Vechten, Library of Congress
> Frédéric Soulié: Musée des familles, lectures du soir, 2e série, t. 5, Paris, 1847-1848.
> Hector Fleishmann: unknown, public domain

ISBN 978-1-937667-21-4

Contents

The Batignolles Murder

Le Petit Vieux Des Batignolles
(The Little Old Man From Batignolles)

Emile Gaboriau

Emile Gaboriau

Emile Gaboriau is frequently credited with creating the modern detective story with his "roman judiciaire" and his detective Monsieur Lecoq, precursor of Sir Arthur Conan Doyle's Sherlock Holmes.

He was born in Saujon in the Maritime region of France, November 9, 1832. After a short period as an apprentice to a notary and a second class infantry man in Africa, he settled in Paris to begin life as a writer. He contributed short articles and popularized historical articles on French royal mistresses to various newspaper *feuilles*, insertions in newspapers appearing over a period of months. Once the *feuilles* had completed their run in newspapers, they were published as 400 to 500 page novels. He worked as secretary and sometimes as a ghost writer to Paul Féval, the most popular *feuilletoniste* of the period.

He became well known when the banker, Moise Millaud, owner and publisher of *Le Petit Journal*, a newspaper begun in 1863 directed toward the man in the street, and running until 1944, published *The Lerouge Affair*. The novel launched Gaboriau as a major *feuilletoniste*, and led to The Lecoq Series of novels featuring one of its characters, Monsieur Lecoq.

Note: The Lecoq Series by Emile Gaboriau: *L'Affaire Lerouge* 1866, *Le Crime d'Orcival* 1867, *Le Dossier No. 113* 1867, *Les Esclaves de Paris* 1868, *Monsieur Lecoq* 1869.

Chapter I

When I was finishing my studies to become a Civil Service Public Health Officer—those were good days—I was 23—I was living on Rue Monsieur le Prince, almost at the corner of the Rue Racine. There I had a furnished room for 30 francs a month, including maid service, which would cost a good 100 francs today. It was so big I could put my legs into my pants without opening the window.

Leaving early in the morning to go about my hospital rounds, coming back very late because the Café Leroy had an irresistible attraction for me, I scarcely came to know the other lodgers in my apartment building by sight. They were all quiet, retired persons or small business people. There was one, however, with whom, little by little, I finally struck up an acquaintance.

He was a man of middle height, insignificant-looking, always very clean shaven, a very important man they called Monsieur Méchinet. The house porter treated him with particular respect and never failed to take off his hat quickly when he passed by his station.

Monsieur Méchinet's apartment opened onto my landing right in front of my door. On several occasions we found ourselves face to face. At those times we usually greeted each other. One evening, he came over to my place to ask me for some matches. One night I borrowed some tobacco from him. One morning we happened to leave at the same time and walked side by side to the end of the street, chatting.

Those were our first relations. Without being either nosey or impertinent—you aren't at the age I was then—you like to know what to make of the people you form a friendship with. Naturally, therefore, I began to observe not only my neighbor's existence, but also to take an interest in his comings and goings.

He was married and Madame Caroline Méchinet, blonde, fair, petite, good-natured and plump, seemed to adore her husband. But her husband's schedule wasn't regular. Frequently he went out before daylight and often the sun was up when I heard him come back to his place. Sometimes he disappeared for whole weeks at a time. How the pretty, little Madame Méchinet could tolerate that, that's what I couldn't understand.

Intrigued, I thought our house porter, usually as talkative as a magpie, could enlighten me somewhat. Error! Hardly had I pronounced Méchinet's name than he sent me on my way in no uncertain terms. He told me, lifting his eyebrows, that he wasn't in the habit of "squealing" on his tenants. That reception so added to my curiosity that, becoming totally shameless, I started spying on my neighbor. Then I discovered some things that seemed to me of enormous importance. One time I saw him come back dressed in the latest fashion, in his Sunday best, with five or six decorations on the front of his suit. The next day I saw him on the stairway dressed in a dirty shirt and wearing a ragged cloth hat which gave him a sinister look. And that wasn't all. One fine afternoon, as he was leaving, I saw his wife come with him as far as the doorway of their apartment, and there, kissing him passionately, saying:

"I beg you, Méchinet, be careful. Think about your little wife!"

Be careful! Why?…For what reason? What did that mean? Then, the wife was his accomplice!…My amazement wasn't long in becoming twice as great.

One night I was soundly asleep when suddenly someone knocked hurriedly on my door. I got up. I opened the door…Monsieur Méchinet came in, or, rather, rushed into my room. His clothes were torn and in disorder, his tie and the front of his shirt pulled apart. He was bareheaded, his face completely bloody….

Alarmed, "What's happened?" I cried out.

But he, motioning me to be quiet, said:

"Not so loud. Someone could hear you. This is probably nothing, although I'm suffering like the devil. I told myself that you, a medical student, would probably know how to take care of this…"

Not saying a word, I made him sit down, examined him quickly, and gave him the necessary attention. Although there had been a great loss of blood, the wound was slight. To tell the truth, it was nothing but a superficial graze starting at the left ear and stopping at the corner of the mouth.

The wound dressed, Monsieur Méchinet said to me:

"So, for this time I'm well and healthy again. Thanks a million Monsieur Godeuil. But, please, most of all, don't tell anybody about this little accident…. and, Good Night."

"Good Night!" As if I really could think about sleeping! When I remember what sort of absurd hypotheses and romantic notions went through my head, I can't keep from laughing. Monsieur Méchinet took on fantastic proportions in my mind.

He, himself, came over quietly the next day to thank me and to invite me to dinner. You can well imagine that, going into my neighbors' house, I was all eyes and all ears. But I concentrated all my attention in vain. I found nothing of a nature to dissipate the mystery that so strongly intrigued me. However, dating from this dinner, our relationship went forward. Decidedly, Monsieur Méchinet had taken a liking to me. Rarely a week went by without his inviting me to "eat his soup," in his expression. And almost every day at the time to drink absinthe he came to meet me at the Café Leroy and we played a game of dominoes.

So it was that on a certain evening in the month of July, a Friday, about 5:00 p.m., he was in the process of beating me with a double-six domino, when a rather, I must admit, dangerous-looking, tall armed guard suddenly entered and came to whisper in his ear some words I couldn't hear.

All at once, with a deeply distressed expression, Monsieur Méchinet stood up.

"I'm coming," he said. "Run ahead and say I'm coming."

The man left as fast as his legs could carry him and Méchinet then held out his hand to me.

"Excuse me," my old neighbor added. "Duty comes first....We'll take up our game again tomorrow."

And burning up with curiosity, I showed a great deal of vexation, saying I really regretted not being able to go with him.

"Actually," he muttered, "Why not? Would you like to come along? You might find that interesting..."

As my only answer, I picked up my hat and we left.

Chapter II

Certainly, I was far from suspecting that I was taking one of those steps, apparently insignificant, which have a decisive influence on one's entire life.

I'm being let in on it, I thought to myself, *I've got the key to the puzzle.*

And filled with a silly, adolescent satisfaction, I trotted along like a skinny cat beside Monsieur Méchinet. I say: "I trotted," because I had a hard time not letting myself be outdistanced by that good man. He rushed along, he hurried along, the length of the Rue Racine, pushing aside passers-by as if his fortune depended on his legs. Fortunately, at the Place de l'Odéon, we came across a carriage. Monsieur Méchinet hailed it and opening the door:

"Get in, Monsieur Godeuil," he said to me.

I did as he said and he took a place beside me after having shouted to the coachman in a commanding tone:

"39, Rue Lécluse, in the Batignolles....and hurry!"

The distance of the trip brought out a chain of swear words from the coachman. That didn't matter. He whipped up his nags with a masterful crack of his whip and the carriage started off.

"Ah! Then we're going to the Batignolles?" I asked with a winning smile. But Monsieur Méchinet didn't answer me. I doubt that he even heard me. A total metamorphosis had taken place in him. He didn't seem to me to be exactly emotional, but his pinched lips and the contraction of his bushy eyebrows betrayed a painfully distressing preoccupation. His gaze, lost in the void, seemed to be studying the terms of some insoluble problem. He had taken out his snuff box and constantly took enormous pinches that he rubbed between his index finger and his thumb, formed into lumps, and carried to his nose. Nevertheless he didn't inhale it.

This was a tic he had which amused me a great deal. This worthy man, who had a horror of tobacco, always carried a snuff box like a vaudeville financier. If something pleasant or troublesome happened to him unexpectedly, crack, he took it out of his pocket and appeared to sniff and snort furiously. Often the snuff box was empty. The gesture was the same. I later learned that this was his own system to hide his impressions or to turn aside the attention of those questioning him.

Even so, we were still moving along...

Not without some trouble, the carriage went up the Rue de Clichy. It went up the outside boulevard, took the Rue de Lécluse and wasn't long in stopping some distance from the address indicated. The street was so obstructed by a thick crowd to go further was physically impossible. There were 200 to 300 people stationed in front of the house bearing the number 39. Their necks craning, their eyes shining, panting with curiosity, they were with difficulty held back by a half-dozen city policemen, raising their harshest voices in vain: "Move on, Messieurs, move on!..."

Out of the carriage, we moved forward, painfully slipping through the on-lookers. We had already reached the door of Number 39, when a city policeman rudely pushed us back.

"Get back! Nobody goes through here!"

My companion looked him up and down and raising himself to his full height:

"So you don't recognize me? "he asked. "I'm Méchinet and this young man— he pointed to me—is with me."

"Pardon! Excuse me!" stammered the agent, raising his hand to his hat. "I didn't know; please come in."

We went in. In the vestibule, a heavy-set, talkative woman, the concierge apparently, redder than a peony, was gesticulating and holding forth to a group of the building's renters.

"Where is it?" Monsieur Méchinet asked her roughly.

"On the fourth floor, dear Monsieur," she answered, "on the fourth floor, the door on the right. *Jesus! Mon Dieu!* What a tragedy! In an establishment like ours! Such a nice man!"

I didn't hear any more of that. Monsieur Méchinet had rushed to the stairs and I was following him, climbing four steps at a time, my heart beating so fast my breathing was cut off.

On the fourth floor, the door on the right was open. We went in. We went through an antechamber, a dining room, a living room, and finally we came to a bedroom. If I live a thousand years I'll never forget the sight that struck my eyes. And even at this moment that I'm writing, after so many years, I can see it even in its smallest details. Two men were kneeling at the fireplace facing the door: a Police Commissioner, wearing his official sash, and an Investigating Magistrate. On the right, seated at a table, a young man, the stenographer, was writing.

On the floor in the middle of the room, was the cadaver of an old white-haired man lying in a sea of black, coagulated blood. He was stretched out on his back, his arms crossed. Terrified, I remained nailed to the threshold, so close to fainting that, in order not to fall, I was obliged to lean against the door frame.

My profession had made me familiar with death. I had long since gotten over the repugnance of the amphitheatre but this was the first time that I'd found myself faced with a crime. Because it was apparent that an abominable crime had been committed. Less easy to impress than I, my neighbor had entered with a firm step.

"Ah! It's you, Méchinet, the Commissioner of Police said to him. "I'm very sorry to have had you disturbed."

"Why?"

"Because we won't need your expertise...We know the guilty person. I've given arrest orders and he must be under arrest right now."

Ah! Such a strange thing! From the gesture Monsieur Méchinet made, you'd have thought that assurance displeased him. He took out his snuff box, took two or three of his imaginary pinches, and said:

"Ah! The guilty person is known!..."

It was the Investigating Magistrate who answered.

"And known in a certain and positive manner, yes, Monsieur Méchinet... The crime committed, the murderer fled, thinking his victim was not alive. He was mistaken. Providence was watching...This unfortunate old man was still alive. Bringing together all his strength, he dipped one of his fingers in the blood escaping in floods from his wound, and there, on the floor, he wrote the name of his murderer with his blood, thus denouncing him to human justice. See for yourself."

Thus pointed out, I saw what I had not at first noticed. On the floor, in badly formed big letters, readable, however, had been written in blood: MONIS...

"And so?" asked Monsieur Méchinet.

13

The Commissioner of Police answered: "That's the name of a nephew of the poor dead man…a nephew he was fond of, and whose name is Monistrol…"

"The devil!" burst out my neighbor.

"I don't suppose," continued the Investigating Magistrate, "that the miserable man will try to deny it…The five letters are an overwhelming indictment against him. Besides, who profits by such a cowardly crime as this? Only he, the sole heir of this old man who leaves, they say, a large fortune. There's more. The crime was committed yesterday. Well! Yesterday evening nobody visited this poor old man but his nephew. The concierge saw him arrive about 9:00 p.m. and leave a little before midnight.

"It's clear," agreed Monsieur Méchinet, "it's very clear, this Monistrol was nothing but an imbecile."

And shrugging:

"Did he even steal anything? Did he break some piece of furniture to give pretense for a motive for the crime?"

"Until now, nothing seems to us to be out of place," answered the Commissioner of Police. "You've said it, the miserable man isn't very smart. As soon as he sees he's been found out, he'll confess."

And on that, the Commissioner of Police and Monsieur Méchinet went over to a window opening and conferred in a low voice, while the Investigating Magistrate gave some instructions to his stenographer.

Chapter III

From then on, I had the picture. I'd wanted to know exactly what my enigmatic neighbor did…I knew. Now the irregular nature of his life was explained: his absences, his late night returns, his sudden disappearance, the fears and the complicity of his young wife, the wound that I'd dressed.

But what did my discovery mean to me! I had come to myself little by little. The ability to think and deliberate had returned to me and I was examining everything around me with bitter curiosity. From where I was, leaning against the door jamb, my glance took in the whole apartment. Nothing, absolutely nothing betrayed a murder scene there. On the contrary, everything revealed comfort, and at the same time, parsimonious and methodical habits. Everything was in its place. There was not one bad fold in the drapes, and the wood furniture gleamed, proving daily care. Besides, it appeared evident that the conjectures of the Investigating Magistrate and the Police Commissioner were correct and that the poor old man had been murdered the evening before at the time he was getting ready for bed.

In fact, the bed sheets were laid back and a night shirt and cap were laid out on the bed covering. On the table at the head of the bed I saw a glass of sugar-water, a box of matches, and an evening newspaper, the *Patrie*. A heavy and solid brass candlestick was shining on one corner of the fireplace mantle. But the candle that had lit the crime had had been used up. The murderer had fled without snuffing it out and it had burned down right to the end, blackening the pointed alabaster disk to which it had been affixed.

I noticed these details at a glance without my will having anything to do with it, you might say. My eyes took the place of some sort of photographic object. The theatre of the murder was engraved on my mind as if on a prepared plaque, with such precision that no circumstance was missing. It had such solidity that even today I could sketch the apartment of "the little old man of Batignolles" without forgetting anything, without even forgetting a wine cork half covered with green wax that I think I can still see on the floor under the stenographer's chair.

This was an extraordinary faculty that has left me, my most important faculty, which I no longer have the occasion to exercise, which suddenly is coming back. Then I was too strongly moved to analyze my impressions.

I had only one desire, stubborn, burning, irresistible: to approach the cadaver stretched out two meters from me. At first I fought. I shielded myself against the obsession of that desire. But fate took a hand in it…I moved toward it.

Had anyone noticed my presence? I don't think so. In any case, nobody paid any attention to me. Monsieur Méchinet and the Commissioner of Police were still chatting near the window. The stenographer was re-reading his criminal indictment to the Investigating Magistrate. So nothing stood in the way of the accomplishment of my plan.

In addition, I must confess a sort of fever had gotten hold of me, which made me insensitive to exterior circumstances and absolutely isolated me. That was so true that I dared kneel down near the cadaver to see better and closer.

Far from thinking that someone was going to shout at me: "What are you doing there?" I acted slowly and calmly, like a man who, having been given a mission, was accomplishing it.

This unfortunate old man seemed to me to be about 70 or 75-years old. He was short and very thin, but certainly healthy and built to last until 100. He still had a lot of hair, of a yellowish-white hue, curling at the neck. His gray beard, full and thick, seemed not to have been cared for in five or six days. It must have grown after his death. That circumstance that I had often noticed among our subjects at the medical amphitheatre didn't astonish me. What surprised me was the facial expression of the unfortunate man. It was calm; I would say more than that, smiling. His lips were half opened as if for a friendly greeting. Death must have come terribly quickly for him to have kept that welcoming expression!...That was the first idea that came to my mind.

Yes, but how could you reconcile these two circumstances which were irreconcilable: a sudden death and those five letters: *Monis,* that I was looking at in bloody strokes on the floor? To write that, what effort it must have taken a dying man! Only the hope of vengeance would have been able to lend him such strength. And what rage must have been his to feel himself dying without having been able to trace the entire name of his assassin. And nevertheless the cadaver's face seemed to be smiling at me.

The poor old man had been struck in the throat and the weapon had gone through the neck from one side to the other. The instrument of the crime must have been a dagger or rather one of those formidable Catalan knives, big as the hand, which cut from both sides and which are also as pointed as a needle.

I have never in my life been shaken by such strange sensations.

My temples were beating with an unbelievable violence, and my heart in my chest swelled to almost break.

Then what was I about to discover?

Pushed by a mysterious and irresistible force which destroyed my free will, I took the still and icy hands of the cadaver between my hands in order to examine them better. The right one was clean. It was one of the fingers of the left hand, the index finger, that was stained with blood. What! It was with the left hand the old man had written! What about that! Stricken with a sort of vertigo, with wild eyes, my hair bristling on my head, and assuredly paler than the dead man stretched out at my feet, I stood up uttering a terrible cry.

"*Grand Dieu!*"

All the others jumped at this cry, surprised, frightened:

"What is it?" they all asked me at the same time. "What's going on?"

I tried to answer, but emotion was strangling me. It seemed to me as if my mouth was full of sand. I could only point to the hands of the dead man stammering: "There! There!"

As fast as lightening, Monsieur Méchinet threw himself on his knees near the cadaver. What I had seen, he saw, and my impression was his also, because standing up quickly:

"That poor old man wasn't the one who traced those letters there," he declared.

And as the Investigating Magistrate and the Police Commissioner looked at him with their mouths open, he explained to them the significance of only the left hand being stained with blood.

"And to think that I hadn't paid attention to that!" the Commissioner, distressed, kept repeating.

Monsieur Méchinet was gripped with fury.

"That's how it is," he said, "The things that stare you in the face are those you don't see at all. But that doesn't make any difference! Now the situation has devilishly changed. From the moment that it's no longer the old man who wrote, it's the one who killed him who did."

"Obviously," approved the Commissioner.

My neighbor continued: "Now can you imagine a murderer stupid enough to incriminate himself by writing his name beside the body of his victim? No, right? Now, we conclude…."

The Investigating Magistrate had become worried.

"It's clear," he stated, "appearances have misled us. Monistrol isn't the guilty one…Who is he? It's up to you, Monsieur Méchinet to find him."

He stopped… A policeman was entering. Speaking to the Commissioner he said:

"Your orders have been carried out, Monsieur …Monistrol has been arrested and booked at the Depot. He has confessed everything."

Chapter IV

The shock was so much more severe because it was unexpected. It's impossible to describe the stupor of us all. What! While we were there striving to find proofs of Monistrol's innocence, he had admitted he was guilty!

Monsieur Méchinet was the first one to recover. Quickly, five or six times, he carried full fingers from his snuff box to his nose, and was advancing toward the policeman.

"You're mistaken or you're misleading us," he said to him. "There's no middle ground."

"I swear to you, Monsieur Méchinet…."

"Shut up! Either you've misunderstood what Monistrol said, or you've gotten drunk on the hope of astonishing us by telling us the crime is solved."

Humble and respectful up until then, the policeman refused to take any more.

"Excuse me!" he interrupted, "I'm neither an imbecile nor a liar, and I know what I'm saying…."

The discussion was turning into an argument so fast that the Investigating Magistrate thought he should step in.

"Cool down, Monsieur Méchinet," he declared, "and before pronouncing judgment, wait to hear what he has to say."

Then, turning to the policeman:

"And you, my friend," he continued, "tell us what you know and your reasons for what you're saying."

With this support, the policeman crushed Monsieur Méchinet with an ironic look and said, with a very discernible nuance of complaisant stupidity:

"Well," he began, "here's the thing: Monsieur the Investigating Magistrate and Monsieur the Commissioner here charged us, Inspector Goulard, my colleague Poltin and me, to arrest the accused Monistrol, a dealer in costume jewelry, living at 75 Rue Vivienne, the before-mentioned Monistrol being accused of assassination on the person of his uncle.

"That's accurate," the Commissioner approved in a low voice.

"Thereupon," the policeman continued, "we took a carriage and had us taken to address indicated. We arrived and we found the gentleman, Monistrol, in the back of the shop on the point of sitting down to dinner with his wife, a woman 25 to 30-years old of admirable beauty.

"Seeing all three of us standing in a single line, my fellow stood up. 'What do you want?' he asked us. On that, the Brigadier Goulard took the arrest warrant out of his pocket and answered: 'In the name of the law, I arrest you...'"

Monsieur Méchinet seemed on pins and needles.

"Can't you cut it short?" he asked the policeman.

But the other man continued in the same calm tone as if he hadn't heard him.

"I've arrested quite a few individuals in my lifetime. Well, I've never seen any of them fall apart like that one. 'You're joking,' he said to us, 'or you've made a mistake.' "No, we haven't made a mistake." 'But really, why are you arresting me?'"

Goulard shrugged his shoulders. "Don't act like a child,' he said. "What about your uncle? The cadaver has been found and there are overwhelming proofs against you."

"Ah! The criminal, what a nasty situation! He began trembling and finally fell into a chair sobbing and stammering some answer it was impossible to understand."

"Seeing that Goulard shook him by the collar of his suit, saying to him: 'Believe me, the fastest way is to confess everything.'"

He looked at us with a dazed air and murmured: "'All right! Yes! I confess everything!'"

"Good maneuveur, Goulard!" the Commissioner approved.

The policeman was triumphing. "It was a matter of not staying very long in the shop," he continued. "It had been recommended that we avoid any scandal, and the on-lookers were already gathering. Goulard grabbed the accused by the arm, yelling at him:

'Come on, let's go! They're waiting for us at the Prefecture.' Monsistrol, stood up on his wobbly legs as well as he could and in the tone of a man who's taking his courage in both hands, said: "Let's get started!"

"We thought the worst was over. We hadn't counted on the wife. Until then she had stayed in an armchair as if in a faint, without saying a word, without even seeming to understand what was happening. But when she saw that we were very definitely taking away her man, she bounded up like a lioness and threw herself across the door, crying out: 'You won't leave!' On my word of honor, she was superb. But Goulard had seen a great many others like her.

"'Come now, come now, little mother,' he said, 'Don't give us any trouble. You'll get him back, your husband!'"

"Nevertheless, far from letting us pass, she clutched the door facing even harder, swearing that her husband was innocent, declaring that if he was taken to prison, she would follow him, sometimes threatening us and sometimes heaping curses on us, sometimes begging us in her sweetest voice…"

"Then, when she saw that nothing would keep us from fulfilling our duty, she turned loose of the door and threw herself around her husband's neck.

'Oh! Dearly beloved," she moaned, 'is it possible that they're accusing you of a crime? You…you!…Speak to them, to these men, tell them you're innocent!'"

"It's true. We were all moved, but he, more insensitive than we were, he was barbarous enough to push his poor wife away so brutally that she went to fall down in a heap in a corner of the back shop. Fortunately, that was the end of it."

"The wife being prostrate, we took advantage of it to wrap up the husband in the carriage that we'd brought along. 'Wrap up' is really the right word, because he'd become like something inert, he couldn't stand up; we had to carry him. And, not to forget anything, I have to say that his dog, a kind of black, bad-tempered little runt, wanted absolutely to jump into the carriage with us, and we had a lot of trouble getting rid of him. On the way, as he should have, Goulard tried to distract our prisoner and to make him blab…But it was impossible to get a word out of his throat. It was only on arriving at the Prefecture that he seemed to come to himself. When he was solidly and completely installed in a cell in solitary confinement, he threw himself helplessly on the bed repeating: 'What have I done to you, Oh *Mon Dieu*, What have I done to you!'

"At this moment Goulard went up to him and for the second time: 'So,' he interrogated him, 'You confess you're guilty!' Monistrol nodded and said: 'Yes, Yes….then, in a harsh voice: 'Please, leave me alone,' he said."

"That's what we did, after having taken care, however, to place a guard to watch through the window in the cell's door, just in case the fellow tried to put an end to his days. Goulard and Poltin stayed there, and here I am!"

"That does it," the Commissioner muttered. "Nothing could be clearer."

That was also the opinion of the Investigating Magistrate because he mumbled:

"After that, how could you doubt the guilt of Monistrol?"

Me, I was confused, and nevertheless my convictions remained unshaken. And I was even opening my mouth to hazard an objection when Monsieur Méchinet stopped me.

"All that's well and good!" he burst out. "Only, if we admit that Monistrol is the murderer, we're also forced to admit that he wrote his name there on the floor...and *Damn!* That's tough..."

"*Bast!*" interrupted the Commissioner, "From the moment the accused confessed, what's the good of being preoccupied with a circumstance the investigation will explain..."

But my neighbor's observation had raised the Investigating Magistrate's uncertainty. So, without making a decision:

"I'm going back to the Prefecture," he said. "I'm going to interrogate Monistrol right this evening."

And after having charged the Commissioner with filling out all the paperwork carefully and waiting for the doctors called to do the autopsy, he left, followed by his stenographer and the policeman who had come to tell us of the success of the arrest.

"Provided these medical devils don't make us wait too long!" grumbled the Commissioner, who was thinking of his dinner.

Neither Monsieur Méchinet nor I answered him. We remained standing, facing each other, obviously obsessed by the same idea.

"After all," murmured my neighbor, "maybe it was the old man who wrote it."

"Then with the left hand? Is that possible! Without considering the fact that the death of the poor good man must have been instantaneous."

"Are you sure of that?"

"Considering his wound, I'd swear to it...Besides the doctors who're coming will tell you whether I'm right or wrong."

Monsieur Méchinet rubbed his nose with a veritable frenzy.

"Maybe, in fact, there is some mystery in all this," he said. "This needs to be looked into. That would mean an investigation to be started over....So be it; let's redo it...And to begin with, let's interrogate the porter."

And running to the stairwell, he leaned over the ramp, shouting:

"Concierge!...Hey! Concierge! Come up a little while, please..."

Chapter V

While waiting for the concierge to come upstairs, Monsieur Méchinet began a rapid and knowledgeable examination of the crime scene. But it was above all the lock of the apartment's entry door that attracted his attention. It was intact and the key turned in the lock without difficulty. That fact act absolutely did away with the idea that an unknown robber had entered during the night with the help of false keys. On my side, mechanically, or rather by means of the astonishing instinct that had been brought out of me, I went to pick up the wine cork on the floor half covered with wax that I'd noticed. It had been used, and on the wax side it still had traces of the bottle opener. But on the other side could be seen a rather deep sort of nick, evidently produced by a sharp cutting instrument.

Suspecting the importance of my discovery, I communicated it to Monsieur Méchinet, and he couldn't hold back an expression of pleasure.

"Finally," he cried out, "finally, we have a clue. This wine cork, it's the murderer who let it fall here. He stuck the fragile point of the weapon he used in it. Conclusion: The murder weapon is a dagger with a fixed handle, and not one of those knives that can be closed. With this cork, I'm sure of getting to the guilty man, whoever he is."

The Commissioner of Police was finishing up his duties in the bedroom. We, Monsieur Méchinet and I, still in the living room, were interrupted by the sound of panting. Almost immediately there showed up the powerfully built woman I had noticed in the vestibule holding forth in the middle of the renters. It was the woman porter, redder, if that was possible, than she was when we arrived.

""What can I do to help you, Monsieur?"

"Sit down, Madame," he answered.

"But, Monsieur, the fact is, I have people downstairs...."

"They'll wait for you. I told you to sit down."

Taken aback by Monsieur Méchinet's tone, she obeyed. Then, fixing her with his terrible little gray eyes, he said:

"I need certain information," he said, "and I'm going to question you. In your own interest, I advise you to answer straightforwardly. And first of all, what is the name of this poor fellow who's been murdered?"

"His name was Pigoreau, good Monsieur, but he was mainly known under the name of Anténor,. He took that in the past as more fitting to his line of work."

"Had he been living in this house very long?"

"For eight years."

"Where did he live before that?"

"Where did he live before? Rue Richelieu, where his shop was….because he was known there. He had been a hairdresser and that's how he'd earned his fortune."

"He was reputed to be rich?"

"I have it from his niece that he was worth at least a million."

In that regard, the general opinion would have to be verified, since they had inventoried the poor old man's papers.

"Now," Monsieur Méchinet continued, "what type of man was this Monsieur Pigoreau, called Anténor?"

" Oh, the cream of the crop of men, dear, good Monsieur," answered the concierge. "He was a great worrier, cranky, so miserly you couldn't believe it, but he wasn't proud. And so amusing in addition to all that! You could spend entire nights listening to him when he was in good form. What tales he knew! Just think about it, a former hairdresser who had, as he used to say, curled the hair of the most beautiful women in Paris."

"What was his life style like?"

"Like everybody…like people who have an income, that's understood, and who, nevertheless, hold on to their money."

"Can you give me some details?"

"Oh! As for that, I certainly think so, seeing that I was the one who took care of his housekeeping. That wasn't hard for me to do, since he did almost everything, sweeping, dusting, and polishing himself. That was really his mania! So, every day the good God made, I brought him up a cup of chocolate. He drank it. After that he swallowed a big glass of water and that was his lunch. After that he got dressed, and that took him up to 2:00 p.m. because he was more coquettish and careful of his person than a bride. As soon as he was decked out, he went out to take a walk about Paris. At 6:00 p.m. he went to eat dinner in a middle class pension run by the Gomet ladies, on the Rue de la Paix. After his dinner he hurried to drink his demitasse of coffee and a little cognac at the Guerbois Café. And at 11:00 p.m. he came back to go to bed. Finally, he had only one fault, the poor fellow. He was drawn to the opposite sex. Many times I said to him: 'At your age, have you no shame!…But no one's perfect and you can understand that in a former perfume salesman who's had a heap of good opportunities in his lifetime."

A flattering smile played across the sturdy concierge's lips, but nothing was capable of amusing Monsieur Méchinet.

"Did Monsieur Pigoreau have a lot of visitors?" he continued.

"Very few...I hardly ever saw anyone come to visit him except his nephew, Monsieur Monistrol, whom he took to dinner at Father Lathuile's every Sunday."

"And how were they together, the uncle and the nephew?"

"Like two peas in a pod."

"They never had any arguments?"

"Never! Except they were always squabbling because of Madame Clara."

"Who is this Madame Clara?"

"The wife of Monsieur Monistrol, really a superb creature...The departed Father Anténor couldn't stand her. He said his nephew loved her too much, that woman, and that she led him about by his nose. He said she made him see things through rose-colored glasses. He claimed she didn't love her husband, that she had a lifestyle too exalted for her position and that she would wind up doing stupid things. Madame Clara and her Uncle had even fallen out at the end of last year. She wanted the good uncle to lend Monsieur Monistrol 100,000 francs to buy the stock of a jeweler in the Palais-Royale. But he refused, saying they could do with his fortune whatever they liked after his death, but, until then, having earned it, he claimed he wanted to keep it and enjoy it."

I thought Monsieur Méchinet was going to make a point of that circumstance, which seem very serious to me, but...not at all. I motioned to him in vain. He went on.

"We still need to know: who discovered the crime?"

"It was discovered by me, my good Monsieur, by me!" moaned the woman porter. "Ah! It was terrible! Just imagine that this morning, on the stroke of noon, I came upstairs as usual to bring Père Anténor his cup of chocolate... Since I do the housekeeping, I have a key to the apartment. I opened the door, I entered, and what did I see..Ah! *Mon Dieu!*"

And she began to let out piercing cries...

"This grief is proof of your good heart, Madame," Monsieur Méchinet said gravely." However, I'm in a great hurry. Try to control yourself. What did you think on seeing your tenant murdered?"

"I've told whoever would listen: It was his nephew, the robber, who did it in order to inherit."

"What gave you that certainty? Because, after all, to accuse a man of such a serious crime is to push him toward the scaffold."

"Eh, Monsieur, then who could it be? Monsieur Monistrol came to see his uncle last evening and when he left it was almost midnight. And what's more, he, who always speaks to me, said nothing to me when arriving or when leaving. And from that moment right up to when I discovered everything, nobody,

I'm sure, went up to Monsieur Anténor's apartment."

I admit that deposition confused me. Still naïve, I would not have thought of continuing that interrogation. Fortunately, Monsieur Méchinet had great experience and he possessed to the utmost degree that very difficult art of drawing the whole truth from witnesses.

"So, Madame," he insisted, "You're certain that Monsieur Monistrol came last evening?"

"Certain."

"You saw him clearly, really recognized him?"

"Ah! Let me explain, please. I didn't stare at him. He went by very quickly, trying to hide himself like the thief he is, and the corridor is poorly lit…"

At that answer of an importance that couldn't be overestimated, I jumped. And going up to the concierge:

"If that's how it was," I burst out, "how dare you swear you recognized Monsieur Monistrol?"

She looked me up and down and answered with an ironic smile:

"If I didn't see the master's face, I did see the dog's muzzle. As I always pet it, he came into my quarters. I was going to give him a mutton bone when his master whistled for him."

I was looking at Monsieur Méchinet, anxious to know what he thought of these answers, but his face kept the secret of his impressions faithfully. He only added:

"What breed is Monsieur Monistrol's dog?"

"He's a Spitz, like the conductors used to have, completely black, with a white spot above his ear. His name is Pluton."

Monsieur Mechinet got up.

"You may leave," he said to the woman porter. "I have what I need to know."

And when she had left:

"It seems to me impossible that the nephew is the guilty one. "

However, the doctors had arrived during this long interrogation. When they had finished the autopsy their conclusion was:

"The death of the Pigoreau individual was certainly instantaneous. Therefore, he wasn't the one who traced these five letters, *Monis,* that we've seen on the floor near the cadaver."

So, I wasn't mistaken.

"But if he wasn't the one, then who was it?" Monsieur Méchinet exclaimed. "Monistrol, that's what they'll never convince me of."

And when the Commissioner, delighted to be able finally to go to dinner, was joking to him about what was puzzling him, ridiculous perplexities, since Monistrol had confessed, he admitted:

24

"Maybe, in fact, I'm just an imbecile," he said. "Only time will tell. And while we're waiting, my dear Monsieur Godeuil, come with me to the Préfecture."

Chapter VI

We took a carriage to go to the Préfecture of Police, just as we had done to come to the Batignolles. Monsieur Méchinet's was greatly preoccupied. His fingers never stopped traveling from his empty snuff box to his nose and I heard him mutter between his teeth:

"I must have a clear conscience. I have to have a clear conscience."

Then he took from his pocket the wine cork I'd turned over to him. He turned it over and over with the expression of a monkey trying to crack a walnut, muttering:

"It looks like an open and shut case; however, there must be something to get out of this green wax."

Me, sunken in my corner, I didn't say a word. Assuredly, my situation was one of the most bizarre, but I wasn't thinking about that. Everything I had of mental ability was absorbed by that affair. I ruminated in my mind the diverse and contradictory elements. I wore myself out trying to penetrate the secret of the drama I felt coming on.

When our carriage stopped, it was dark night. The Quai des Orfèvres were deserted and silent: not a sound, not a passer-by. The rare shops in the area were closed. All life in the neighborhood had taken refuge in the little restaurant which took up almost the whole corner of the Rue de Jérusalem. The shadows of the customers could be seen through the red curtains of the front window.

"Will they let you go in to where the accused is?" I asked Monsieur Méchinet.

"Certainly," he answered me, "Am I not in charge of following this business?" Isn't it necessary that, according to the unforeseen necessities of the investigation, I can interrogate the detainee at all hours of the day and night?"

And walking rapidly, he went under the entry arch, saying to me:

"Hurry, hurry, we have no time to lose."

He had no need to encourage me. I followed him, agitated by indefinable emotions and quivering with a vague curiosity. This was the first time I'd crossed the threshold of the Préfecture of Police. God knows what my prejudices were then.

There, I was saying to myself, not without some fright, *there is the secret of Paris.*

I was so engrossed in my own thoughts that, forgetting to look where I was going, I almost fell. The shock brought me back to the realization of the situation. We were going along an immense corridor with humid walls and rough paving stones. Soon my companion went into a little room where two men were playing cards while three or four others, stretched out on camp beds, were smoking their pipe. He exchanged some words with them, which I couldn't hear, since I'd stayed outside. Then he came back out and we started walking again. Having gone across a courtyard, we had picked up another corridor. We weren't long in arriving in front of an iron grill gate with heavy bolts and a strong lock. On a word from Monsieur Méchinet, a guard opened that gate. We passed a vast room on the right, where I seemed to see policemen and Paris city guards, and finally we climbed a rather steep staircase.

At the top of that staircase, at the entrance of a narrow corridor pierced with a large number of small doors, was a rather fat man with a jovial face, who certainly looked nothing like the classical jailor. As soon as he saw my companion:

"Eh! It's Monsieur Méchinet!" he cried out. *"Ma foi!* I was expecting you. Let's bet you've come for the murderer of the little old Batignolles man."

"Precisely. Is there anything new?"

"No."

"Nevertheless, the Investigating Magistrate must have come."

"He's left here."

"Well?"

"He didn't stay three minutes with the accused man. On leaving him, he seemed to be very satisfied. At the bottom of the stairway, he met Monsieur the Director and said to him: 'It's an affair in the bag. The murderer didn't even try to deny it.' Monsieur Méchinet jumped about three feet but the guard didn't notice it, because he continued:

"What's more, that didn't surprise me. Just by looking at this individual when they brought him to me, I said: 'There's one who won't be able to hold up.'"

"And what's he doing now?"

"He's whining. Now, they ordered me to keep a watch on him, fearing he'd commit suicide. And as I should, I'm watching him, but it's totally useless. He's just another one of those sly customers who think more of their own skin than they do of others."

"Let's look at him," interrupted Monsieur Méchinet. "And above all, don't make any noise."

At that, all three of us, on tip-toe, went up to the solid oak door with a window grill opening at the height of a man. Through this opening you could see what was happening in the cell, which was lit by a puny gas jet. The guard glanced in first, Monsieur Méchinet looked next, and then came my turn. On a little narrow iron bed with a covering of gray wool cloth with yellow stripes, I saw a man lying on his stomach, his head hidden in his half-folded arms. He was crying. The dull sound of his sobs came as far as me and at times a convulsive quivering shook him from head to foot.

"Let us in now," Monsieur Méchinet commanded the guard.

He obeyed and we entered.

At the creaking of the key in the lock, the prisoner raised up and seated on his miserable bed, his legs and his arms hanging down, his head bowed toward his chest, he looked at us with a dazed expression. He was a man from 25 to 38-years old, with a height a little below medium, but robust, with an apoplectic neck sunk between large shoulders. He was ugly. Smallpox had disfigured him. His long straight nose and his receding forehead gave him something of the stupid facial expression of sheep. However, his eyes were very beautiful and he had teeth of remarkable whiteness.

"Well! Monsieur Monistrol, we're distressed, aren't we?" Monsieur Méchinet began. And the unfortunate man not answering: "I agree the situation isn't very cheerful," he continued. "However, if I were in your place I'd prove I was a man. I'd give myself an alibi and I'd try to show my innocence."

"I'm not innocent."

This time, there was no equivocation and no suspecting the intelligence of a policeman. We had gathered the terrible confession from the mouth of the accused man.

"What!" Monsieur Méchinet exclaimed: "You're the one who...."

The man had gotten up on his legs, staggering, his eyes bloodshot, his mouth slobbering, in prey to a veritable excess of rage.

"Yes, it was me," he interrupted. "Just me. How many times do I have to repeat it? An Investigating Magistrate already came in a while ago. I confessed everything and signed my confession....What more do you want? Go away. I know what I'm in for, and I'm not afraid. I killed, I must be killed. Cut off my neck. As fast as possible would be best."

At first a little dazed, Monsieur Méchinet quickly recovered.

"Just a moment! What the devil! They don't cut off people's neck just like that. First of all they have to prove they're guilty. Then the law understands certain things that lead one astray, certain inevitabilities, if you like. That's the reason they invented extenuating circumstances."

Monistrol's only reply was an inarticulate groaning, and Monsieur Méchinet continued:

"You were really terribly mad at your uncle?"

"Oh! No!"

"Then why?…"

"In order to inherit. My business was in bad shape. Go check that out. I needed money. My uncle, who was very rich, refused to give me any."

"I understand. You were hoping not to get caught."

"I was hoping so."

Up to that point, I was astonished at the way Monsieur Méchinet was conducting this rapid interrogation. But now, I could explain it. I was guessing what would come next. I saw what trap he was setting for the accused.

"One thing more," he began again suddenly. "Where did you buy the revolver you used to commit the murder?"

"I've had it in my possession a long time," he answered.

"What did you do with it after the crime?"

"I threw it on the outside boulevard."

"That's good," Monsieur Méchinet said gravely. "They'll make a search and they'll certainly find it."

And after a moment of silence:

"What I can't explain to myself," he added, "is why you had your dog come with you."

"What! How! My dog…"

"Yes, Pluton…The concierge recognized it."

Monistrol's hands clinched. He opened his mouth to answer, but a sudden thought crossed his mind. He threw himself on his bed, saying in an accent of unshakeable resolution:

"You've tortured me enough. You won't get another word out of me."

It was clear that to insist would have been a waste of time. So we left and once outside on the quay, seizing Monsieur Méchinet's arm, I said:

"You heard him," I said to him. "This unfortunate man doesn't even know how his uncle died. Is it still possible to doubt his innocence!"

But this old policeman was a terrible skeptic.

"Who knows," he answered. "I've seen some remarkable actors in my life. But that's enough of this for today. This evening I'm going to invite you to eat my soup. Tomorrow it'll be daylight and we'll see."

Chapter VII

It was nearly 10:00 p.m. when Monsieur Méchinet, that I was still with, rang at the door of his apartment.

"I never carry my entry key," he said to me. "In our confounded profession, you never know what can happen. There're a lot of scoundrels who have it in for me, and if I'm not always careful for myself, I must be so for my wife."

My worthy neighbor's explanation wasn't needed. I had even observed that he knocked in a certain way, which must have been a signal agreed on between his wife and himself. It was the very nice Madame Méchinet who came to open the door for us. With a movement as nimble and gracious as that of a cat, she jumped to her husband's neck, crying out:

"You're really here! I don't know why, but I was almost worried."

But she suddenly stopped. She had just seen me. Her happy expression darkened, and she stepped backward, addressing me as much as her husband.

"What!" she continued. "You're coming from the café at this hour! That doesn't make sense!"

Monsieur Méchinet had on his lips the indulgent smile of the man who's sure he's loved, who knows how to calm with a single word the quarrel about to start.

"Don't scold us, Caroline," he answered. "My associate has his reason for there being two of us. We're not coming from the café and we haven't wasted our time. They came to get me for an affair, for a murder committed in the Batignolles."

The young woman examined alternately, her husband and me, with a suspicious look, and when she was persuaded that we weren't deceiving her, she said only: "Ah!"

But it would take a whole page to detail all that was contained in that brief exclamation.

She was addressing Monsieur Méchinet and clearly meant:

"What! You took this man into your confidence. You revealed your situation to him. You let him in on our secrets!"

That was how I interpreted that very eloquent "Ah!" and my worthy neighbor interpreted it just as I did, because he answered:

"Well! Yes! Where's the problem? If I have to fear the vengeance of miserable men I've delivered up to justice, what do I have to fear from honest people? Do you imagine I'm hiding, that I'm ashamed of my job?"

"You've misunderstood me, my love," the young woman objected.

Monsieur didn't even hear her. He had just gotten on his favorite hobby-horse—I noticed this detail later—which always carried him away.

Parbleu! You have unusual ideas, Madame, my wife. What! I'm one of the lost guardians of civilization! At the price of my repose and at the risk of my life I protect society's security and I should be ashamed of it! That would be really too funny! You'll tell me there exists, against us policemen, a large number of silly prejudices bequeathed to us from the past. What does that matter to me! Yes, I know there are touchy gentlemen who look down on us from high up. But, *Sacrebleu!* I'd like very much to see their faces if tomorrow my colleagues and I went on strike leaving the pavement free for the army of criminals that we hold in check."

Probably accustomed to sorties of this sort, Madame Méchinet didn't say a word, and she was right, because my good neighbor, not meeting any contradiction, became calm as if by magic.

"But that's enough of that," he said to his wife. "It's a matter right now of something of very different importance. We haven't eaten dinner. We're dying of hunger. Do you have anything for us to eat?"

What happened that evening must have happened too often for Madame Méchinet to let herself be taken by surprise.

"In five minutes these Messieurs will be served," she answered with the nicest smile.

In fact, we shortly sat down at the table in front of a piece of cold beef, served by Madame Méchinet, who never stopped filling our glasses with an excellent little Mâcon wine. And I, while my worthy neighbor worked his fork industriously, considering the interior peace which was his, that pretty little attentive wife which was his, I wondered if there was here one of those "fierce" Sûreté agents who have been the heroes of so many absurd stories.

Nevertheless that enormous hunger wasn't long in being satisfied and Monsieur Méchinet undertook to tell his wife about our expedition. And he didn't tell it sketchily. He went into the minutest details. She was sitting beside him and from the way in which she was listening, with a little competent expression, asking for explanations when she hadn't understood, you could see she was a bourgeoise Egéria* accustomed to being consulted and who had a decisive say.

When Monsieur Méchinet had finished:

"You made a big mistake," she said, "an irreparable mistake."

"What?"

"You shouldn't have gone to the Préfécture when you left the Batignolles."

"However, Monistrol…."

"Yes, you wanted to question him. What good did that do you?"

"That helped me, my dear love…."

"To do nothing. You should have run to the Rue Vivienne, to the wife. You would have surprised her while she was still feeling the emotion which she must necessarily have felt about her husband's arrest. If she's an accomplice, as you must suppose she is, with a little cleverness you could get her to confess."

---

* Wife and instructress of Numa Pompilius; a woman counselor

At these words, I jumped out of my chair.

"What, Madame, you believe Monistrol is guilty?"

After a moment's hesitation, she answered.

"Yes."

Then more strongly:

"But please understand that I'm sure, absolutely sure, that the idea of the murder came from the wife. Of 20 crimes committed by men, 15 have been conceived, mulled over and inspired by women. Ask Méchinet about that. The concierge's deposition should have enlightened you. What sort of person is that Madame Monistrol? A remarkably beautiful person, she told you, coquettish, ambitious, eaten up with covetousness and someone who leads her husband around by the nose. What's her situation now? Shabby, constrained, precarious. She is suffering because of that. And the proof is that she asked his uncle to lend him 100,000 francs. He refused to give them to him, destroying all her hopes. Don't you know she held that against him mortally! Don't you see, she must have repeated very often: 'Nevertheless, if he should die, that old miser, we'd be rich, my husband and me.' And when she saw him in good health and strong as an oak, she said to herself with fatality: 'He'll live to be a hundred and when he leaves us his inheritance, we'll be toothless and too old to enjoy it. And who knows, he may even bury both of us!' From that point to the idea of a crime, is that so far? And once she'd made up her mind, she would have taken a long time to prepare her husband. She would have familiarized him with the thought of a murder. You might say she would have put the knife in his hand. And one day, threatened with bankruptcy, driven crazy by his wife's complaints, he did the deed."

"All that is logical," Monsieur Méchinet approved.

Very logical, perhaps, but what had become of the facts we had revealed?

"Then, Madame," I said, "you think Monistrol is stupid enough to have incriminated himself by writing his name…?"

She shrugged slightly and answered:

"Was that stupid? Me, I don't think so, because that's your strongest argument in favor of his innocence."

The reasoning was so plausible but lacking in real merit that I remained a moment without saying anything. Then I began again:

"But he admits he's guilty, Madame," I insisted.

"That's an excellent way to get the law to point out his innocence."

"Oh!"

"You're the proof of that, Monsieur Godeuil."

"Eh! Madame, the poor man doesn't even know how his uncle was killed."

"Pardon, he appeared not to know that. That's not the same thing."

The discussion became livelier and it would have lasted even longer if Monsieur Méchinet hadn't put an end to it.

"Come now, come now," he said to his wife gently. "You're a great deal too romantic this evening." And speaking to me:

"As for you, I'll come get you tomorrow and we'll go together to see Madame Monistrol. And this settled, since I'm falling asleep, …Good Night…"

He himself must have slept. But as for me, I couldn't close my eyes. A secret voice rising from my deepest being cried out to me that Monistrol was innocent. My imagination represented to me with sad vividness the tortures of this unfortunate man alone in his cell at the holding Depot.

"But why had he confessed?"

Chapter VIII

What I lacked then—a hundred times since then I've had the occasion to realize that—was experience, practice in the profession, above all, the exact understanding of police methodology and investigation. I vaguely sensed that the investigation had been conducted badly, or rather conducted carelessly, but I would have been embarrassed to say why, most of all to say what should have been done.

I was no less passionately interested in Monistrol. It seemed to me his cause was my own. And that was very understandable. My youthful vanity had come into play. Wasn't it one of my remarks that raised the first doubts as to the culpability of this unfortunate man?

I owe it to myself to demonstrate his innocence, I told myself.

Unfortunately, the discussions of the evening had so troubled me that I no longer knew on what exact fact to raise the scaffolding of my theory. So, as it always happens when you apply your mind to the solution of a problem, my thoughts became as tangled as a ball of thread in the hands of a child. I could no longer see clearly. It was chaos.

Sunk into the depths of my armchair, I was torturing my head when at 9:00 a.m. Monsieur Méchinet, faithful to his promise of the evening before, came to pick me up.

"Come on! Come on!" he said, shaking me brusquely, since I hadn't heard him enter. "Let's go!"

"I'm ready," I said, standing up.

We went downstairs in haste, and I noticed then that my worthy neighbor had dressed with more care than usual. He had managed to give himself those debonair and rich appearances which most seduce the Parisian shopkeeper. His gaiety was that of a man sure of himself, who marches to certain victory.

Soon we were in the street and while we were walking along:

"Well!" he asked me, "What do you think of my wife? At the Préfecture I have a reputation for being difficult, and, even so, I consult her—Molière often consulted his maid—and often I've found good advice. She has one weakness. For her, there are no stupid crimes and her imagination attributes diabolical plots to every scoundrel. And, since I have exactly the opposite failing, as I'm a little too matter-of-fact, it's rare that our consultations don't bring out the truth."

"What's that!" I exclaimed. "You think you've solved the mystery of the Monistrol affair!

He stopped short, took out his snuff box, and inhaled three or four of his imaginary pinches and in a tone of discreet vanity:

"I at least have the way to solve it," he answered.

However, we were coming to the top of the Rue Vivienne, not far from Monistrol's establishment.

"Be careful," Monsieur Méchinet said to me, "Follow me, and whatever happens, don't be surprised."

He was right to warn me. Without that warning I would have been unusually surprised to see him suddenly enter the shop of an umbrella merchant. Stiff and serious as an Englishman, he had himself shown everything in the shop. Not finding anything to his liking, he ended up asking if it wasn't possible to have an umbrellas made for him using a model he would furnish. He was told that would be the simplest thing in the world and he left saying he would be back the next day.

And certainly the half-hour he had spent in the store hadn't been wasted. While at the same time as he was examining the objects shown him, he had the art to draw from the merchants all they knew about the Monistrol couple. Actually, an easy talent, because the affair of "the little old man of the Batignolles," had profoundly affected the neighborhood and had become the subject of every conversation.

"There, you see how you get exact information," he said to me when we were outside. "As soon as people know who they're dealing with, they strike a pose, they compose fancy sentences, and then good-bye to the real truth."

Monsieur Méchinet repeated that comedy in seven or eight stores in the vicinity. And in one of them, where the owners were cantankerous and not very talkative, he even made a 20 franc purchase.

But after two hours of that unusual exercise, which amused me very much, we knew the public opinion exactly. We knew precisely what people thought of Monsieur and Madame Monistrol in the neighborhood where they had lived since their marriage, that is for the last four years.

On the subject of the husband, they all spoke with one voice. He was, they affirmed the best of men, helpful, honest, intelligent and hardworking. If his business hadn't succeeded, that was because luck doesn't always favor those who merit it the most. He was wrong to take on a shop which was bound to fail, since in the last 15 years four businesses had gone under there.

He adored his wife. Everybody knew that and said it, but this great love hadn't gone beyond conventional limits. There had been no backlash of ridicule towards him. Nobody could believe he was guilty. His arrest, they said, was a police mistake.

As for Madame Monistrol, the opinions were divided. Some found her too elegant for her social position; others held that a fashionable outfit was one of the obligations, one of the necessities of the commerce in items of luxury she provided. In general, people were persuaded that she loved her husband very much. Because, for example, with one voice they praised her upright behavior. Her proper behavior was so much more meritorious because she was remarkably beautiful and she was besieged by many admirers. But she had never been talked about. The slightest suspicion had never touched her spotless reputation.

I could see that threw Monsieur Méchinet off the track.

"This is astounding," he told me. "Not one bit of gossip, not one malicious rumor, not one slander. Ah! That wasn't what Caroline was thinking. According to her, we should have found one of those little shop girls, who stay behind the counter and show off their beauty more than their merchandise, who relegate their husband to the back of the shop—their husband either a blind imbecile or a dirty man who turns a blind eye. And that's not it at all!"

And I didn't answer, being hardly less disconcerted than my neighbor. We were now far from the deposition of the concierge of the Rue Lécluse. The point of view, it's true, varied so much depending on the neighborhood. What in the Batignolles was considered damnable flirtation was no more in the Rue Vivienne but a job requirement.

But we had already spent so much time in our investigation for us to be able to stop and exchange our impressions and discuss our conjectures.

"Now," said Monsieur Méchinet, "before going into the shop, let's study the outside of it."

And breaking the practice of discreet investigations, in the middle of Paris activity, he motioned me to follow him under a carriage door entry exactly across from the Monistrol store. It was a modest boutique, almost poor when compared with those around it. The front window craved the attention of an artist's brush. Below, in letters gilded in the past, now smoked and blackened, the name Monistrol was exhibited. On the glass could be read: "Gold and Gold filled."

Helas! It was primarily imitation gold which shone in the display case. Hung along rods were a great number of gold-filled chains, jet costume jewelry, tiaras spangled with rhinestones, then necklaces set with coral, broaches, rings, and cuff buttons enhanced with false stones in every color.

In short, a poor display. I recognized it at a glance. Nothing to tempt robbers to break in.

"Let's go in," I said to Monsieur Méchinet.

He was less impatient than I was, or knew how better to contain his impatience, because he held me back by the arm, saying:

"An instant, I'd at least like to get a look at Madame Monistrol."

But for more than 20 minutes more, we waited in vain planted in our observation post: the boutique remained empty. Madame Monistrol did not appear.

"Decidedly, this is enough of standing on one foot and then the other," my worthy neighbor finally exclaimed. "Come on, Monsieur Godeuil, let's take a chance... ."

Chapter IX

We had only to cross the street to enter Monistrol's shop. That was done in four strides. At the noise of the door opening, a little servant girl, 15 or 16-years old, dirty and ill-kempt came from the rear of the shop.

"How may I help these Messieurs," she asked.

"Madame Monistrol?"

"She's here, Messieurs, and I'll go tell her, because, you see...."

Monsieur Méchinet didn't give her chance to finish. With a fairly brutal gesture, he pushed her out of the passageway and went into the back of the boutique, saying:

"That's good. Since she's here, I'm going to talk to her."

Me, I followed on the heels of my worthy neighbor, persuaded that we wouldn't leave without the key to the enigma.

That back part of the boutique was a sad room, serving as a living room, a dining room and a bedroom, all at the same time. Disorder reigned there, and even more so that lack of unity or harmony noticed among the poor who try to appear rich. At the back was a bed with damask curtains, with lace pillow covers and in front of the fireplace there was a table completely encumbered with a more than modest lunch. In a big armchair was a young, very blonde woman, holding in her hand a piece of paper with a stamp on it. That was Madame Monistrol.

And of a certainty, when they talked about her beauty, all the neighbors had stayed well below reality…I was astounded. Only one circumstance displeased me. She was in full mourning, wearing a crepe dress slightly décolleté which fit her marvelously. That was too much presence of mind for great sadness. It seemed to me that I saw the artfulness of an actress wearing in advance the costume of a role she was to play.

At our entry, she stood up with the movement of a startled deer and in a voice that seemed broken by tears:

"What do you want, Messieurs?" she asked.

Monsieur Méchinet had seen everything as I had.

"Madame," he answered harshly, "I've been sent by the law. I'm an agent of the Sûreté service."

At that declaration, she at first fell back in her armchair with a moan that would have softened a tiger. Then, suddenly, seized with a kind of wildness, her eyes shining and her lips trembling:

"Then have you come to arrest me?" she cried out. "Then bless you. Take me; I'm ready. Lead me away. So I'll go join that honest man you arrested yesterday evening. Whatever his fate, I want to share it. He's innocent, as I am too. That doesn't matter. If he must be the victim in an error of human justice, it would be a final joy for me to die with him."

She was interrupted by a muffled growl which came from one of the corners at the rear of the boutique. I looked and I saw a black dog, his hair standing up, and his eyes bloodshot, who was about to jump on us.

"Be quiet, Pluton," said Madame Monistrol. "All right, go lie down. These Messieurs don't mean me any harm."

Slowly, and not ceasing to fix us with a furious look, the dog took refuge under the bed.

"You were right to say we didn't mean you any harm, Madame," Monsieur Méchinet began again. "We haven't come to arrest you."

If she heard him, it hardly appeared so.

She went on, "I've already received this letter I'm holding this morning. It orders me to show up, this afternoon at 3:00 p.m. at the Palais de Justice, in the office of the Investigating Magistrate. What do they want with me, *Oh! mon Dieu!* What do they want with me!"

"To clear up some matters which will demonstrate, I hope, your husband's innocence. So, Madame, don't consider me an enemy. What I want is to bring out the truth."

He took out his snuff box and rummaged around in it hastily with his fingers, and with a solemn tone I'd never heard him use:

"I must tell you, dear Madame, how important will be your answers to the questions I'm going to have the honor of asking you. Do you agree to answer me frankly?"

She stared a long time at my worthy neighbor with her big blue eyes, wet with tears, and in a tone of sad resignation:

"Question me, Monsieur," she said.

For the third time, I repeat: I was absolutely inexperienced. Nevertheless, I suffered from the way Monsieur Méchinet conducted that interrogation. It seemed to me he revealed his perplexities and instead of following an end decided in advance, he made his points by chance. Oh! If I'd been allowed to do it!...Ah! If I'd dared!...

He, inscrutable, had sat down across from Madame Monistrol.

"You must know, Madame," he began, "that evening before last, about 11:00 p.m. the honorable Pigoreau, known as Anténor, your husband's uncle, was murdered."

"Alas!..."

"Where was Monsieur Monistrol at that hour?"

"*Mon Dieu!* It's a catastrophe!"

Monsieur Méchinet didn't move a muscle.

"I asked you, Madame," he insisted, "where your husband spent evening before last."

It took the young woman some time to answer because sobs seemed to stifle her voice. Finally, getting hold of herself:

"Day before yesterday," she moaned, "my husband spent the evening away from home."

"Do you know where he was?"

"Oh! As for as that goes, yes. One of our workers, who lives in Montrouge, was supposed to deliver a set of false pearls to us and he didn't deliver it. We risked keeping the order on the books, which would have been a disaster, because we're not rich. That's why, while we were dining, my husband said to me: 'I'm going right to that fellow's house!' And in fact, toward 9:00 p.m. he left. And I even took him as far as the omnibus, where he got on in front of me, on the Rue Richelieu."

I breathed easier. That could be an alibi, after all.

Monsieur Méchinet had the same idea, and said more gently:

"If that's how it was," he continued, "your worker will be able to swear he saw Monsieur Monistrol at his house at 11:00 p.m."

"Alas! No..."

"What do you mean? Why?"

"Because he had gone out. My husband didn't see him."

"In fact, that is a misfortune...But it could be that the concierge noticed Monsieur Monistrol..."

"Our worker lives in a house where there isn't a concierge."

That might be the truth. It was surely a terrible charge against the unfortunate detainee.

"And what time did your husband get home?" continued Monsieur Méchinet.

"A little after midnight."

"You didn't find he'd been gone a long time?"

"Oh! Yes, I did and I even reproached him for it. To excuse himself he told me that he'd taken the long way home, that he'd strolled along, and that he'd stopped at a café to drink a glass of beer."

"What did he look like when he came back in?"

"He seemed vexed, but that was very understandable."

"What clothes was he wearing?"

"The ones he was wearing when he was arrested."

"You didn't notice anything unusual about him?"

"Nothing."

Chapter X

"Standing up, a little behind Monsieur Méchinet, I could observe Madame Monistrol's facial expressions at my leisure and catch the most fleeting telltale signs of her impressions. She seemed crushed by an immense sadness. Big tears were rolling down her pale cheeks. And nevertheless it seemed to me that I found, at moments, something like a gleam of joy at the bottom of her big blue eyes.

Could she be guilty, then? I was thinking.

And that thought, that had just come to me, persisting in my mind, I went forward quickly and in a harsh tone:

"But you, Madame," I asked. "You. Where were you during that fatal evening, at the time your husband was running uselessly to Montrouge, looking for your worker?"

She stared at me a long moment with a look full of stupor and said softly; "I was here, Monsieur," she answered. "Witnesses will confirm it. "

"Witnesses!"

"Yes, Monsieur. It was so hot that evening that I wanted to have something cold, an ice. But to have something by myself bored me. So, I sent my maid to invite two of my neighbors, Madame Dorstrich, the wife of the shoemaker whose shop joins ours, and Madame Rivaille, the glove seller across the street. These two ladies accepted my invitation and they stayed here right up to 11:30

38

p.m. Ask them. They'll tell you so. In the middle of the very cruel tests I'm undergoing, that fortunate circumstance is the gift of the *bon Dieu.*"

Was this really a chance circumstance?"

With a glance faster than lightening, that's what we both asked ourselves, Monsieur Méchinet and I. When chance is as intelligent as that, when it serves a cause so conveniently, it's very difficult not to suspect its having been prepared for and brought about. But the moment was badly chosen to follow our thought to its conclusion.

"You've never been a suspect, you yourself, Madame," Monsieur Méchinet shamelessly declared. "The worse that could be supposed is that your husband told you about the crime before committing it."

"Monsieur, if you knew us...."

"Wait a moment. Your business isn't doing very well, we've been told. You were in financial straits...."

"Momentarily, yes, in fact...."

"Your husband must be unhappy and worried about that precarious situation. More than anything, he must suffer for you, whom he adores, for you who're young and beautiful. For you more than for himself, he must ardently desire the pleasures of luxury and the well-being that fortune can buy."

"Monsieur, one more time, my husband is innocent."

Seeming to be thinking, Monsieur Méchinet appeared to fill his nose with snuff, then he suddenly said:

"Then, *Sacrebleu!* How do you explain these confessions! An innocent man who declares he's guilty just at the mention of the crime he's suspected of. That's rare, Madame, that's prodigious!"

The young woman blushed slightly. For the first time her look, up until then straightforward and clear, became troubled and shifty.

"I suppose," she answered with a faint voice and beginning to cry again, "I suppose my husband, frightened and amazed at seeing himself accused of so great a crime, lost his head...."

Monsieur Méchinet shook his head.

"If we absolutely had to," he pronounced, "we could admit temporary insanity. But this morning, after a long night in which to think it over, Monsieur Monistrol persists in his first confessions."

Was this true? Was my worthy neighbor making that up or, before coming to pick me up, had he gone to the Depot holding cells to have a conference.

Whichever it was, the young woman appeared about to faint, and hiding her head between her hands, she murmured:

"*Seigneur Dieu!* My husband has gone crazy!"

I'll have to say that wasn't my opinion. From then on I was persuaded that

I was witnessing an act and that the young woman's great despair was nothing but a lie. I wondered if, for certain reasons which escaped me, she hadn't been responsible for the terrible decision taken by her husband, and if, him innocent, she didn't know the real murderer. But Monsieur Méchinet didn't look like a man who would go that far. After having addressed some words of consolation to the young woman, too banal to encourage her to say anything further, he gave her to understand that she would dispel a great number of suspicions if she willing allowed a careful search of her domicile.

She seized that suggestion with a rapidity which wasn't faked.

"Go ahead and search, Messieurs," she told us. "Examine, pry into everything. You'd be doing me a favor. And it won't take very long. We own only the shop, the section behind the shop where we are, our maid's room on the seventh floor and a little cellar. Here are the keys to everything."

To my great astonishment, Monsieur Méchinet accepted. He appeared to conduct the most exact and the most patient investigation. What was his purpose? He must have some secret aim, because this search, obviously, couldn't turn up anything. As soon as he had, apparently, finished:

"We have only the cellar left to explore," he said.

"I'll take you there," Madame Monistrol said.

And with that, armed with a lighted candle, she had us go through a back entry of the shop, cross a courtyard and guided us down a very slippery staircase, to a door she opened, saying:

"There it is. Go in, Messieurs."

With a quick and trained eye, my worthy neighbor examined the cellar. It was poorly kept and even more poorly filled. There was a little keg of beer in one corner and right in front of it, supported on a wooden framework, was a wine cask. It had a wooden butt cock to draw out wine. On the right, lined up on iron racks were some fifty full bottles. Monsieur Méchinet didn't lose sight of those bottles and he found an opportunity to move them, one by one. And what I saw, he saw. Not one of them had been sealed with green wax. So, the cork I'd picked up which had been used to protect the murderer's weapon had not come from the Monistrol cellar.

"Decidedly," Monsieur Méchinet said, pretending some disappointment, "I don't find anything. We can go back upstairs."

That's what we did, but not in the same order as when we went down. On the return trip I walked ahead. Because of that, I was the one who opened the door of the back shop. As soon as I did, the Monistrol couple's dog jumped toward me, barking so furiously that I jumped back.

"*Diable!* Your dog is mean!" Monsieur Méchinet said to the young woman.

With a gesture of her hand, she had already ordered the dog to one side.

40

"No, he's certainly not mean," she said. "He's just a good guard dog…We're jewelers, more open to robbers than other people. We trained him."

Mechanically, as you always do when threatened by a dog, I called this one by his name: "Pluton! Pluton!" But he, instead of coming to me, recoiled, growling, showing his sharp teeth.

"Oh! It's useless to call him," Madame Monistrol said in an off-handed way. "He won't obey you."

"Is that so? Why not?"

"Ah! That's because he's faithful, like all those of his race. He knows only his master and me…."

That sentence, nothing on the surface, was for me like a bolt of lightening. .And without thinking, quicker than I would be today, I asked:

"Then where was this very faithful dog, Madame, the evening of the crime?"

The effect that point-blank question produced was such that she almost dropped the candlestick she was still holding.

"I don't know," she stammered. "I can't remember."

"Maybe he followed your husband…."

"In fact, yes, it seems to me now that I remember…."

"Then he's been trained to follow vehicles, since you told us that you went with your husband right to the omnibus."

She stopped talking and I was going to follow up, when Monsieur Méchinet interrupted me. Very far from taking advantage of the young woman's trouble, he seemed to make it a point of reassuring her. After having instructed her to obey the Investigating Magistrate's citation, he drew me outside.

"Have you lost your mind?" he asked me.

The reproach wounded me.

"Is finding the solution to the problem loosing your mind? I now have that solution….The Monistrol dog will lead us to the truth!"

My enthusiasm made my worthy neighbor smile and he said in a fatherly tone:

"You're right," he told me, "and I understood you very well. Only, if Madame Monistrol saw your suspicions, before this evening, the dog would be dead or would have disappeared."

Chapter XI

I had committed an enormous indiscretion, that's true. I had nonetheless found the chink in the armor, that joint through which the most solid defense can be broken apart. Me, a volunteer, I had seen clearly there where the old professional, groping about, had gone astray. Anyone else would have been jealous of me. He was not. He thought only of taking advantage of my fortunate discovery. As he told it, that shouldn't be something taking a long time and difficult to do now that the arrest was based on a single positive starting point.

We went into a neighborhood restaurant to talk it over while having lunch. And here was the problem which the hour before had seemed insolvable. Just the evidence had proved to us that Monistrol was innocent. Why did he admit he was guilty? We thought we could guess, but that wasn't the question for the moment. We were equally sure that Madame Monistrol hadn't budged from her house the evening of the murder. But everything indicated that she was morally an accomplice of the crime, that she had known about it. And even if she hadn't advised and prepared for it, on the other hand, she knew the murderer very well.

Then who was this murderer? A man Monistrol's dog obeyed as he would his masters, since he had followed him when he went to the Batignolles. Therefore, he was someone familiar with the Monistrol household.

However, he must hate the husband, since he had put everything together with a hellish cleverness so that suspicion of the crime would fall on that unfortunate man. On the other hand, he had to be someone dear to the wife, since she knew him and didn't denounce him. She was thus without hesitation sacrificing her husband.

Therefore…*Oh! Mon Dieu!* It was a foregone conclusion. The criminal could only be some miserable hypocrite who had taken advantage of the affection and confidence of the husband to take possession of the wife. In sort, Madame Monistrol, belying her reputation, certainly had a lover and that lover was the guilty person.

Full of that certainty, I began torturing my mind to try to imagine what infallible ruse would lead us to that miserable man.

"Here's how I think we ought to operate," I said to Monsieur Méchinet. "Madame Monistrol and the murderer must have agreed that after the crime they'd remain a certain amount of time without seeing each other. That would be the most elementary caution. But you can believe that before long the woman will get impatient and want to see her accomplice. Put someone to watch her who will follow her everywhere. Before twice two forty-eight hours have gone by, the affaire will be in the bag."

Furiously digging into his empty snuff box, Monsieur Mechinet didn't answer for a moment. He was mumbling between his teeth I don't know what unintelligible words. Then suddenly leaning toward me:

"You haven't got it right," he said to me. "The genius of the profession, you have it, that's for sure. I grant you that. But it's practice you lack. Fortunately, me, I'm here."

"What! A sentence relating to the crime puts you on the trail and you don't follow up on it. How's that?"

"We must use this faithful poodle."

"I'm not following your reasoning."

"Then learn how to wait. Madame Monistrol will leave at about 2:00 p.m. to be at the Palais de Justice by 3:00 p.m. The little maid will be alone in the shop. You'll see. That's all I'll tell you."

And in fact I insisted in vain. He wouldn't say anything more, avenging himself for his defeat with that very innocent malice. Willingly or unwillingly, I had to follow him to the nearest café, where he forced me to play a game of dominoes. Preoccupied as I was, I played badly. He was shamelessly taking advantage of that fact to beat me when the clock struck 2:00 p.m.

"Come to attention, men on guard duty!" he said to me, putting down his dominoes.

He paid. We left and an instant afterwards we were again on sentry duty under the couch entry door where we had studied the outside of the Monistrol store.

We hadn't been there ten minutes when Madame Monistrol appeared on the threshold of her shop, dressed in black, wearing a large crepe veil, like a widow.

"Pretty get-up for an interview!" grumbled Monsieur Méchinet.

She gave some instructions to her little maid and wasn't long in leaving.

My companion waited patiently five long minutes, and when he supposed the young woman already far away:

"It's time," he told me.

And for the second time, we went into the jewelry store. The little maid was alone there, seated behind the counter. To distract herself, she was nibbling on some morsels of sugar stolen from her employer. She recognized us as soon as we appeared. Embarrassed and a little frightened, she stood up.

But without giving her time to open her mouth:

"Where is Madame Monistrol?" Monsieur Méchinet demanded.

"Out, Monsieur."

"You're deceiving me. She's back there, in the back of the shop."

"Messieurs, I swear to you she's not. Go look for yourselves."

Monsieur Méchinet slapped his forehead with the most annoyed air, repeating:

Mon Dieu! How disagreeable this is. How upset that poor Madame Monistrol is going to be."

And the little maid was looking at him with her mouth open, her eyes wide with astonishment.

"But in fact," he continued, "you, my good girl can perhaps take the place of your mistress. If I've come back, it's because I've lost the address of the Monsieur that she'd asked me to visit."

"What Monsieur?"

"You know very well. Monsieur….Come now! Well! Now I've forgotten his name. Monsieur….*Parbleu!* He's the only one you know…That Monsieur your devil of a dog obeys so well."

"Ah! Monsieur Victor…."

"That's right, exactly. What does this Monsieur do?"

"He makes jewelry. He's a great friend of Monsieur. They were working together when Monsieur was a jewelry worker before becoming an owner. And that's why he can do whatever he wants to with Pluton."

"Then you can tell me where this Monsieur Victor lives…."

"Certainly, He lives on the Rue du Roi-Doré, number 23.

The poor girl appeared very happy to be so well informed. Me, I was suffering to hear her in this way denounce her mistress without knowing it."

More hard-hearted, Monsieur Méchinet had none of this delicacy. And when we'd gotten our information, he even terminated the scene with a sad joke:

"Thank you," he said to the young girl. "Thank you! You've just done Madame Monsitrol a great service and she'll be very happy."

Chapter XII

As soon as we were on the sidewalk, I had only one thought. To take to our running legs and dash to the Rue du Roi-Doré and arrest this Victor, the real guilty man, obviously.

A word from Monsieur Méchinet fell like a cold shower on my head.

"And the law!" he said to me. "Without an arrest warrant from the Investigating Magistrate, I can't do anything. We have to go to the Palais de Justice."

"But we'll meet Madame Monistrol there. And if she sees us, she'll have her accomplice warned."

"So be it!" answered Monsieur Méchinet with badly disguised bitterness, "So be it! The guilty man will get away and the formality will be saved. However, I can prevent this danger. Let's keep walking; let's walk faster."

And in fact the hope of success gave him the gait of a deer. Arrived at the Palais de Justice, he climbed the steep staircase which leads to the Investigating Magistrates' gallery four steps at a time. Speaking to the head of the bailiffs, he asked him if the Magistrate in charge of the *Little Old Batignolles Man affair* was in his office.

"He's there with a witness, a young lady in black," answered the bailiff.

"That's certainly her!" my companion told me.

Then to the bailiff:

"You know me," he continued. "Quick! Give me something to write a short note to the Magistrate with. You'll carry it to him."

The bailiff left with the note, dragging his shoes on the dusty tiles. He wasn't long in coming back to announce to us that the Magistrate was waiting in No. 9.

In order to receive Monsieur Méchinet, the Magistrate had left Madame Monistrol in his office, watched by his stenographer, and had borrowed the office of one of his colleagues.

"What is it?" he asked in a tone that allowed me to measure the abyss which separates an Investigating Magistrate from a poor Sûreté agent.

Briefly and clearly, Monsieur Méchinet laid out what we'd been doing, the results, and our hopes.

It must be said that the Investigating Magistrate hardly seemed to share our convictions.

"But since Monistrol confesses!" he kept repeating with a stubbornness which exasperated me.

Nevertheless, after a great deal of explanation:

"I'm going to sign a warrant, nevertheless," he said.

In possession of that indispensable document, Monsieur Méchinet flew so lightly that I almost fell in rushing down the stairways after him. A carriage horse couldn't have followed us. I don't know if it took us a quarter of an hour to get to the Rue du Roi-Doré. But once there:

"Be careful," Monsieur Méchinet said to me.

And it was with the calmest air that he started into the narrow pathway of the building bearing the number 23.

"Monsieur Victor?" he asked the concierge.

"On the fifth floor, the door on the right in the corridor."

"Is he at home?"

"Yes."

Monsieur Méchinet took a step toward the stairs and then seemed to change his mind.

"I must bring him a gift of a good bottle of wine, this good Victor," he said to the porter." What wine merchant does he go to around here?"

"To the one across from here."

We were over there in a minute and with the air of a regular customer:

"A bottle of wine, please, and a good year, the one with the green seal.'

Ah! *Par ma foi!* That thought would never have come to me at that time! Nevertheless, it was so simple. When the bottle was brought to us, my companion compared it with the cork found at the apartment of Pigoreau, called Anténor, and we were happy to confirm the identity of the wax.

From this point, a material certainty was joined to our moral certainty. Monsieur Méchinet knocked confidently at Victor's door.

"Come in!" a deep voice yelled out.

The key was in the door. We went in. In a very orderly room I saw a man about 30 years old, slim, pale and blond, behind a workbench. Our presence didn't seem to bother him.

"What do you want?" he asked politely.

Monsieur Méchinet went right up to him. Grabbing him by the arm, he said:

"I'm arresting you in the name of the law!"

The man became livid but didn't lower his eyes.

"Are you joking?" he asked in an insolent tone. "What have I done?"

Monsieur Méchinet shrugged.

"Don't act innocent! We know everything. You were seen leaving Père Anténor's. In my pocket I have the cork you used to protect the point of your dagger."

This was like a blow to the neck of the miserable man. He collapsed in his chair stammering:

"I'm innocent...."

"You can tell that to the Magistrate," Monsieur Méchinet said calmly. "But I doubt very much that he'll believe you. Your accomplice, Madame Méchinet, has admitted everything."

Victor stood up as if on a spring.

"That's impossible!" he cried out. "She didn't know anything about it."

"Then you did the job all alone. Very good! That's as good as a confession." Then speaking to me as a man sure of his facts:

"Go look in the drawers, dear Monsieur Godeuil," Monsieur Méchinet continued. "You'll probably find this pretty fellow's dagger. And you'll certainly find his love letters and the portrait of his lady love."

A gleam of fury shown in the murderer's eyes and he ground his teeth, but

Monsieur Méchinet's broad shoulders and iron fist snuffed out in him all attempts at resistance. In addition, I found what my companion said I would in a drawer of a chest. And 20 minutes later, Victor was "properly wrapped up" —that's the expression—in a carriage between Monsieur Méchinet and me, rolling toward the Prefécture.

Well! What do you know, I said to myself, stunned at the simplicity of the scene, at the arrest of a murderer, of a man promised to the scaffold, *Is that all it is!* Later I was to learn at my expense that there are more terrible criminals. This one, as soon as he was locked up in the Depot holding cells, feeling himself lost, fell apart and told us about his crime in detail.

He said he had known Père Pigoreau for a long time and was known to him. His goal in the murder was, above all, to make the accusation and punishment for the crime fall back on Monistrol. That's why he dressed up like Monistrol and had Pluton follow him. And once the old man was murdered, he had the horrible courage to dip the cadaver's finger in the blood in order to trace those five letters: *MONIS,* which had almost condemned an innocent man.

"And it was nicely set up, don't you agree?" he said with bragging cynicism. "If I had succeeded, I would have killed two birds with one stone. I would have gotten rid of my friend Monistrol, that I hated and that I was jealous of, and I would have made the woman I love rich."

It was, in fact, simple and terrible.

"Unfortunately, my boy," Monsieur Méchinet objected, "you lost your head at the last moment. What do you expect! You can't be perfect! You dipped the cadaver's left hand in the blood…."

With a start, Victor stood up straight.

"What!" he exclaimed. "Is that what gave me away!"

"Exactly!"

With the gesture of a misunderstood genius, the miserable man lifted his arms toward heaven.

"*Soyez donc artiste!*" he cried out.

And looking us up and down with pity, he added:

"Père Pigoreau was left-handed!"

So it was as a result of an investigation mistake that the very prompt discovery of the guilty man came about. That lesson wasn't lost on me. Fortunately, I remember it in circumstances a great deal more dramatic that I'll talk about later.

Monistrol was set free the next day. And when the Investigating Magistrate reproached him for his lying confession which set up the law for a terrible error, he got out of him only this:

"I love my wife. I wanted to sacrifice myself for her. I thought she was guilty."

Was she guilty? I would swear she was.

She was arrested, but she was acquitted with the same judgment that condemned Victor to life at hard labor.

Monsieur and Madame Monistrol are today the owners of a wine shop with a bad reputation on the Avenue Vincennes. Their uncle's inheritance has long since been spent. They are in terrible poverty.

The Cursed House

Badmouthing or slandering, for years people have said worse than "hang the landlords." It's time to try to rehabilitate them, if it can be done. In essence, what do people accuse them of? Of continually raising rents without a reason. All right! There's one man who won't raise them. Positively, he exists in flesh and blood. Giving his address would be easy. And here's his story.

Le Vicomte de B...... a young man, likable, charming, peacefully enjoying an income of 30,000, when, lately,—about six months ago—his uncle, the worst type of miser, died, leaving him all his wealth, nearly 2,000,000. While looking over the papers of the inheritance, the Vicomte de B...... also discovered that he found himself the proprietor of a house on Victory Street. He also discovered that this magnificent building, bought for 300,000 francs in 1849 brought in a net income of 82,000 francs per year.

Oh, obviously, that's too much, thought the generous Vicomte. *My uncle was a good deal too hard to rent at this price. That's usury, that can't be denied. When one bears a great name such as mine, he can't give way to such exploitation. Beginning tomorrow, I'll diminish my rents and my renters will bless me for it.*

With that good thought, the Vicomte de B...... sent for the custodian of the house in question.

The manager presented himself with his head bowed very low.

"Bernard, my friend," the Vicomte said to him, "you are going to let all your tenants know, as if coming from me, that I'm lowering rent by one-third."

This word, "diminish," unheard of, fantastic, fell like an enormous roof tile on Bernard's head. But he recovered quickly. He must not have heard correctly, must have misunderstood.

"Lower," he stammered, "Monsieur le Vicomte must be joking. Lower!" It's raise the Vicomte means.

"On my life, I've never spoken more seriously. I've said, and I repeat: "Diminish." This time the rental agent was at this point surprised, stunned, astonished, so much so that he lost all control of himself.

"Monsieur has not thought about it," he insisted, "by this evening Monsieur will have regrets. Lower the rents! That's never been seen and will never again be seen! If it gets around, what will people think of Monsieur? What will people in the neighborhood say? Because, finally, it's clear...."

"Monsieur Bernard," interrupted the Vicomte, "when I give an order, I like to be obeyed without any talking back. You heard me. Go on."

It was with the staggering steps of a drunk man that Monsieur Bernard left his proprietor's home. All his ideas had been turned upside down, overthrown, all jumbled up together. Hadn't he been the plaything of a dream, of a ridiculous nightmare? He was at the point of asking if he was awake or sleeping.

Lower rents, that's unbelievable, he thought. *"It's not as if the tenants were complaining! But they're not complaining, on the contrary. They're all good payers! Ah! If the departed Monsieur could see this from the bottom of his tomb he must be happy! His nephew has gone crazy! That's for sure. Lower the rent! This young man needs to be taken to family counseling; he's going to wind up badly. After this, who knows? He must have had too much to eat this morning.*

That honorable Bernard was pale with emotion when he returned to his dwelling. He was so pale and so undone that, on seeing him, his wife and his daughter, Amanda, both asked him at the same time:

"What's wrong with you? What is it?"

"Nothing," he answered, "absolutely nothing."

"You're not telling me the truth," insisted Madame Bernard: "Come now, speak; I'm strong. What did the new owner tell you? Is he thinking of replacing us?"

"If that was all it is! But look here, he told me with his own mouth, speaking to me in person he told me…. Ah! You won't believe me."

"Will you speak up?"

"You want it? All right, here it is. He told me to alert all the tenants that he was lowering the rents by a third. You understand me, don't you? He is 'lowering' them."

But neither Madame nor Mademoiselle Bernard understood. They were dying laughing.

"Lowering," they repeated, "That's a good joke, how funny, really! Lowering…."

And Mademoiselle Bernard ran to her piano—because she had a piano, as a student of the Conservatory—and she began to sing the great aria of Verdi:

> *"Etrange aventure,"*
> *Bizarre imposture*
> *Jamais, je le jure*
> *On ne te croira*
> *Nous fais-tu l'injure*
> *"Strange happening*
> *Bizarre imposture*
> *Never, I swear it*

People would never believe it
You're kidding us!"

But Bernard meant to be taken seriously in his own household. He became very red and angry; his wife responded in kind, and a quarrel followed. Madame Bernard accused Monsieur Bernard of having taken that order from the bottom of a liter in the shop of the wine merchant at the corner.

Without Mademoiselle Amanda the couple would have come to blows. So much so that Madame Bernard, who didn't want to be contradicted, threw her shawl over her shoulders and ran to the house of the landowner. Bernard had told the truth; she saw it only too well. With her two ears, ornamented with golden earrings, she heard the unbelievable word. However, as she was a strong and prudent woman, she asked for it in writing, wanting to be sure of her responsibility. This "written word" the proprietor, laughing, gave it to her.

She too, she came back stunned. And all evening long, the father, the mother, and the daughter deliberated. Did they have to obey? Should they warn some relative of the young man, where wisdom opposed so much folly? After serious reflection, it was agreed that they would obey.

The next day, Bernard, acting as the best levite bill collector, made the rounds of the 23 tenants announcing the big news. One minute afterwards, the house on Victory Street was in an uproar impossible to describe. People, who, during the four years that they had lived on the same floor, had not honored each other with a greeting, got together, spoke to each other.

"Do you understand, Monsieur?"

"It's very extraordinary!"

"Really, unheard of."

"The owner is lowering my rent."

"By one-third, right? Mine too."

"That's amazing."

"There must be some mistake."

In spite of affirmation by the Bernard couple, in spite of the written word, there were some Saint Thomas renters who doubted. There were three who wrote to the landlord to warn him about what was happening and to charitably warn him that his custodian had absolutely lost his reason.

The landowner answered these skeptics. He confirmed what Bernard had said. It was impossible henceforth to doubt. Then the reflections and the commentaries began.

"Why is the landlord lowering the rents?"

"Yes, Why?"

"What reasons," they asked, "motivate this strange man? Surely he must have serious motives. An intelligent man who has good sense doesn't deprive himself of big, secure revenues just for the pleasure of doing so. Nobody acts this way without having to, forced by powerful, terrible circumstances."

And everybody repeated: "There's something at the bottom of this."

"But what?"

From the first floor to the sixth, they searched, they guessed, they conjectured, they exhausted their reasoning ability. Every tenant looked like a man preoccupied at all costs with deciphering an impossible puzzle. Everywhere they began to be vaguely disturbed, as happens when one finds oneself in the presence of a mystery. Some of them began making guesses such as:

"This man must have committed some great secret crime. Remorse is pushing him to this philanthropy."

"It's not nice living side by side with a reformed scoundrel because, after all, there are those who return to that type of life."

On the other hand people asked: "Is the house really solid?"

"Hum! So-so, just barely."

"However, it isn't very old."

"That's true; but they had to prop it up when they dug the sewage system last March."

Others supposed that the danger came from the roof. Still others claimed to have strong reasons for believing that he was making counterfeit money in the basement and claimed to hear sometimes the dull and deep noise of the presses. Some of those on the second floor were of the opinion that he must be hiding some Russian or Prussian spies in the house. The gentleman on the first floor was inclined to believe that the proprietor meant secretly to set fire to his building just to draw huge sums from the insurance companies, which are, as everybody knows, delighted to pay for fires. Then extraordinary and even frightening things were happening, they claimed. On the sixth floor, in the attics it appears strange and absolutely inexplicable noises were once heard. Some people claimed that they had seen ghosts that dragged chains down the stairs. One evening the maid of the spinster on the fourth floor, while going to steal some wine from the cellar, encountered the specter of the former proprietor—he was even holding a rent receipt in his hand.

And the refrain was: "There's something in all this."

They went from being disturbed to being frightened and from there they passed quickly to terror. So much so that the gentleman on the first floor, who had valuable things in his apartment, gave notice by way of a bailiff.

Bernard went to notify the proprietor, who answered:

"All right! Let him leave, that imbecile!"

But the next day, the podiatrist, although he had nothing to fear concerning valuables, imitated this gentleman.

The renters from the second and the little households on the fifth bravely followed this example.

From that moment there was a general panic. At the end of the week everybody had given notice. Everybody expected some terrible catastrophe.

The terrified domestic servants wanted absolutely to leave that cursed house. To stay they demanded that their salaries be tripled.

Bernard was no longer anything but the shadow of himself. The result of fear had made him grow thin. Mademoiselle Bernard gave up her piano.

"No," repeated the manager to each new lodger giving notice, "this is not natural!"

However, 23 FOR RENT signs, affixed to the front of the house, brought forth people in quest of lodgings. Bernard, without grumbling, climbed the stairs and let them visit the apartments.

"You can take your choice," he said to the people who came, "the entire house is vacant. All the tenants gave notice, in mass, like a single man. We don't know exactly why, but some things happened, Oh! Such things. Really a mystery! A story like you've never heard. To tell the truth, the owner is lowering the rents." And the potential renters, frightened, fled.

The end came: 23 Bailly moving vans carried away the furniture of the 23 renters. Everybody left. From the foundation to the attics, the house remained empty.

The rats themselves, no longer finding anything to live on, abandoned it. Only the manager remained, turning pale with fear in his apartment. Frightful visions haunted his nights. He seemed to hear mournful howls. At certain sinister murmurs, his teeth chattered with terror and the hair on his head stood up under his cotton night cap. Madame Bernard no longer closed her eyes.

In her fright, Amanda, renouncing the glories of the theatre, married a young wig-maker that she couldn't abide just to leave the paternal apartment. Finally, one morning, after a sleepless night more harrowing than the others, Bernard made a great resolution. He went to find the landlord, gave him back his money sack, and left.

And now if you pass Victory Street, you will see an abandoned house. That's the one I have just told you the history of. Dust is stacking up on the closed shutters; grass is growing in the courtyard. No tenant presents himself anymore, and in the neighborhood the haunted house has such an unsavory reputation that the neighboring buildings are losing some of their value.

So, therefore, LOWER YOUR RENTS!!!!

(Le Lion Amoureux)

The Dandy in Love and Other Stories

Melchior-Frédéric Soulié
Une Nouvelle Collection Michel Levy
(Oeuvres Complètes)
Neuvième Edition) Calman Levy, editeur
Ancienne Maison Michel Levy Frères
3, rue Auber, 3
1886

Melchoir Frédéric Soulié

During his relatively short life (1800–1847), Melchoir Frédéric Soulié was a friend and colleague of Honoré de Balzac, Alexandre Dumas, the elder, and Paul Féval. He was as well-known as any of them. He entered the Paris literary world as a poet and dramatist. His first publication was a volume of poems, *Amours françaises*, composed during his leisure hours before he came to Paris when he was 24. The poems were praised by Casimir Delavigne, and, although the collection did not find a wide public, its publication introduced Soulié to Alexandre Dumas, who became his friend. His first play, an adaptation of Romeo and Juliette (1827), was a success. And although his second, *Christine à Fontainebleau* (1829), was a total failure, it is important historically and was followed by two successes: *Lucigny* (1831) and *Clothilde* (1832). Encouraged by Dumas, he began contributing to Paris newspapers as a *feuilletoniste*. This method of publication benefited both the publisher and the author. It increased newspaper circulation and the writer was well paid. He could thereafter have the work printed and sold as a book. André Maurois is quoted as saying: "… The real masters of this particular technique were Eugène Sue, Alexandre Dumas and Frédéric Soulié." He quotes Joseph Méry as saying: "If I were King Louis Philippe, I would subsidize Dumas, Eugène Sue, and Soulié, on condition that they kept the *Muskeeters, The Mysteries of Paris,* and *The Memoirs of the Devil* going indefinitely. Revolutions would be a thing of the past."

Chapter I*

The name *lion* as applied to a part of French young manhood has been made so commonplace that I don't think it's necessary to go into long explanations in order for my readers to take it to mean anything other than the terrible king of the forest or the slave obeying Monsieur Van Amburgh.** But what else is it? In general people have a vague idea, useful enough to talk about it. They know that the race the lion belongs to has always lived in France under diverse names. So the lion in the past has been called the sophisticate, the essence of lily man, the lucky man, a cunning devil. Later he was called a Muscadin (name given to elegantly dressed Royalists in 1793), the unbelievable, the marvelous, and finally, last of all, the dandy and the fashion plate. Today he's called the lion.

Why?

Is it because he is the king of that little piece of society that's called the fashionable world? Is it because he takes three-fourths of the prey that others helped him catch?

I can't tell you, but I'm going to try to sketch his appearance for you, and then you can work it out, if you can.

The lion is, in general, a handsome fellow who has gone from the state of childhood to that of a full-grown man. The claim to being a young man was long ago given over to forty or fifty-year-old men, since in our days the state of young manhood is almost as much looked down on as that of old man.

Now, the lion, never having been a young man, has almost never done any of the youthful foolishness which comes from the heart, although he loves gambling, women and wine, as the songs of the time of the Empire say, one of the things the lions despises the most. But that love is not love, because it isn't for themselves that these gentlemen have these three passions, to which they join, when they can, that of horses.

True passion is, by its nature, personal, hidden, discreet. Theirs, on the contrary, is all show and profusion. They possess their mistress the same way they do their carriage, in order to dazzle the passers-by, and they dine sitting at Parisian cafe windows because that's the most easily seen place in the capital. In fact, they don't pretend to drink, but to have emptied a great number of bottles, which is a very different thing.

---

* Soulié begins *Le Lion Amoureux* with a short explanation of the origin of the word LION as used in the mid-XIX century to describe the rich, idle, dissolute man about town in Paris.
** One of the first traveling menageries. Traveled the US in the mid and late 1800s.

Lions are, therefore, very ignorant about love, about its most passionate fool-ishness, about its most delicate happiness, about its most unreasonable hopes, about its frivolous fears, and especially about its charming silliness. On the other hand, they have acquired the right (the word right is correctly chosen) to use the familiar "tu" when speaking to the majority of the singers of the chorus line or opera singers.

What's more, they have this in common with the young nobility of sixty years ago: they have one foot in the best society in Paris and one foot in the worst. But they differ from those of sixty years ago in that today's great ladies no longer compete, as they did in the past, with kept prostitutes and leave them to intrigues behind the scenes in the theatre. It may happen that even in the theatre some woman is encountered who had only to have someone love her to lose her reputation if she had given herself to some poor boy in love that they had branded in advance with the epithet of bourgeois. bad, and probably inaccurate translation.

That said, we can begin our story.

Chapter II

Several days ago, at noon, a most beautifully decked out lion stepped out of his carriage and went into the *Cafe de Paris*. His entry caused very lively astonishment for two main reasons; the first because he was formally dressed; the second because he ordered his lunch like a man who's in a hurry and has something to do. One of his friends looked at him carefully out of the eye in which he wore his *lorgnon*, and said to him:

"Where the devil are you going dressed like that, Sterny?"

"I'm going to a marriage."

"So who's getting married?" the questioner asked.

And immediately a half-dozen heads were lifted. They looked at each other. They looked at the ceiling and each one asked himself the question, *Who's getting married?*

Sterny saw that pantomime and hastened to answer in an indifferent tone, saying:

"Nobody, gentlemen, nobody. It's a private affair."

"And what time will you be through with it?"

"I have no idea, but I'll duck out of the church when I'm no longer needed."

"Then you have to be there?"

"I'm a witness for the bridegroom."

"A witness for the bridegroom," everybody on all sides repeated.

"Yes," answered Sterny, who saw astonishment painted on all the faces. "Yes, a witness for my father's godson. He wrote me a letter on this subject which doesn't allow me to refuse this nice boy a pleasure that he considers a great honor. That's what it's all about. And now, added Sterny, finish eating your lunch in peace. Until this evening!"

As he was leaving, one of his friends shouted after him:

"Where is it taking place, your marriage?"

"Ma foi,I have no idea. The meeting is at the home of the future bride. ...Rue St. Martin, at 12:00 noon and it's 12:15 p.m. now. Good bye!"

He left, and though that event was of very little importance, it was nonetheless the subject of a rather long conversation.

"The old Marquis de Sterny, the son of a pottery maker grown rich, who professed a great respect for hereditary traditions, the old Marquis de Sterny has kept a few of the patronage habits of the old nobility. So what Sterny is doing should be in rather good taste. But despite his great name, he doesn't know anything in this case. Instead of being considered kind and affectionate toward these poor people, he going to bring an air of boredom and mockery, and nevertheless...."

"However," said a forty-year-old elegant and very ugly ex-beau, a sort of opulent podiatrist who called all women, *la petite,* and to whom the title of lion was questionable, "that could be amusing. There are some very pretty women in all that."

"Pretty, yes," exclaimed a true lion no one knew anything about whose specialty had a certain artistic side consisting of protecting oddities and art. *"Pretty, yes, but they're middle-class women."*

"Ah! Messieurs," the son of the pottery maker continued, *"the ancient aristocracy set great store by middle-class women."*

"Pardieu," the artistic lion continued, "middle-class women of the past, that's understandable. Those were young girls who didn't know anything about anything, women who scarcely knew anything more, for whom the pleasures of society, the arts, literature, were a domain to which they couldn't aspire, who looked on the aristocratic man as the tempting serpent from the Book of Genesis." Middle-class women of the past, that's understandable. To enter that life, to throw love, disorder, there, to take advantage of that ignorance of everything, to astonish it as one does a child with a fairy tale, that might be amusing. I understand perfectly the Maréchal de Richelieu's passion for Madame Michelin. But today's bourgeois women, gifted as they are with a small amount of false education which they use with an unshakeable impertinence so as not to be astonished by anything, virtuosi who play Steibelt sonatas, and who argue about Rossini and Meyerbeer in favor of the Postillon de Longi-

umeau, blue stockings who take lessons from reading Madame Sand, and who gladly devour Monsieur Paul de Kock, artists who have themselves painted by Monsieur Dubuffe, who illuminate lithographs, and, finally, women who have opinions about the tax basis and on the immortality of the soul. That's vile and I fully understand Sterny's annnoyance. They're going to look at him as some sort of curious beast, and God knows if they won't judge him by some handsome, dumpy shop keeper who's written a dozen couplets for the marriage, who carves at the table, who sings at the dessert, who'll dance all night, and who'll be considered the nicest man of the gathering."

Having said that, the lion lit his cigar, went to take a chair, putting one under each of his legs, and looked at people passing by on the boulevard. All the other lions were quick to take up occupations of that importance, and it was no longer a question of Léonce Sterny.

Chapter III

However, Sterny had arrived at the Rue Saint-Martin. That day our lion had no appointment. He had neither errands, nor plans to ride in the Blois, and he wasn't missing any pleasure during the two hours he was going to consecrate to Prosper Gobillou, his father's godson. He would have been bored elsewhere; he came there to be bored. Therefore, what he was doing was not important to him and he entered the house of Monsieur Laloine, a maker of pen tips, with no set opinions one way or the other. He was sent to do an errand. He was carrying it out. Nothing more was expected of him. He was aware of that without needing it pointed out to him in the slightest way and he thought he didn't need to apologize. He was introduced to the bride, who didn't dare look at him, then to the parents, and he saw that the young people milled about so as to give a view of him when he answered an introduction or when he spoke. He looked about for someone he could stand next to and saw no one in that conversation whom he could use to hide him from that curiosity. Sterny retreated into a corner while the family was taking a great deal of care to organize the departure, when suddenly a tall young girl entered, exclaiming:

"But I told you I wanted to change dresses before your Marquis arrived!"

"Lise," Monsieur Laloine said severely, while everyone was stupefied by that indiscretion.

Monsieur Laloine's glance directed toward Léonce showed the young girl what an impropriety she had just committed, and she blushed as the handsome lion had never seen anyone blush.

"Forgive me, Father, I didn't know…." she said, bowing her head as Monsieur Laloine approached Sterny, saying to him in a fatherly way:

"She's a child who's not yet sixteen and doesn't know how to behave."

Sterny looked at that child, who was as beautiful as an angel.

"She's your daughter also?" Léonce asked.

"Yes, Marquis, my spoiled child that a terrible heart problem almost took from us, and that we still have to be careful about. That's the reason I didn't scold her."

"Well, will you please introduce me to her and excuse me for being late."

"No, there's no reason to do that," Monsieur Laloine replied. "Don't pay any attention to that child who's still wet behind the ears*."

But that wasn't at all Sterny's opinion. He had never seen anything more charming than that very beautiful girl. While her mother was gently scolding her and seemed to be advising her behave better, she threw a furtive look at the lion, a questioning and not very friendly look. She had concluded her mother's lecture with a little impatient gesture which meant very clearly:

"I was sure that he would spoil the party!"

However, they were leaving for the Mayor's office and they had put Léonce in the bride's carriage with Madame Laloine and one of the witnesses for the family. Fortunately, the trip wasn't long, because the four people were very ill at ease. Léonce's colleague, the other witness, couldn't find anything to say to him but:

"What is your opinion, Sir, about the question of sugar (cane)?"

Sterny had no idea, but he answered coldly: "I'm for the Colonies."

"I understand," the witness said bitterly. "You're afraid of the progress of national industry. But the government finally intends to ruin everything in France. That's a given fact."

Thereupon, the gentleman held forth on the question, and that lasted until they reached the Mayor's office without anyone else having to say a word.

Léonce was already no longer thinking about the beautiful Lise and was beginning to find the task tiring. They had arrived, and when Léonce had just gotten out of the carriage, he saw Lise, her face shining, who had just gotten out of hers. At this moment there occurred a kind of small awkward situation which was probably the first cause of all this story. Lise was holding on to the arm of a tall young man dignified with the name of best man who was standing next to Sterny. Lise, called to by another girl walking behind her, turned around to fix a badly placed flower in her coiffure while the best man remained immobile holding arm open in a semi-circle waiting to receive the beautiful arm of the young girl. But just as she finished what she was doing,

---

* French idiom: has a runny nose.

a voice called the young man to the head of the cortège. He walked off, while Lise passed her arm through the one she found beside her and which turned out to be that of the handsome lion. Then she turned around quickly, saying:

"Come on, let's hurry!"

When she saw Léonce's face, she uttered a little cry and wanted to take her arm away, but Léonce tightened his arm, kept the hand, and, smiling, said:

"Since luck is giving it to me, I want to keep it."

"Pardon, Monsieur, Lise answered, but I'm maid of honor. I can't. Monsieur Tirlot would be angry."

"Monsieur Tirlot, who's that?"

"Well! The best man. That's a right...."

"That's a right I'll dispute with him in hand to hand combat," said the young lion, who thought he was saying the most insignificant thing in the world.

Lise looked at him wide-eyed and answered in an emotional voice:

"If that's how it is, Monsieur, come along. I'll tell him I was the one who wished it."

That sentence and the emotion with which she had said it proved to Léonce that Lise had taken "hand to hand combat" seriously and that she was persuaded that the marquis would have killed the best man if he had been allowed to complain. However, everyone having gone into the municipal office, Léonce and Lise went in last and the young girl was quick to say:

"Since Monsieur Tirlot left me there on the sidewalk, without Monsieur le Marquis, whose arm I was forced to ask, I wouldn't have had an escort."

The word "escort" somewhat disenchanted Léonce, but the Mayor not having yet arrived, and for lack of anything better to do, he sat down beside Mademoiselle Lise. At first, he didn't know what to say to her and obviously his presence bother her a great deal.

Léonce want to act the nice fellow, and smiling sweetly, he said:

"This is a day that starts young girls' hearts to beating...."

Lise didn't answer.

"This is a big day..."

Same silence.

"And one that will soon come for you?"

"Ah! How annoying this Mayor is!" Lise said. "He keeps everyone waiting."

Léonce understood that he was having very little success. But, seated as he was near that beautiful child, he admired with a great deal of pleasure the marvelous purity of her profile, the grace of that very gently curving shoulder, and then he felt wafted toward him for the very first time that freshness of life sweeter than the perfumed atmosphere surrounding a beautiful woman. He didn't get discouraged, and seizing Lise's words on the fly, he said in his most caressing voice:

"You're speaking very casually about such a grave magistrate."

"Who's that?" Lise asked. *"Monsieur le Maire, is he a magistrate?"*

It's useless to create quite admirable Constitutions. Until they have been sanctioned by time, they don't enter the sentiments of the masses. That the Mayor is the one and only person who can legally consecrate a marriage, that's how the law wants it. But the act over which he presides, although serious, however indissoluble it may be, is only in the eyes of the people a contract which carries an official stamp. The real marriage ceremony, the one where there is thought, respect, prayer, can only take place in the church. Sterny was a little of that opinion. He understood perfectly Lise's outburst, and to make her talk answered:

"Certainly, he's a magistrate. He's the one who's really going to marry your sister. The marriage in the church is only a formality."

At these words, Lise raised a frightened glance at Léonce and drew back gently from him and then she lowered her eyes and answered.

"I know, Monsieur, that there are some men who think this way, but I would never be the wife of a man who would not commit himself to me before God."

Ah! Léonce said to himself. *The little one is devout. But she is so beautiful! I'll try again....*

"And this oath," he said, "will never bind you to anything very important, because the one you get will never do everything you want."

"I certainly hope it will," Lise said in a mischievous tone.

"Ah! "Léonce continued. "You're a despot."

"Oh yes!" she answered, picking up again all her youthful jauntiness.

"But don't you know that's wicked? "Léonce asked her.

"What does that matter to you?" she said, laughing in his face. "You're not the one who'll have to suffer from it."

"That doesn't keep me from being sorry for the man that you'll one day tyrannize," Léonce retorted, laughing also.

"But I believe he won't complain. That's enough for me."

"Has he already told you so?"

"No, but I'm sure of it."

"Then he loves you very much?"

"Who's that?" Lise asked, with an astonished look.

"But this future spouse, this future slave, who will be so happy in his chains."

"How do I know who he is?"

"But you were saying that you were sure…"

"Ah!" said Lise. "I'm sure that I'll love him very much, Monsieur. I'm sure that he'll be a gentleman, and as I'll be a lady, I hope that he'll be happy."

That was said in a tone so sincere and so truthful that Léonce believed in the faith of that young girl and said to her with conviction:

"You're right. He will be."

"Ah!" said Lise, standing up. "Here's your magistrate."

The Mayor entered and the ceremony began.

Chapter IV

The Mayor read to the future spouses the articles of the Civil Code which covered their mutual understanding: they swore to conform to it, declared they accepted one another, and they passed into the private room where signatures were given.

To sign a register seems a very easy thing to do, but it happened that this was a small situation where Lise noticed Léonce, and still in a way not advantageous to him. When the two spouses and their parents had signed, it was the turn of the witnesses. Léonce did the same thing as the others and he was greatly surprised, when passing the pen to the person following him, to see Lise who was shaking her head with a little disapproving pout.

Was it because he had signed *Marquis de Sterny*? But omitting his title had seemed to him to be not very complimentary to Prosper Gobillou, who prided himself on having a marquis as a witness. Had he signed before it was his turn or taken up more space than was necessary?

Sterny remained completely intrigued by having brought about the displeasure of a little shop girl, he who thought he had all the polish of a man of the world and he wanted to know how he had failed in her eyes. He found that amusing. Because of that, he remained standing near the office, looking sometimes at Lise, sometimes at those signing after him. They seemed to be doing exactly as he had done, without the young girl finding it badly done. But when it was Lise's turn to sign, she showed him how gauche he had been. So, when the clerk gave her the pen, she stopped, saying in a voice more than a little mocking:

"Pardon. Let me take off my glove."

And her glove removed, she signed with her very slender, white hand.

Léonce understood. He had signed with his glove on. To swear an oath before a judge with a gloved hand! Do you sign a marriage contract wearing a glove! Léonce thought about it and said to himself:

These people have definite sensitivity about what they consider good taste. What does a glove more or less matter to the sanctity of an oath or a signature on a contract? Nothing probably. And nevertheless, it seems there is more sin-

cerity in that naked hand lifted before God which affixes the signature of a man testifying to the truth That's one of the imperceptible sentiments you can't exactly understand, and which, nevertheless, exist.

Léonce was still thinking about it when they began to line up to leave. Monsieur Tirlot, the best man, and as a consequence grand master of the ceremonies, had gone downstairs to have the carriages brought to the door. Léonce therefore thought he could again offer his arm to Lise. She took it with a not very delighted expression, but without noticing that she had forgotten to put her glove back on. And there was Léonce walking beside her, his head lowered, his eyes attached to that charming hand gently holding on to his arm.

On first sight, Lise had seemed a beautiful, young girl. But everything in him struck first of all by dazzling youth and freshness, he hadn't thought about the fact that she possessed all the details of grace of the privileged, by mean of which women of society take their revenge for being pale, thin, and faded. He was looking at that very silky, very tapered hand as at a precious rarity which had gotten lost among the people of Auvergny, and little by little his glance stopped at a ring worn on her index finger which had a little gold plate on top. Engraved on that plate in imperceptible letters was a motto that Léonce was persistently trying to read. He was so absorbed that he didn't notice people had arrived downstairs and were getting into carriages. Lise didn't seem to be absorbed in such profound contemplation, because her pretty little fingers Léonce had been admiring so intently, were moving impatiently, and at last tapped an infinitely prolonged trill on Léonce's arm.

At this moment Léonce looked at Lise. At he started to lift his head, she looked at him, but with such a mocking expression that Léonce didn't want to be stopped doing so, and he said to her:

"It appears Mademoselle is a great musician?"

"And how is that?" Lise asked, with a little look of disdain.

"That's because Mademoiselle has just played a delightful dance rhythm on my arm."

Lise blushed, but this time with painful embarrassment. She quickly withdrew her naked arm from Léonce's arm, and no longer knew what she was doing nor what she was saying. She stammered very low:

"Oh! Pardon, Monsieur. I forgot to put my glove back on."

"As I forgot to take mine off," retorted Sterny. "You see, anybody can make a mistake."

Lise didn't find anything to answer. The footboard of a carriage having been let down in front of her, she got in quickly, so rapidly that Léonce was able to see her very narrow, arched foot, attached gracefully to her very dainty ankle. Sterny wanted to get in beside her, but he had the good sense not to do so.

Without being aware of it, Lise had gotten into Léonce's carriage. He backed off, saying quickly to the groom:

"Close the door and follow the other carriages." And he immediately bounded into the hired carriage holding Madame Laloine.

"Well!" exclaimed the mother. "And Lise, what have you done with her?"

"I put her in a carriage."

"With whom?" asked the prudent mother.

"Alas! By herself, Madame."

"What do you mean, by herself?"

"Yes, Madame. Without being aware of it, she got into my carriage, I believe."

"Ah!" said Madame Laloine. "I don't know what's wrong with her. She's been completely flustered since this morning."

"It's my coupe," Léonce said modestly. "It has only two seats and I didn't dare…"

Madame Laloine thanked Léonce for his discretion with a silent and solemn nod and added:

"She's going to be bored all alone."

Léonce secretly thought she wouldn't be bored.

Chapter V

In fact, Lise was at first astonished to find herself alone. But she took advantage of the fact to regain her composure from the embarrassment which Léonce's words had caused her. And answering her thoughts concerning the comments made to her, she shook her pretty head, saying to herself:

Bah! What does that matter to me?

That said, she began to examine that splendid coach upholstered in satin, the whole decorated with silk tassels and whose ride was so silent and gentle. She sat on one side and then on the other in order to feel the soft flexibility of the cushions, half raised one glass in order to admire its thickness, and began to smile with comfort in finding herself there.

Then she recalled that the beautiful carriages of the great ladies she saw riding in the Champs Elysees must have been resembled this one. And without thinking that she could occupy one as beautiful as the most noble among them, she leaned back in imitation of the nonchalant abandon with which they rested in a corner of their equipage.

The silly child leaned back like them, half reclining, pressing her cool cheek and her white shoulders against that silk which caressed her so gently with its suppleness, softly sinking into the movements of the vehicle, blinking her eyes to look down on the poor people on foot who turned their head to look at her, then, seeing at a distance someone she knew, gently biting her lower lip while smiling gently, and nodding imperceptivity to address a private greeting to a handsome horseman passing by, and in that little improvised daydream it so happened that the handsome horseman was Léonce Sterny.

Actually, who else but the handsome dandy could Lise imagine passing by on a beautiful English horse, gracefully riding beside her? It certainly was not Monsieur Tirlot, that she had seen fall off a donkey at a Montmorency party. So it was therefore Sterny to whom she addressed her sweetest smile, her softest look as he passed in front of her.

But imagine what must have been her amazement when she saw the actual face of Léonce, not mounted, but on foot and offering his hand to help her out of the carriage. She at first trembled at seeing herself thus surprised in this nonchalant position, like a child who has sat down in a seat that doesn't belong to him. And then, when Léonce said to her while helping her to descend:

"So, who were you greeting that way with such a sweet look and with such a sweet smile?"

Ashamed and very upset, she would have wished to go hide somewhere far off. So she entered the church sadly and slowly. And Léonce could see she took little interest in the ceremony taking place. Lise didn't notice out of the corner of her eyes the face of the bride nor the embarrassed behavior of the groom. She didn't follow with curiosity the ring to see if it slipped across the second knuckle of the finger, which predicted obedience. Lise prayed, and sincerely prayed. You would have said that there was remorse in her little heart and that she was asking God real pardon for her sin.

God gave it to her because at the end she rose calm, happy, strong. And just as they passed into the sacristy she turned toward Sterny, who was watching her with marked attention, and without seeming to be aware of it, she walked up to him, took his arm, and with a very different tone than the one in which she had spoken to him up until that time:

"All this must bore you a great deal, Monsieur?"

"Bore me! Why?"

"Because this upsets your habits and your pleasures, but you will very soon be delivered."

Chapter VI

Up until then Sterny, despite the urging of Prosper Gobillou and Monsieur Laloine, had kept in reserve the resolution not to stay one minute after the signing at the church. All the grace, even all the beauty of Lise, by occupying him a great deal, hadn't made him decide to brave the boredom of a bourgeois wedding, because he had understood perfectly that to have admired that beautiful child some few hours more would not have led him to anything.

But it seemed to him that he was being given a kind of dismissal by Lise's words. He therefore thought, and justly so, that he wasn't the one who would be delivered from boredom, and he didn't want to accept that way of being evicted. Therefore, he answered Lise.

"I'm experiencing no boredom, Mademoiselle, doing a proper thing which Prosper seems to have wanted and was acceptable to him. If it isn't so for everybody, I'm not the one who made a mistake; it's your brother-in-law. And he's the one you need to be scolded for my presence."

This time also Lise was very annoyed at having brought on herself that reprimand made with serious politeness and to which she couldn't respond because Léonce immediately took leave of her and retired into a corner of the sacristy. Lise hid among her young friends, not listening to their whispered chatter. She was completely absorbed in her thoughts when another girl pushed her shoulder sharply, saying:

"Look!"

She looked and saw Léonce, who was signing.

He took off his glove, the girl added in a little triumphal tone as if to congratulate Lise on the success of the lesson she had given the handsome Marquis.

Léonce, who had heard the exclamation, glanced toward Lise and met her look which had something uneasy in it.

Lise felt as if by some unspoken instinct that something had occurred between her and the young man, something that should not have been so, and when it was her turn to sign, her eyes were full of tears, her hand trembled, and when her mother, who was near her, asked her what was wrong, she answered:

"Nothing, nothing, a thought."

And taking advantage of the alarm she had caused her mother, she clung to her arm.

"Take me in your carriage Mama," she said in the voice of a child who is afraid and is asking for protection.

"Come! Come! My poor Lise," her mother said to her, embracing her and leading her into a little corner, while the serious men of the assembly smiled at each other with a capable expression, while the young people looked on without understanding, and while Léonce, in a corner, said to himself:

Most certainly I'll go back for the dinner and the dance.

Everyone went downstairs and Lise watched Léonce get into his carriage. The coachman, humiliated by having been so long in the bad company of hired carriages, began to make the horses rear in such a way that it was feared he would break everything; he then disappeared quickly. Lise breathed a great sigh and, getting back in the carriage, she found herself comfortable for the first time since the morning. She began to talk about the beautiful outfit she was going to wear for the evening. But in the middle of that important discussion, she suddenly raised her hand to her neck.

"Ah! *Mon Dieu!* I've lost my medallion. *Mon Dieu! Mon Dieu!* I had it; I'm sure."

"It might have fallen at the Mayor's office; maybe it fell at the church, maybe in a carriage."

"Ah!" said Lise, Hopefully it wasn't in that of Monsieur Sterny.

"Why?" her mother asked her. "He'll find it and return it to us."

"Then he's coming back?"

"He promised us."

Lise didn't answer, but she became sad again, didn't talk any more and thought that her dress, that she had at first believed so ravishing, perhaps wasn't as charming as she had thought. But Lise wasn't of an age nor of a personality for such a preoccupation to last a very long time and she was scarcely in the house before she had put aside all her vague fears, and she announced to herself:

Ah! No. I want to be happy today.

And without the need of any more long arguments, she got rid of the thought of the handsome Marquis and promised herself to amuse herself at his expense just as if he were any other young man.

As for Léonce, as soon as he was alone, he again hesitated to reappear at the wedding.

However high an opinion he had of himself, he was well aware that there was nothing that day for him near that little girl, and that day couldn't have a tomorrow. What would he do in that family of pen makers? And if no one dared show him the door, how would he be received there?

Decidedly, that made no sense. The best thing for him to do was to write a letter of excuse when he returned home and to eat dinner at six o'clock at the Cafe de Paris instead of going to the Cadran-Bleu where the wedding party was.

But this logic reached Sterny's head only through the image of Lise, and that image was so charming!

Chapter VII

It would be hard to describe all the dreams that passed through the dandy's head as he recalled that precious beauty: to make that beautiful girl fall in love with him, to snatch her away from her family; to fight with some unknown brother, even submit to a scandalous lawsuit against her family, get himself talked about in the newspapers, be found guilty of seduction by the law courts and be found innocent by society, for whom such a marvelous beauty made such a crime excusable, to find in that passion a reputation that would be the despair of all his friends. All that tempted him greatly, but almost immediately he measured the obstacles, counted the insurmountable difficulties, and put such an idea very far away, not as sinful, but as impossible.

Finally he had settled on the position of not returning when he saw on the cushion of his carriage a little golden medallion suspended on a slender, small cord of hair. That was exactly like the one Lise had on her ring. Like it, that one carried a motto which said: *What you want to do, you can do.*

At this moment, the dandy looked himself in the face and found himself completely contemptible and unimportant.

What! A little girl from the Rue Saint-Martin dared give herself as a motto: What you want to do, you can do. And he, a dandy, didn't feel he had the strength either to will anything or do anything!

Pardieu! He said to himself. *I will wish and I will act!!*

And to encourage himself in that noble resolution, he recalled all the women he had seduced or taken away from his friends.

Nevertheless, having gone over everything, he found that none of the methods that he had succeeded with right up to that time could be used in his new enterprise, and that he would have to find something else.

In the midst of all that, he arrived at his house, where he found installed four or five of his friends, heatedly arguing about the unconstitutionality of allowing government horses to race at the Champs-de-Mars.

Sterny's arrival put an end to the argument.

Seeing him, the fat beau Lingart, the chiropodist we spoke about, swaggered up acting important.

"Well?"

"Well! I lost," retorted Aymar de Rabut, the artistic dandy.

"How the devil!" added Marinet, the son of the pottery maker. "So how the devil are you going to bet against this great gambler? You know very well that he knows about good business deals, and he just has to touch the worst thing

70

for it to turn into something good as soon as there's something in it for him."

"Oh, yes, I'm rather fortunate," said Lingart, in a tone that meant "I'm rather clever," while licking with the tip of his tongue the few hairs of his beard near the corner of his mouth.

"So what's this about?" Sterny asked.

"It's about the fact," said Lingart, "that we're having dinner at the Rocher de Cancale, and that it's Aynar de Rabut who's treating us."

"So there was a bet?" asked Léonce, who pointed his ears like a warhorse who hears the trumpet.

"Yes," said Aymar de Rabut. "I don't know how that happened. I maintained for an hour that you would be bored to death at your marriage, that the men and the women would weary you to death and finally I was the one who bet that you would let yourself get entangled with the family of the future bride and groom and that you'd stay for the dinner and the dance. And it was Lingart who bet you'd come back."

"But when I tell you," exclaimed Marinet, "that if you go to get him to repay a hundred louis, and he doesn't want to pay them, he will prove to you as clearly as two and two make four that you owe him ten thousands francs."!

"Ah bah!" said Lingart, "and do you think it's perfectly clear that two and two make four?"

They looked at him as if he had said something stupid. But he added with an arrogance of nonsense so stupendous that he astounded those assembled.

"All right! Kindly prove to me that two and two make four."

"All this, my dear fellow, is pure Odry.* "

"There's a little bit of Odry, but I offer to bet twenty-five louis that none of you can prove to me that two and two make four."

"Pardieu!" said Aymar de Rabut, "that doesn't need to be proved; that is, because…"

He stopped and Lingart continued with a triumphant expression.

"Well! Why is that?"

He waited for an answer that didn't come and continued in a doctoral tone.

"Go order our dinner, and…"

"And let it be splendid," said Sterny, laughing, "because it's Lingart who's paying."

"How's that?" asked the gambler.

"Because Aymar won. I'm going back to the dinner and I'll stay for the dance."

"Is that to make me lose?" asked Lingart.

At these words, Sterny's conscience as a gambler was troubled and he reflected. Then he said:

---

* Jacques-Charles Odry, 1778/1781-1853, famous clown, created character of Bilboquet.

"I call off the bet."

"Why do that?"

"That's because when I came in here, I wasn't too sure what I would do, and I still don't know what I would have done if you hadn't talked about a bet."

"And for what reason did you suddenly decide?"

"None. I just can't do anything else."

"Why is that?" asked Lingart.

"Ah! That can't be proved anymore than two and two make four," Sterny answered.

"Nevertheless you've proved it to yourself, since you were doubting it."

"I say! You've become terribly boring, with your mania for pontificating."

"He's practicing for the Chamber of Deputies," said Marinet.

Lingart, who had just spent thirty thousand francs to buy three votes, bit his lips and pretended to shrug his shoulders. They began to feel sorry for Sterny, who went along with it with the best grace in the world and didn't pay much attention so long as it was only about himself. But it happened that the conversation casually drifted to the daily occupation of those gentlemen. They talked about a girl who had shown up in the Opera corridors the night before, and that they proclaimed delightful.

From there, they started in on all the details of that young beauty, whom Sterny himself had applauded. By making a rather ordinary inventory of his memories, he found that praise turned everything to Lise's advantage. In fact, what was admired about that perfect beauty? An almost pretty face, almost elegant hands, a corseted figure, a foot cruelly confined to make it look small, while with Lise everything was truly perfect, sincerely beautiful. The daughter of the pen maker became each moment more charming in Léonce's mind. And by another coincidence he began to repent of the vague ideas of seduction he had had about her, because the artistic dandy, Aymar, exclaimed in the middle of the conversation:

"I say," Lingart, "I hope you'll leave that little girl alone?"

"Yes," said the fat beau, "yes, until after her debut."

A very particular meaning must have appeared on Lingart's face, because it caused Sterny a movement of disgust. It would be hard for us to explain the mystery of that sentence. But Sterny was thinking that if he found it odious that if they were putting off the fall of a girl of the theatre until a time set in advance for her to be worth the trouble of being seduced, he was guilty in another way. He himself was thinking about that of a child who at least didn't face the danger. But what happens to people who have a conscience easily salved happened to Sterny. He persuaded himself so well that he wouldn't succeed that he believed himself permitted to attempt success without too many scruples.

They soon left and as six o'clock struck, Sterny entered the Cadran-Bleu.

Chapter VIII

Love is a beautiful passion for storytellers like us. It has this excellent advantage; we can carry it along at the speed we wish without anyone asking us to account for the verisimilitude of its actions.

It's in love most of all that the most unlikely things are the truest: sudden and irresistible passions which burst into the heart at the sight of an unknown being, like the light that God commanded to be, and it was; passions slow and strong which penetrate the soul with imperceptible progress, like heat into metal, without there being an apparent difference between the minute which precedes and the minute which follows, until both become boiling from the cool state they were in; and those which go by leaps and bounds, dashing foolishly ahead, then recoiling with timidity; and those which go obscurely back and forth; those which beg and those which demand. All are true in their greatest variations, in their most apparent contradictions.

All this, you understand, without taking into account personalities, bending the stiffest, making the weakest stand upright, tyrannizing the most over-bearing.

Now that's why Léonce returned to the Cadran-Bleu.

When he entered, no one had arrived except the newly-married couple and Monsieur Laloine, who had just started having the dinner preparations set up. Prosper at first wanted to leave Sterny in the company of Madame Laloine, but Sterny so insistently begged both of them not to bother with him, that they went on about their affairs. He remained alone in the small room adjoining the big party room, while the father-in-law and the son-in-law went to check out the dance floor. But, really, people will ask us, is this actually Léonce de Sterny you're talking about, a dandy who knows all the advantages of arriving late, who's arrived before the time to sit down at table, like a dumpy shopkeeper or a literary man invited to the home of a great lord? Truly, yes, it's Léonce de Sterny, one of the maddest of his group. And do you know what he was doing while his hosts were absent? He was walking around the table reading each place card to find out where he would be seated. And when he saw he had been placed between Madame Laloine and some unknown lady, he changed his place card to steal that of Monsieur Tirlot, and found himself seated beside Lise.

Take a good look at him, trembling with fear of being surprised in the middle of his substitution, like a child who puts his finger into a plate of cream to see if it tastes good. Look at him, when a waiter enters, suddenly turning toward the wall to look at an old engraving of Aeneas carrying his father Anchises on his back. Then, when the waiter has left, finishing his clever maneuver that he would have thought the most utter stupidity if he had read it that morning in a newspaper insert.

Nevertheless, he had succeeded, and now he's worried about the success of his ruse.

Monsieur Laloine comes back in and wants to inspect the place card distribution one last time. Léonce immediately goes up to him and begins talking about bird feathers to trim writing pens. Prosper appears and wants to make sure everything is properly done, and Léonce throws him off the track by departing so far from his usual self as to make bad jokes about how much work Prosper's done on such a day.

He chats, he talks, he laughs. He asks Monsieur Laloine, who find him charming, for some tobacco. With him, he pokes fun at Prosper's acting busy. He sends Prosper to help the ladies getting out of carriages which have stopped at the door. Prosper dashes there. It's a gentleman and a lady who ask for a private room. Prosper comes back and Sterny unleashes a tirade to him about the morality of private dining rooms.

What's he up to? What does he want? I tell you truly, in love nothing resembles reality, because, look, there's our dandy who's gone to a great deal of trouble for something. Well! Why, Mon Dieu! To sit next to a girl.

As success wipes out the worst actions and almost wipes out ridicule, then Léonce was right because he succeeded.

Everybody arrived. They greeted each other. They talked to each other. They had to be served. That was Gobillou's job while Monsieur Laloine was obliged to stay at the door to greet guests. But Lise must be curious. She would probably want to know where she would be seated. And she would be surprised. So there's the dandy who stands between the door which opens from the little waiting room into the dining room, very confident that Lise wouldn't dare go in before him because when she arrived with her mother and her sister, Madame Laloine very graciously said to Sterny:

"What! Already here, Monsieur le Marquis?"

And he answered, looking at Lise.

"One mistake is enough for one day."

Lise, who had arrived glowing and proud, felt the reproach and retired angrily into a corner of the waiting room. No one had spoiled pleasure for her so persistently as Monsieur de Sterny, and for such a small thing.

Léonce seemed to her unsupportable. So, a very amusing little comedy took place when it was time to sit down around the table. Léonce, who knew his seat, made his way there and stood behind his chair, while Lise was looking on the other side.

"Over there!" Prosper cried out to her, pointing to the side of Léonce, whom Prosper was very surprised to find at the end of his finger.

Prosper exchanged a look with Monsieur Laloine, who pinched his lips together in a way that meant:

My son-in-law is an idiot.

On the other side, Madame Laloine, who was counting on being near the Marquis, gave Monsieur Tirlot a startled look when he, proud of the place of honor he had been given, sat down beside her, looking proud of meriting the seat assigned him.

Lise came forward timidly, not knowing how she should behave, because she had seen all that imperceptible dialog of looks. As for Léonce, his eyes were fixed on the ceiling, he was seeing nothing; he was looking at nothing. He was a complete stranger to what was happening.

The embarrassment was coming to an end, however. He heard Monsieur Laloine say to his daughter:

"Come now, Lise. Go take your seat."

The tone in which these words were pronounced forced resignation to the clumsy mistake of Gobillou and Léonce thought everyone would attribute it to Prosper. But when he moved his chair to make way for Lise, she greeted him with such a hard look that he saw very well she understood that her brother-in-law was innocent of that mistake.

At the first sentence he tried, Léonce recognized that Lise had decided not to answer him except with monosyllables. But he had two hours ahead of him, and that was more than he needed to fulfill that resolution.

First of all, he let the poor child compose herself and gather confidence. To accomplish that, he paid no attention to her. But he became extremely attentive to the fat gentleman who was seated on the other side of the young girl, and who was none other than the fat haberdasher who had intruded himself that morning with the question of sugar cane.

Sterny dauntlessly continued the discussion, which was forced to pass in front of or behind the young girl, but in a way that she would not lose a word of it. It was such that it would have bored a Deputy himself. Finally, Lise couldn't help showing her impatience by very small, significant movements. But Sterny was without pity. He went on, warming up to the subject, and causing his questioner to warm up and exert himself in return, so much so that Monsieur Laloine, who saw them speaking with such heat, exclaimed:

"What are you talking about, gentlemen?"

"About sugar cane and beets," Lise answered in an irritated voice.

"Ah!" said Monsieur Laloine, and satisfied with such a virtuous conversation, he thought about something else.

But the moment was badly chosen, because immediately, Sterny, hoping this was the moment to begin the attack, spoke to his questioner, saying:

"Really, Monsieur, I fear we have bored Mademoiselle a great deal. We'll continue out conversation later."

"Gladly," said the haberdasher, who noticed he had let the first course be served without touching it, and he wanted to make up for lost time.

Nevertheless, Lise made no observation, and the fat haberdasher continued between two mouthfuls:

"Isn't your mother right, Mademoiselle Lise, that men are no longer gallant? And so here we are, two cavaliers beside a pretty woman, and we don't find anything better to do than to talk about molasses instead of saying nice things to her. But me, I can be excused…a papa…I forgot myself, but this gentleman, who's a young man, must have a lot to say."

Then find some nice things, animal, Léonce, who didn't know what to say, was thinking. And seeing the young girl's disdainful little pout, he ended up offering her something to drink.

She accepted and thanked him and the conversation didn't go any further.

Well, the dandy said to himself, *I've become as dumb as a rock. I'd bet Monsieur Tirlot would do better than I'm doing.*

Then he made a desperate effort, but one of the most ordinary. He had to talk about himself in order for her to take notice of him and he said:

"Really, Mademoiselle, I'm very unhappy."

"And why's that, Monsieur?"

"I've had the honor of seeing you only twice and I've already found the way to displease you three or four times."

"Me, Monsieur?" Lise asked, looking surprised.

"You. First of all this morning, by arriving too late; at the Mayor's office by not taking off my glove; here, perhaps, by arriving too soon…and…"

"Well, noble lion, by not having tried this time to be subtle, you have succeeded." Lise had, in fact, understood what he meant to say.

"And…?" looking at him, she asked.

"And," added Léonce, with a real young man's expression, "in stealing Monsieur Tirlot's place."

Lise blushed, but while smiling.

Chapter IX

First of all, she had guessed correctly, which flattered her, and then the Marquis, to be near her, had acted like a schoolboy, and that flattered her more. But this time there was some reason to be afraid, because for what purpose had the handsome Marquis approached her? The smile begun disappeared immediately to give way to great embarrassment.

Lise was too innocent to think of attempts at seduction. But in her position as a member of the petite bourgeoisie, faced with an aristocrat, she told herself: *He wants to make fun of me, and she put on a little prim and prudish expression.*

"You can certainly see that I've displeased you," Léonce said.

"Ah! *Mon Dieu!* Monsieur, you or Monsieur Tirlot, it's all the same thing."

Léonce made a face. The analogy was cruel. Then he added, somewhat impertinently:

"I don't think so."

"Ah!" said Lise, who thought he was excessively fatuous.

"Yes," said Léonce, skirting the pitfall rather well. "I believe you would have preferred Monsieur Tirlot."

Lise didn't answer.

"Is he one of your relatives?" Léonce asked.

"No, Monsieur."

"He's one of your friends?"

"No, Monsieur."

"Then he's one of Prosper's friends!"

"Yes, Monsieur."

"So much the better," said Léonce, "there'll be an even exchange and Prosper will be pardoned for his friend Sterny in favor of his friend Tirlot."

"Oh!" Lise said, "you aren't Prosper's friend."

"Me? And why not? I like him a lot."

"Oh! That doesn't mean anything."

"I'm very ready to help him."

"I don't doubt it, but that's not what I mean."

"And I believe he has a great deal of affection for me."

"I'm sure of that," Lise said, "but you know you're not friends."

"But, then why?"

"Because," Lise said, "you're Monsieur le Marquis de Sterny, and he's Prosper Gobillou, who manufactures writing pens. "

"That's very wicked, Mademoiselle, what you've just said," Léonce answered, with a liberal expression.

"And why is that?"

"Isn't that the same as saying that the title I wear makes me proud, haughty, maybe impertinent?"

"Ah! Monsieur."

To believe that is to believe that I don't know how to appreciate the honor and the probity of those who don't have such a title. That's almost to make me regret having been born in what's called an elevated rank, as if we don't live in a time when each one is valued only through his merit and his works.

Ah! lion, master lion, what's happened to your noble gentleman's mane? What! There you are uttering sentimental sentences from the Constitutionelle, or from melodrama, and that in a serious voice. Where are your friends to laugh at you as you would laugh at yourself if you could see yourself??"

But there you are, taking the thing seriously, because Lise answers in a friendly tone:

"I thank you for Prosper, for what you've just told me. That would please him very much."

"Oh! Prosper has known me a long time. We were children together. He's not like you. He doesn't think that I'm a dandy, a lion."

"What's that--a lion?" Lise asked, laughing.

"Oh!" Sterny continued, "those are young men in society who think they're clever because they mock everything, who pretend to despise everything which isn't part of their circle, and who have no other occupation except doing nothing."

The lion was denying his religion and his brothers.

"Ah!" exclaimed Lise, "I know what you mean. But I ask you to believe that I don't have such a bad opinion of you, Monsieur le Marquis."

"Not totally as bad, but hardly favorable, however."

"I can't tell...I don't know..." said Lise, hesitating.

"Ah! You owe me an answer. What's your opinion of me?"

Lise still hesitated, and finally she said, looking the lion in the face, with an expression of childish mischievousness.

"Well, I'll tell you, if you'll tell me why you took Monsieur Tirlot's place."

Léonce was embarrassed. The answer would have been decisive. He was fortunate to find something stupid, and answered:

"I don't know."

Lise burst out with loud laughter, which made the whole assembly turn their heads.

"What's wrong with you, Lise?" … "What's wrong with you, Mademoiselle?" came from all sides of the assembly.

Still laughing, Lise said: "It's because Monsieur le Mar—"

"Oh!" said Léonce, very low, trembling that Lise would recount his prank. "Oh! Don't betray me!"

"What is it," people continued to ask.

"Oh! It's nothing, just a thought, "she answered.

"Well, really, Lise!" her mother said to her, with a frown that carried with it a whole sermon.

"Eh! Let her laugh," said Monsieur Laloine. "That's the age for it. She'll have to be serious soon enough."

The time had already come. Lise felt that she had gone too far, when Léonce said to her, very low:

"I thank you for having kept our secret."

"What secret, Monsieur?"

"The one about the trick that let me sit near you."

"Oh! That had no importance," she said coldly.

"And nevertheless that meant a lot to me."

And immediately he began painting a picture, gay, grotesque, amusing, about his campaign, his alarms when he heard a noise at the door. Lise listened to him, half laughing, half annoyed, and finally answered:

"And all that without knowing why?"

"Ah! I know why, however," Léonce, almost moved, said.

"Ah!" Lise said.

"But I don't dare tell you."

"You, tell me!"

"Yes, tell you!"

"You're making fun of me, Monsieur le Marquis."

"If I tell you, will you hold it against me?"

"But…," Lise continued. "I don't know. It depends on what you tell me…Ah! no," she added quickly, "I don't want to know."

Therefore she knew.

But that didn't satisfy the lion. He wanted to talk, if only to be listened to. He began and said very low:

"It's because this morning…"

"Look! Look!" Lise said, interrupting him sharply. "Monsieur Tirlot is going to sing."

"This gentleman is very ridiculous," said Lénoce, very annoyed at seeing himself stopped when he thought he believed himself coming to the beginning of a declaration.

"Ridiculous!" Lise said to him with a dignified look, "And why, Monsieur le Marquis?"

Léonce saw his mistake. He had reverted to being a lion without knowing it. And once again, embarrassed, he responded rather quickly. "I don't like Monsieur Tirlot."

"And why not?"

"I have something against him."

"But the reason?"

Léonce began to laugh at himself, and saving himself as well as he could from the mistake into which he had gotten entangled, he answered:

"First of all because he was the best man and had the right to give you his arm this morning."

"It seems to me that right didn't help him very much," Lise said, smiling.

"And then because they seated him at the table next to you."

"And he really kept his seat!" Lise said, still smiling.

"And finally because he'll dance the first dance with you."

"Alas! He forgot to ask me."

"In that case, I'll take it."

"What do you mean, you'll take it?"

"Yes," Léonce said with open gaiety. "I want to take everything away from him. And if I were sitting beside him, I would steal every thing off his plate and drink his wine."

"Ah! Poor Monsieur Tirlot," said Lise, laughing with real ease.

"We'll dance the first dance together, won't we?"

"Since it's agreed on."

"This Monsieur Tirlot," Sterny continued, carried away by the success of his gaiety, "I would even like to steal his song."

"That would be difficult," said Lise. "He's beginning."

"That's all right," said Sterny, "I want to compete with him."

"Really!"

"You'll see!"

Monsieur Tirlot began. There were four couplets, which lacked neither measure nor rhyme and which praised:

1. Madame Laloine;
2. Monsieur Laloine;
3. Mademoiselle Laloine, now Madame Gobillou
4. Gobillou

There was something there for everybody. There was applause and touching compliments. Monsieur Tirlot triumphed. Lise was impressed; she was applauding. She was sorry she had stolen his dance from him.

But Sterny was in good form and he gently touched Lise's shoulder, saying to her:

"Say that I want to sing also."

Lise got up, held up her pretty hand and everyone stopped talking, waiting for some new song by the young girl. But when she asked for silence for Monsieur le Marquis, there were cries of astonishment and congratulations on his friendliness.

Sterny pulled out all the stops. He could be ridiculous even for these bourgeois. It was so to himself and he felt it. He threw himself head-first into danger and wanted to bring on the catastrophe.

"Pardon, gentlemen," he said. "This is not a song, but couplets, which it seems to me were lacking in Monsieur Tirlot's very special song. "

Monsieur Tirlot bowed.

"Let's hear it! Let's hear it! they said on all sides."

Sterny immediately began to perform, almost as swaggeringly as Monsieur Tirlot himself. Addressing himself first to Monsieur and Madame Laloine:

> "The sacred right to make people happy
> Is so beautiful that God envies us."

And pointing to Prosper Gobillou and his wife:

> "And like you, when two have been made happy
> That's enough, our task is completed"

To Monsieur and Madame Laloine, alone

> "And, nevertheless, this blessed right
> Is not finished for you on the earth."

And turning toward Lise,

> "Because, when seeing Lise, everyone says to himself:
> They still have one more to make happy."

Oh! Lion, what shame! a couplet improvised at the table, at a sanctified marriage! Lion, what a little boy you are! Poor lion.

Léonce didn't have time to think, because no sooner had he finished the couplets than the whole table broke out in applause, in stomping, in bravos. Lise, who wasn't expecting that conclusion, hid her embarrassment by ducking her head. Madame Laloine, all in tears, got up to go hug Lise, saying to Monsieur Tirlot:

"It's true, Monsieur Tirlot, you forgot my Lise!"

Monsieur Laloine, full of emotion, came into the middle of these embraces, and held out his hand to Léonce, saying from the bottom of his heart:

"Thank you, Monsieur le Marquis. Thank you! Thank you!"

Then the mother thanked him, and they congratulated him from all sides. That caused a moment of confusion where everybody got up from the table, while Gobillou was shouting:

"To the salon! To the salon! There are already people there!"

Léonce offered his arm to Lise. She took it, but he felt her hand trembling. She was confused, embarrassed; but she was neither sad nor annoyed.

"Do you also hold my couplets against me?" Léonce asked her.

"Oh! no," she said softly, "that pleased my father and mama. "

"And you?"

"Me? I think it was very pretty," she said, lowering her eyes.

And she gently took away her hand to go meet some of her young girlfriends who were in the salon that Monsieur and Madame Laloine had already greeted and to whom they had already explained the reason for the loud applause which shook the Cadran-Bleu.

"Is it true?" taking Lise aside, the young girls asked. "Is it true the handsome Marquis made couplets for you?"

If that had been asked in a friendly voice, Lise would perhaps have denied it. But they had pronounced, the handsome Marquis, with such an envious tone, that she answered with affectation.

"Yes, it's true."

"It seems you made his conquest," said one who was very ugly.

"And probably he made yours?"

"Who knows?" said Lise, who found her good friends very impertinent.

"And first of all," said another, "I'm going to get myself invited to dance for the whole evening so I can refuse him."

"Ah! That's not worth the trouble," said the ugly girl. "These aristocrats don't dance."

"They dance, Mesdemoiselles," said Sterny, who had approached quietly by going around a group of men. And he offered his hand to Lise, saying to her with profound respect:

"Mademoiselle hasn't forgotten she promised me the first dance?"

"No, Monsieur, no," Lise said, holding out her hand.

That hand was still trembling.

Chapter XI

Fortunately for Sterny, who had been so carried away by the charm that emanated from that beautiful child, and perhaps by his success also, that he hadn't had time to reflect on all he had just done. But he would perhaps have been terrified if he had had a moment of peace and quiet to consider what he had dared by going beyond his usual behavior. Fate would decide otherwise.

The orchestra had given the signal to begin the dance and Sterny took his place with Lise.

Lise was beautiful, beautiful as one dreams the angels are with the holy serenity of innocence and the guiltless peace of happiness. That beauty had astounded Sterny and he had contemplated it a long time with just the pleasure of the eyes, like a work that glorifies, you might say, the human form by show-ing how it can be magnificent and graceful.

But at this moment, Lise, trembling at his side seemed to him even more charming than he had yet seen her. On that very innocent face there was such an unspeakable expression of happiness, of fear, and of astonishment. Some-thing unaccustomed which delighted and frightened her was taking place in that child's heart. Her heart had just fluttered in her breast and it seemed to her that there was something in her being which had not yet lived and which was coming alive.

God has given that emotion twice to the woman, the first time she feels her-self loved and the first time she becomes a mother. But no paint brush, no pen can express the ecstasy spreading over Lise's face. And Sterny, who was look-ing at her, let it flow into him without himself being aware of the unknown intoxication which was overcoming him. He wanted to speak to her and his voice wouldn't come, and her voice hesitated as Leónce's did.

That whole dance passed thus between them. And it was only in conducting Lise back to her seat that Sterny thought he was going to be separated from her. So, he said to her very low:

"Does Mademoiselle waltz?"

"Oh! No, Monsieur," she answered, with a head shake meaning that a waltz was a pleasure beyond the hopes of a young girl.

"Then," Léonce continued, "I'll ask you for another quadrille."

"But I've already promised a great number of them," Lise continued. "But… but…Mama has allowed me to do the galoppe."

"Then it will be for a galoppe."

"Yes, the first," Lise said, "but until then, won't you dance with some other young ladies?"

"Only with you!"

"At least with my sister, please," Lise said in an uneasy and begging voice.

"With the bride? You're right. I thank you for reminding me of it," Léonce responded.

"And I thank you for agreeing," Lise said to him with a sweet smile of un-derstanding.

Léonce left her near her mother and went into another room. In spite of himself he was happy! Happy about what? About having troubled that little girl!

A poor triumph for a man whose lion eye had made intrepid women used to scoffing and daring everything, even scandal, tremble.

Chapter XII

Don't ask Léonce why he was happy. He wouldn't know how to tell you, because that emotion was as new to him as for Lise. He was thinking neither of examining it nor of fighting it. He found himself comfortable as he was. He looked at everything with a friendly eye and if sometimes he didn't see complete grace in the things that were happening, he found they had a good faith which charmed him. These people were sincerely having a good time.

He tried to stay far away from the dance floor where Lise was, but despite himself he returned and glanced between two men standing in the doorway. Lise was dancing, but she was not at the dance. She either kept her eyes lowered or she glanced rapidly and furtively around the salon.

Who was she looking for?

Léonce was afraid it wasn't for him, but when he saw that since he was there she was no longer glancing around, he felt a new happiness, a happiness so strong that in his turn he was afraid.

That fear couldn't remain unexplained in Léonce's heart as well as in Lise's heart. He wondered what he was experiencing and blushed at himself.

Ah, ça, he said to himself. *I'm acting like a child. I'm becoming very ridiculous. Their doctored wine has gone to my head. The devil take me if I'm not drunk! That's not possible.*

And to make sure that he wasn't a man to let himself be dominated by a childish emotion, he began to look at Lise.

Lise was dancing with a handsome young man with simple elegance, as handsome as the lion, and who was speaking to his partner with perfect self-assurance. He must have been telling her some rather interesting things, since she was listening to him carefully; he must have been rather well spoken, since she answered by little signs of agreement.

Seeing that, a complete revolution took place in Léonce's heart. He compared himself to someone. He compared himself to that man who could be a cotton fabric merchant and he found that nothing assured him he had an advantage over that man.

Léonce's disappointment was even crueler when he saw Lise's face tranquil, happy. The poor child had no other happiness than having seen Léonce glancing at her, than having felt a joy, a pride, a delight that she no longer feared, because he wasn't beside her, and the contact of his hand, the sound of his voice no longer made her tremble.

An odd doubt entered Sterny's heart.

Could that candid child be a behind the counter boutique coquette?

Ah! Really! You're too ambitious, my lovely. You're pretty, but your pretensions are too impertinent.

As he was thinking that, looking at Lise, Léonce's face took on an expression of haughtiness and disdain. Having looked at him at this moment, the sweet child was so surprised to see herself so regarded that she became pale and her eyes, fixed on Léonce, seemed to say:

Well! What's wrong with you! What have I done to you, Mon Dieu?

And immediately she was no longer listening to her dance partner and stumbled three times while dancing.

Léonce saw all that and wanted to see if it wasn't a game. He didn't want a man of his kind duped by a trick of a false Agnès.* Consequently, when the quadrille was finished, he put on his most self-assured air, the most indifferent, the most lion, and approached Lise and her mother. He said to Madame Laloine, without looking at Lise:

"Madame, I owe you a great number of apologizes for my thoughtlessness. When I got back to my house, I found this little cord of hair and this little golden medallion in my carriage. It must belong to someone of your guests and I forgot to return it to you, Madame."

At the words: "someone of your guests," Lise looked at Léonce as if to say to him: *Didn't you know that it was mine?*

"You see I was right to tell you that Monsieur le Marquis would return it to you."

"Ah! It belongs to Mademoiselle?" Léonce said in a cold tone, with a disdainful expression, handing her the little pendant.

"Yes, Monsieur," Lise said, stretching out her hand to take it, looking at Léonce as if saying to herself:

Am I mad?

Léonce gave it to her, holding it by the tips of his fingers.

"Give it to me," her mother said, "so I can fasten it around your neck."

"In just a minute," said Lise, hardly able to contain her impatience. And she wrapped it in her handkerchief, which was tightly gripped in her clasped hand.

Lise was pale and her lips trembled.

Léonce was satisfied with the test and continued with an affected politeness.

Mademoiselle hasn't forgotten that she is supposed to dance a galoppe with me?

"I don't know, Lise said in an unhappy voice. If Mama wishes…"

"With Monsieur le Marquis? Of course," said Madame Laloine.

The orchestra played the first measures of a galoppe.

---

* Allusion to Molière's innocent girl in *L'Ecole des Femmes*.

85

Lise gave her hand to Léonce. They stood up and went across the salon, while the crowd moved to give way to the dancers.

"Why didn't you want to put your charming necklace back on?"

"Ah! Charming! You don't mean what you're saying, but it's very important to me," Lise said with effort.

"Is it a souvenir, perhaps?"

"Ah! Yes, it's a good souvenir," she answered, lifting her eyes toward heaven.

"And the motto written on the pendant, you undoubtedly recall what it is?"

"Yes, Monsieur le Marquis," Lise replied with gentle dignity.

"What you want to do, you can do, that motto says."

"Yes, Monsieur le Marquis, 'What you want to do, you can do'," Lise repeated with a barely stifled sigh.

"You must have great confidence in your strength to adopt such a motto," Léonce added.

"It hasn't failed me right up to the present, and I hope it won't fail me," Lise answered with great emotion.

"Do you need it?"

"Aren't we going to dance, Monsieur?"

Léonce put one of his arms around the beautiful child and took in his other the hand in which she was holding the talisman.

They danced in this fashion, he, devouring her with his eyes; she, her eyes lowered, her face serious.

Suddenly, a tear fell from Lise's eyelashes and rolled down her cheek. Léonce was suddenly seized with unhappiness and led Lise into a little nearby room, and said to her:

"Have I offended you, Mademoiselle?"

"No, Monsieur, no."

"But why are you crying?"

"But I'm not crying, Monsieur."

"Listen, Mademoiselle, "Léonce said to her, in a tone full of frankness, "I don't know what I could have done or said to hurt you; but if that happened without my knowing it, I ask you to forgive me, and I swear to you that doing such a thing was very far from my heart."

Lise listened to him attentively and answered with a sad smile:

"Oh, *Mon Dieu*, look, Monsieur, don't pay any attention to what I say or what I do. You see, when I was a child, I was always so weak, so sickly, that no one corrected all my faults, and among those there has to be included a ridiculous sensitivity…silly…"

"But how could I have wounded it, that sensitivity?"

"Don't ask me that, Monsieur. Let's dance, I beg of you. I'm not angry with

you. I swear to you that I'm not angry with you, she said with a nervous movement and an expression of suffering."

Chapter XIII

They finished their galoppe and Léonce again took Lise back to her mother,
Almost immediately Monsieur Tirlot came forward to reclaim his dance, but
Lise said to him with a gentle request:

"Not yet, Monsieur Tirlot. I'm very ill. My heart is palpitating. I'm suffering
a great deal. I'm cold."

Sterny looked at her. She was paler and her lips were trembling convulsively.

Seeing that, her mother seemed very alarmed, and said to her very low:

"Come, come, my child."

"Yes, Mama, yes," she said to her in a broken voice.

And she was led out of the salon, leaning on her mother's arm.

"What's wrong with her?" asked Léonce, speaking to Monsieur Tirlot.

"Ah! *Mon Dieu!*" Monsieur Tirlot answered with an expression of sincere
pity: "It's always the same thing, terrible heart palpitations; the least fatigue
tires her, and a violent emotion could kill her."

Kill her! Léonce said to himself. *And I..., who knows? When I gave her that
disdainful look, when I so stupidly reminded her of that pendant that I knew
couldn't belong to anyone but her, and that she hadn't asked me to return, knowing that I had it, I perhaps terribly wounded that sensitive soul, which was happily giving in to a child-like success! Ah! Poor child! Poor child!...Ah! If I had
thought! That was stupid, an outrageous brutality.*

Chapter XIV

Léonce was angry with himself. To toy with the silliness of a little prude
who worked behind a counter, that could be amusing, but to shock, without
any reason, the sick sensitivity of such a beautiful child, and one the love surrounding her proved so good, so true, so naive, that was odious. Léonce found
himself guilty, beastly, brutal. He was furious with himself. So, it was with real
concern that he remained with some people at the door of the room where Lise
had taken refuge with her mother.

The young girl soon came out, still pale, but calm, serene.

She saw Léonce's alarmed look and her finger, resting gently on her breast, showed Sterny the gold pendant which she had just put back around her neck, and the gesture meant:

What you want to do, you can do.

The smile which accompanied this movement was so sweet, so resigned, that Léonce was touched.

That child had suffered, greatly suffered, and for him, probably because of him.

Sterny would have liked to ask her forgiveness, his heart begging, so as to make her totally understand that he was ashamed and saddened to have wounded her.

Lise had sat down again near her mother and wasn't supposed to dance anymore.

Léonce no longer had a way to approach her just by herself. He was ill at ease. That crowd weighed on him, not just as an assemblage of ridiculous caricatures, as he could have considered them the evening before, but now they clutched his heart. At that moment he wanted to cry out, curse; he almost wanted to weep.

That feeling came over him so powerfully that he was on the point of leaving.

But he didn't want to leave without making known his excuses and his repentance to that weak and sweet creature that he had caused to suffer. Having approached Madame Laloine, he said to her in a serious voice:

"If I had been just someone invited to this party, Madame, I would have thought I could leave without telling you good-bye. But I was Prosper's witness. And I hope you will accept my thanks for having admitted a gentleman into your family who is almost part of mine."

"I thank you, Monsieur," Madame Laloine said to him in an emotional voice, while Lise looked at him with gentle emotion, "I thank you, because only your affection for Prosper could inspire you with such flattering words toward little people like us."

"Madame," said Léonie, "I beg you to believe in the sincere and real respect that I bear toward you and all the persons in your family."

Saying these words, he turned toward Lise and bowed deeply without lifting his eyes toward her. So he could not see the radiant look which lit up Lise's face, but he saw her hand make an involuntary movement as to take his hand and thank him.

Then he left without wanting to see Lise and it was only at the other end of the salon that he turned around. She had her hand resting on her breast and was watching him. He caught her eye. Lise didn't turn her eyes away. They looked thus at each other a long time, both forgetting where they were, both feeling they could read the heart of the other. Madame Lelonie spoke to her daughter. She seemed to awaken from a dream, but before turning toward her mother, a gentle nod had said to Léonce:

"Good-bye and thank you."

The lion left. He was insane, overcome, stupid. He wanted to collect himself and could not. That image of Lise appeared so candid, so pure, saying to him:

Unfortunate man! Why treat you as you treated me? Why insult what you felt to be good, holy, delightful, as you insulted my joy?

And there was Léonce moving about in that carriage where Lise's soft body had leaned, trying to see if a trace of her was still there.

The unhappy man, he had found one and he could have kept it. And to act insulting, he had given it back to someone who wouldn't have asked for it back. He was now sure of that.

As he was in that state of fury against himself, his carriage stopped and the door opened. He got out and looked around. He was in front of the dandies' club. He hesitated to enter, then he walked up the steps rapidly, telling himself:

If that dolt Lingart tells me one bad joke, I'll hit him. And in his anger, he sat down at a gambling table, lost five hundred louis, after having amazed everyone by his bad humor, he who was usually such a good player, and returned to his house at daybreak, thinking no more about his five hundred louis than about his last mistress. And he was saying to himself:

I will see her again; I want to see her; but how?

Chapter XV

No man was ever more perplexed than Sterny was to find a convenient way to see Lise again. By the words he had said to Madame Laloine, he had as much as taken definite leave of that family, who were not at his social level and with whom he could not continue to have social contact without their being surprised. *A la rigeur,* he could make a courtesy call, but that was all he had a right to do. He certainly thought about meeting Lise in church, but in our so little pious century, it's not unusual to see a man like Léonce find such a profanation repugnant..

Just because he never went into a church to pray, he wouldn't have wanted to go into one in pursuit of a woman. What a gentleman of Louis XIV would do, one hour after he left the confessional booth, what a Catholic Spaniard still would do at the moment he had just approached the holy table, the non-believer Léonce wouldn't want to do. It was in all his scrupulous purity that the atheist Canillac explained to the Abbé Dubois in such a pleasant way in a similar circumstance. It was a matter of a rendezvous with a certain abbess, at night, in the chapel at Versailles.

"Go ahead, if you wish to," Canillac said to the Cardinal. "You're a minister of God. It's between the two of you. As for me, I don't know Him well enough to take such liberties in his house."

We wouldn't know how to tell where that difference comes from, but what's sure, it exists for nations and for men. It's in the most fanatical countries that amorous intrigues usually take place in churches. And if, in our France, which isn't very religious, the temple of God still serves as a cover for some adventure of this type, you can be sure that it takes place between people who consider what they're doing a sin. They believe this so much that you would be tempted to believe, like Canillac, that they've set up an account with God and that the assiduity of their praises merits them some indulgence on his part.

However that may be, Sterny rejected the idea of following Lise into the church, not only for himself, but still more for her. There was a delicacy as chaste and as elegant as she was in all that young girl inspired in him. If on one hand he didn't want to give Lise a bad opinion of him in seeming to follow her shamelessly in the middle of her prayers, on the other hand he feared touching by his presence that virginity she must carry to the foot of the altar.

As for utilizing the secondary resources which are available to every man who has gold and audacity, and which he doesn't fear using against the greatest ladies, they horrified him.

He could certainly meet Lise at Prospero's, but going to Prosper's house was almost as improper as going to Monsieur Laloine's. He had nothing to do there, and certainly they would try to find out the reason for his visits. If they managed to discover them, he knew he would be as ashamed of them as of a wicked deed.

However, for several days, and without being too aware of his hopes, Léonce gave up all usual activities. He went to take a walk in the Tuileries.

He told himself: *This is the place the Parisian bourgeois go to take an outing. Perhaps he could find Lise there.*

He went, the same evening, to three or four little theatres, which, according to him, must be the favorite productions of the St. Denis merchant. It was that for him based on the boredom he experienced there. It was the season for the Beaux Arts painting expositions. He found everybody there, except Lise.

Really, he then he told himself, *This is madness. What do I hope for? I don't have any hopes. I don't want to have any.*

He repeated that to himself every day, and every day he had a more ardent desire to see Lise again. Everything that had amused and charmed him before did nothing more than disturb him without satisfying him. He was like a man, accustomed to the noise of the city, to its heavy atmosphere, to its artificial light, to its activity, to its thousand happenings, suddenly transported to a divine countryside illuminated by a soft light, where there floated a vague celestial harmony, where the pure air refreshed the breast, where everything reached the heart like an invisible caress. That man certainly didn't want to live constantly in these thoughts where nothing could satisfy the passion in which he lived. But in an hour of lassitude, he wanted at any cost to go breathe that air, hear those murmurs, and dream under those fresh, perfumed shades, where a man could find the youth of his senses again, as Léonce had again found the youth of his soul near him.

But that hope seemed on the point of escaping Léonce, when one morning his valet presented him with a calling card. It was Prosper's. (It was scarcely ten o'clock, and he was already out of bed, dressed, because that day he was supposed to attend a formidable luncheon at Marly, followed by the carrying out of a most eccentric bet, and ending with a overwhelming supper and frenzied gaming session.)

"Prosper!" Sterny shouted. "Let him come up, let him come in…."

"But, Monsieur, I told him you had gone out."

"Gone out!" Sterny shouted, furious. "Where did you get that impertinence toward my friends? Who told you to say I had gone out?"

"But Monsieur le Count, …I thought…"

Sterny was furious. "Idiot! Animal!" he shouted.

"But this gentleman must scarcely be at the foot of the stairway."

"Then go get him…Ask him to come up…Go quickly!…Go quickly!…."

The servant had hardly left than Sterny became aware of the state he was in. In fact, his hands were trembling, and he felt as if he were suffocating. He had time to compose himself while the valet ran after Prosper, and you might say, forced him to come upstairs so that Léonce could go up to him perfectly calm.

"Pardon me, my dear Prosper, if I had you come back upstairs, but I wanted you to know that if you were told I was out, it wasn't according to my orders."

"Ah!, Monsieur le Count, I'm the one who's sorry to have disturbed you."

"If you were disturbing me, I would have told you so plainly; but perhaps seeing yourself turned away from my door, you might have thought I didn't want to see you, but that isn't the fact."

Then he added, laughing:

"We aren't as impertinent as people say, as we appear, thanks to these gentlemen, our servants. But sit down, Prosper."

"Thank you, Monsieur le Marquis. This is somewhat my fault. I didn't insist very strongly. I'm out paying wedding visits with my wife. She's waiting for me in my carriage with my mother-in-law and Lise and I have to finish on schedule. We have a reservation for one o'clock at the Saint-Germain railway station, where we're joining a party."

"Ah!" said Sterny, "Those ladies are downstairs. It would be very kind of them to do me the honor of coming up to my home."

"Ah!, Monsieur le Marquis," said Prosper.

That exclamation meant at one and the same time: "They wouldn't dare because you're a great lord," and "It wouldn't be proper because you're a bachelor with a rather dubious reputation."

"All right, then," Sterny said to him, "and please give them my regards. But, as a matter of fact, I was going out. I'll go down to their carriage. Come."

And without waiting for Prosper to answer, he put on his hat and went down. His carriage was under the canopy. Seeing him, his coachman shouted to Prosper's hired carriage, which was blocking the carriage way, to move on and he made his horses prance about. The head of an angel, leaning out of the hired carriage's window, was looking at that beautiful carriage. And seeing Sterny, followed by Prosper, coming toward her side, she quickly drew her head back in. It was Lise. Léonce came forward, opened the door, and stood on the footboard. He greeted Madame Laloine, Prosper's wife, and Lise, who was sitting on the back seat of the carriage, while Monsieur Laloine and Monsieur Tirlot the best man, occupied the front seat. The presence of this young man in the middle of Prosper's family irritated Sterny. He was probably a suitor. Nevertheless, he stayed as calm as possible and spoke to Madame Laloine:

"I didn't wish, Madame, to miss the opportunity to renew my gratitude for Prosper, and if I hadn't feared being tiresome to you, I would have myself brought those of my father."

"Of your father?" asked Monsieur Laloine.

"Yes, Monsieur, Sterny. It was he I represented at Prosper's wedding, and I was supposed to give him an account of the mission he had charged me with. I told him, Monsieur, what an honorable alliance his god-son Prosper had been admitted to. He answered me by asking you to accept his thanks."

There wasn't a word of truth in that entire little story, but it was delivered with such good grace that Monsieur and Madame Laloine were overcome with vanity. However, Léonce had hardly dared look at Lise. He didn't have the strength to talk to her. He didn't have anything more to say and he got off the footboard, saying:

"I know you have many visits to pay. I'll leave you."

"Oh! That isn't us," Monsieur Laloine said. "That's Prosper and his wife and we came with them because it would have wasted a lot of time if he had had to come pick us up on the Rue St. Denis."

"And you were going to stay like this in a carriage for two hours, crowded as you are?" Sterny asked, suddenly struck by a bright idea. "Ah! Prosper isn't considerate toward women. Actually, if I dared, I'd suggest to Monsieur and Madame Laloine that they come upstairs to my place. He can come back and pick you up. It's only five minutes to the railway station."

At first Monsieur Laloine and his wife refused but with embarrassment which seemed to indicate that they would gladly have accepted the suggestion from someone other than a marquis like Sterny. Fortunately, Madame Laloine, despite her forty-four years, still had her share of feminine curiosity and she was the first to accept. Monsieur Laloine got out, but neither Lise nor Monsieur Tirlot budged. That wasn't what Sterny was expecting.

"And Mademoiselle Lise…?"

"Oh!" she answered, with a little malicious smile, "we're comfortable now."

"And you, Monsieur," Madame Laloine asked, addressing the best man.

"Me," Monsieur Tirlot said in a sullen voice, "I wasn't invited. "

His bad humor did more to help Sterny than all his cleverness had done. Madame Laloine thought that while Prosper and his wife went upstairs to visit, Lise and Monsieur Tirlot would find themselves alone in the carriage. She certainly understood her daughter and the best man well enough to be sure that there wasn't the least impropriety, but she thought he had thought about that possibility. And as a prudent mother she didn't want him to seem to take advantage without her permission. She said to Lise in a tone whose curtness was aimed more at Monsieur Tirlot than at her daughter.

"Get out of the carriage, Lise."

Lise obeyed, making a little face, apparently sad, but with delight in her heart, because, even more than her mother, she wanted to go into this handsome marquis' house, into the lair of the formidable lion.

As they were going upstairs, Monsieur Laloine suddenly remembered Sterny's carriage.

"But you were going out, Monsieur le Marquis."

"Oh!" Léonce answered. "I have time enough. I was going to visit a country house in the vicinity of Saint-Germain, and it's completely indifferent to me if I arrive at 12:00 or at 2:00 o'clock."

"Ah!" said Monsieur Laloine, "Prosper told us that you owned a very beautiful one at Seine-Port."

"So it isn't for me; it's for my uncle, General R…., who likes the country very much, but being tied up all day in the War Office, he wants to buy something closer to Saint-Germain so that he can come into Paris in the morning and leave in the evening."

Monsieur Laloine didn't ask anything else; as for Lise she looked at Léonce on the sly. He was lying rather cleverly to deceive a father, but too clumsily not to be found out by a young girl. A little situation almost immediately confirmed Lise in her suspicion. Léonce had shown Monsieur and Madame Laloine as well as Lise into his drawing room. Forgetting that just a simple door curtain separated him from her, he said to his valet very low before following her in.

"Go into the reading room and try to get me all the issues of the advertisements for real estate, the Petites Affiches, that you find."

Lise heard him and when Sterny came back in, she looked at him with an expression so mocking that he saw she had guessed. But there was no anger in that look, but almost an approval of his ruse.

Lise had entered Sterny's apartment with the curiosity of a child. But now that she was there, her feelings became more serious and almost timid. It seemed to her she was entering a dangerous place. Under those magnificent paintings, among those trophies, near those shelves covered with gold objects of exquisite taste, in that dwelling where there was nothing a woman would use, she felt uneasy as if she were alone in a group of men. It seemed to her that the air one breathed there was less chaste than in her white bedroom, than that which came across flowers through her windows.

As for Monsieur and Madame Laloine, they were all curiosity about the beautiful things spread out around them. Madame Laloine most of all examined the shelves with a many expressions of amazement, but she didn't dare touch any of the charming objects which ornamented them. At every moment she called Lise to admire them with her. Lise obeyed, but she scarcely looked at them. An unusual feeling of fright had come over her, and she answered in a faltering voice:

"Yes, yes, that's very beautiful."

When Madame Laloine was showing Lise as something precious, or at least unusual, they saw a little house slipper placed among the *objets d'art* and bronzes. Lise frowned and answered in an even more faltering voice,

"Yes, that's very pretty."

Madame Laloine noticed and asked in alarm,

"Are you ill?"

"A little," Lise said, placing her hand over her heart.

"Ah! It's stifling in here," Sterny exclaimed.

"A glass of sugar water and a little orange liqueur, please," said Madame Laloine in a worried voice. "Pardon, Monsieur le Marquis."

Léonce didn't ring for the valet. He opened a door, went himself into his bedroom, took from his bedside table a little plate on which there was a glass of sugared water, and brought it himself into the drawing room.

"Oh! Pardon, …pardon…," Madame Laloine said to him. "That child is truly a great deal of trouble."

Madame Laloine mixed the orange liqueur with the glass of water, and Lise took it, her hand trembling. She drank it, but before putting it down on the table, she looked at two letters incised on the glass in the fashion of Czech glass. Those letters were incised on all the pieces of crystal on the platter. It was an A and a C. Then they didn't belong to Léonce. He saw her attention and taking the glass from Lise's hands, he told her with a sad voice and in an emotional voice that made her tremble.

"Those are the initials of my mother, Mademoiselle."

She raised her eyes to look at him. He had undoubtedly become moved by this memory because he placed the glass back on the platter and said very low:

"That's strange."

"What is?" Madame Laloine asked him.

"Pardon me for this emotion. Four years ago since I was in Nurenburg, I had this crystal made for my mother. I arrived in France with a joyous heart because I knew that that very insignificant attention would please her. She died the day before my arrival, as if struck by lightening. I keep this crystal in memory of her. No one has used it until today. I can't explain to you, but that reminded me of a very sad moment."

Madame Laloine was silent, but Lise looked at Sterny with a gentle expression of joy.

"Monsieur, your mother died very young?" Madame Laloine asked him.

"Too young for me, Madame. She was so noble, so good, so beautiful! I would like to show you her portrait. It's there, in my bedroom. Come, Madame, come, you also Mademoiselle, please. I want you to know my mother."

They went into the bedroom and looked at that portrait. It was a masterpiece of painting, representing a masterpiece of beauty.

"Isn't she beautiful?" asked Sterny.

"Oh! yes," said Lise, in a soft voice, standing in front of that portrait with hands clasped as if in front of the Virgin.

"Here's my father's portrait," Sterny said to Monsieur Laloine.

The husband and wife came forward to look at it, but Lise remained in front of that of Madame de Sterny. That portrait was animated by a sweet and kindly smile, and a deep sigh came from Lise's breast. It seemed to her that a woman with such an heavenly face must have given to her son something of the charming and chaste soul that emanated from her traits. They left that bedroom and Lise came back into the drawing room with her heart comforted and almost happy.

The inspection began again, and Lise returned to the slipper; that slipper intrigued her, but it was hard to ask about its origin. However, the opportunity came of itself. When they came to a certain little table, Sterny had to explain the value of the objects on it. That key was made during the reign of Louis XVI, that serving dish had belonged to Anne of Austria, that book of the mass to Madame de Maintenon.

"And that slipper."

"That's my slipper," Sterny said, laughing.

"What's that? Yours?" said Madame Laloine.

"Ah!" Sterny answered. "That's one of the follies of my youth."

"Ah!" Madame Laloine said in a serious tone, as if she were afraid that folly was of an equivocal nature.

But Lise didn't have that fear. Something assured her that if it had been a hardly proper memoir, Léonce wouldn't have answered in that tone of happy frankness.

"Is that perhaps Cinderella's slipper?" Lise asked, laughing.

"Ah! It's a great deal more extraordinary," said Sterny. "It turned the head of a prince and I was the one wearing it."

"How's that?" asked Monsieur Laloine.

"Ah! It's rather hard to explain, but some ten years ago, I had a small, womanly figure and I resembled my sister. Monsieur d'Auterres was paying court to her and was very jealous of her lack of seriousness. My brother-in-law, because he became so, is most certainly a man of honor, but a little nothing could offend his severity and his mania for etiquette. And one time he had gravely pointed out to my mother that my sister was wearing slippers one day when there were two or three young men in the drawing room. The slippers had struck Monsieur d'Auterres as improper.

"One evening during carnival season, when he had left us saying he was going to the Opera masked ball, I don't know what silly idea made me misbehave. I dressed up like a woman, and remembering his love of formality of dress, I put on, in the place of shoes, my sister's slippers."

"You put on these slippers?" Lise asked with an incredulous expression, forgetting to whom she was speaking.

"But I could wear them in those days, Mademoiselle," Sterny answered, smiling.

In spite of herself, Lise had glanced down at Léonce's feet, and those feet were charming.

"What can I say?" Sterny continued, almost as embarrassed as she was. "I arrived at the Opera masked ball, and having had some of my friends follow me, I suddenly threw myself in Monsieur d'Auterres arms, saying, "Protect my honor!

"Monsieur d'Auterres turned around, and in the trembling voice of a young girl I admitted that, driven by invincible curiosity, I had slipped out of my mother's town house to go see the Opera ball, that I was trembling, confused, lost. Saying that, I drew Monsieur d'Auterres into an isolated corner. I let myself fall down on a seat and while he was lecturing me and asking me who I was, and swearing to protect me, I put my foot forward. He didn't notice. I threw myself about so much that someone bumped me and I cried out, 'Someone just crushed my foot!' I stuck my foot out again. There was no way he could avoid seeing it. Monsieur d'Auterres saw the slipper. He became pale as death and turned toward me shouting,

'That's impossible!'

"Then I pretended to burst into tears, and told him,

"Alas! Yes, it's me! Take me back to my mother. Come.

"He was so stupefied that it was I who led him out of the room, rather then he conducting me. We got into his carriage, and he then seemed to regain his senses. He cried out again, 'That's impossible!' At that moment, certain that the lanterns would light up my face enough for him to see my features, without, however, recognizing them, I snatched off my mask, and he exclaimed:

"It's you….Yes, it's you, Mademoiselle.

"However, a second look might betray me. I hid my confusion and my tears in my handkerchief. We arrived thus at the townhouse. My mother was having a reception. There were still people there. Monsieur d'Auterres had her mysteriously called into her bedroom, where I had thrown myself on a couch without saying anything, my head hidden in a cushion. It was then that Monsieur d'Auterres, in a gloomy and solemn tone tried to explain to my mother his terrible news.

"He first cried out, 'This secret will die in my breast,' but you understand that my plans, that my hopes are destroyed forever.

"'But, what do you mean?' my mother asked.

"'Alas!' he said, pointing to Me, 'there she is. It was imprudent, terribly imprudent, but your advice, the example of your virtue…'

"'Well,' said my mother, 'who is this masked person?'

"'Ah! Madame, don't overwhelm her with your anger. I don't dare tell you…'

"'But who are you,' the Marquise asked me.

"'It's me, Mother,' I said, making my voice deeper.

"'You, Léonce,' my mother said, laughing. 'Ah! I'm not so strict that I would hold it against my son for having gone to the Opera ball.'

"'Léonce,' Monsieur d'Auterres exclaimed. 'Your son….but Madame, your daughter?…'

"'She's in the drawing room.'

"Monsieur d'Auterres hesitated a moment without speaking. He wanted to be angry, and his first glance at me was terrible. But my expression was so modest and my mother had such an amazed look, that he decided that laughter was best, and he recounted the mystification to my mother.

"She was just about to get angry that Monsieur d'Auterres had been able to believe my sister capable of that flighty behavior, but the poor suitor kept repeating,

"'Those are slippers…that slipper,' he was saying, 'so small…'

"'But my daughter! Monsieur,….'

"'Who the devil would have thought that a man could have worn those damned slippers?' he continued.

"I put on a serious look and said to him gravely,

"'Well, Monsieur, here is that slipper; take it, and if you ever come to suspect my sister, let it remind you of your unjust suspicions.'

"'And, me, I'll take the other one, I told him, and I'll keep it until my sister asks me for it back.'

"They've been married ten years, and Monsieur d'Auterres has never dared tell his wife what he dared suspect her of, so I kept it. That's the story of that slipper."

However, time was passing and Lise, completely recovered, was prying about everywhere, like a curious child. At that moment, a servant entered and deposited an enormous packet of small brochures on the table.

"This is what you asked for, Monsieur le Marquis."

"Good," Sterny said, throwing them in a corner cabinet and coming back to Monsieur and Madame Laloine, to keep them from seeing what that might be. At the same time, he said to them,

"Are you curious about these little things? I have a collection of them in this cabinet. Please come over here."

He entered with Monsieur and Madame Laloine, but Lise didn't follow them.

Léonce was on pins and needles. Fortunately, Monsieur Laloine, having seen some objects carefully placed under glass, asked what they were.

"Oh! That one is very valuable. It belonged to the Emperor," Léonce said.

At this name, Monsieur Leloine straightened up.

"Ah! To the Emperor," he repeated. "You're very fortunate."

"That snuff box belonged to him and he used it."

"May I look at it?" Monsieur Laloine asked, in an almost emotional voice.

Léonce took it out from under the class and a fortunate thought suddenly came to him.

"Were you in the army, Monsieur Laloine?"

"Yes, Monsieur," answered Laloine, with a deep sigh, "from 1808 until 1814."

"Well! Monsieur, such an object is only a curiosity for me. It would perhaps mean more to you. Will you allow me to offer you that snuff box?"

"Ah! Monsieur, never,…..I couldn't."

"Please, do."

That went on for five minutes, but Monsieur Laloine accepted.

"Lise, Lise," he shouted, going toward the drawing room. "Come see what Monsieur Sterny has given me."

Lise came in. She was nervous and trembling as if she had done something wrong. Sterny took advantage of this moment to go out. The packet of brochures had spread out and one of the booklets was open on an armchair. He picked it up and looked at it. On the tenth line of the page there was written: Country House for Sale in Saint-Germain. ...He was overcome with happiness. And since he heard Monsieur and Madame Laloine returning, he picked up the brochure and hid it in his jacket.

When Lise reappeared she was triumphant. She threw Sterny such a look of happiness that he didn't know what to think.

Was it chance, a childish curiosity which had made her read the advertisements?

Did she do that to make herself think as he did? Or wasn't it rather a lesson she want to give him? He fell back into cruel incertitude.

However, he wanted to profit by his advantage, and going up to Madame Laloine, he said to graciously,

"But you, Madame, may I not ask you to accept something to take away as a memento of your kind visit?"

Madame Laloine hesitated, but what Sterny was offering her was such a small thing that it would have been ungracious to refuse.

"And," he continued in a casual tone, "Would Mademoiselle Lise also take..."

Lise interrupted him quickly.

"Oh! Thank you, Monsieur, I don't want anything...me...."

That "me" had something meaningful to it, which seemed to say that she didn't want to accept anything in the manner in which he was offering it to her.

"Oh!" said Monsieur Laloine, "This is too much generosity. We seem to be robbing you."

"Thank you for thinking of my daughter. That would be too much."

"Besides," Lise said in a casual voice, "all these things are so fitting in their place that they should be left there."

"There are some that have a priceless value by being moved," said Sterny, looking at her directly, motioning her with his eyes to show her the real estate brochures.

"Yes," said Lise with an effort at gaiety. "But it's the same as with the slipper. You think you see something that isn't there."

Sterny's face showed a moment of irritation. He was silent. And taking the brochure out of his jacket he threw it far away from him. Monsieur and Madame Laloine, busy looking at the Imperial snuffbox, didn't see this gesture. But Lise saw it and was happy about it. But her gaiety dissipated and she followed more attentively Sterny's movements. Léonce, master of himself once again, showed himself as attentive and friendly toward Monsieur and Madame Laloine as before that incident, but with an imperceptible nuance of the great lord and with a studied exquisite politeness. Lise looked at him, listened to him. He pleased her that way. He was so elegant, so gracious. Acting that way he no longer frightened her. She found that was his role.

Finally, Monsieur Laloine seemed to notice the time with impatience and said to Sterny,

"We've kept you. It's growing late and you'll arrive too late at Saint-Germain."

"I probably won't go today," said Sterny.

"We're the cause of that."

"No, Madame, no. Besides, I forgot that I must go locate someone at Saint-Germain to give me the address of that house and it would be boring to wait for me. I would have gone uselessly."

"Oh!" said Lise, hesitating, "I thought all the addresses of the houses for rent were printed in the brochures."

Sterny looked at her. She looked down. There was something in her eyes stronger than her will power, and something which made her blush almost immediately.

"But of course, I have precisely the copy that has the address."

He picked it up and they started talking about country houses.

However, Prosper hadn't come. Impatient, Monsieur and Madame Laloine opened a window, as if seeing him coming from a distance could make him arrive sooner. That was when Sterny approached Lise and said to her,

"You've been very cruel, to refuse a poor memento."

She was silent and seemed very touched.

"Now that you've forgiven me," he continued, "accept something."

She didn't have time to refuse because her father began calling out,

"There's Prosper!"

There was no longer any hope….but just as Monsieur Laloine was picking up his hat, Lise exclaimed.

"I've lost the pin that was holding on my shawl."

Sterny dashed to his bedroom, snatched a pincushion hung by the fireplace, and returned, but the shawl had already been attached by a pin.

"Pardon," said Madame Laloine, "I've just given one to that little scatter-brain."

Sterny threw the pincushion on the table with vexation, but Lise quietly came forward. Without looking, she searched the table with her hand, took a pin from it and attached it to her shawl. Sterny saw it. He would have fallen on his knees to her, if he had dared. He was so happy he was no longer afraid. And he then said,

"But, in fact, now that I think about it, instead of going to Saint-Germain in my carriage, if I took the train there, I would make up for lost time."

"That's true," said Monsieur Laloine.

"Well, then, I ask your permission to take you as far as the railway station. Prosper will follow us, and we can all go together."

The suggestion was accepted. Monsieur and Madame Laloine got into the waiting carriage with Lise and Sterny. Prosper's hired carriage had trouble following the Lion's frisky rig. Sterny had never been so happy in his life.

Chapter XVI

The arrival at the station was less gracious than Sterny had thought it would be. When the friends, and especially the friends of the Laloine family, saw the handsome Léonce enter the large waiting room with the merchants, they whispered and said to each other in a low voice,

"Ah! *ça*, are they bringing that great lord with us?" "The Laloines are fools." "He isn't invited. We don't know him."

With one glance, Sterny saw the disapproval directed toward him, and Lise saw it also. That made her sad, because that was for her a warning of the distance that separated her from the handsome Léonce. At that moment she would almost have begged his pardon for having brought that ungracious reception on him. Sterny wasn't a man to let himself be intimidated by it, nor to be upset by it. He greeted the gentleman with the sugarcane interests in a manner as if charmed to meet him again. Without any ill-humor, without affectation, he told him that he was going to Saint-Germain to see a country house. From the moment they knew he was not a member of the party, they paid no more attention to him. But this wasn't Sterny's intention. He wanted to be part of the group, and he told himself the sugarcane merchant would invite him one way or another.

With that in mind, he came back by a rather clever roundabout maneuver and began a first rate discussion of political economics. The departure time came; Sterny went down the debarkation ramp still discussing and arguing against the position of Monsieur Gurauflot. (That was the name of the sugarcane merchant.) And the discussion continuing, he got into a railway car beside him, without the latter imagining that the Marquis had any other purpose except listening to his learned dissertations. However, Monsieur Gurauflot wasn't drying up, and as it was a short trip, Sterny, who needed to change the subject, began to be impatient. Suddenly, he took out his watch and exclaimed,

"Well, I'm going to miss my appointment."

"What!" said the sugarcane merchant, so rudely interrupted.

"Pardon," said Sterny, "I made an appointment with an architect to visit that house with me and he wouldn't have waited for me."

Sterny took advantage, as a clever storyteller, of the imaginary characters he had invented for Monsieur Leloine.

"Was it then a very important purchase you were going to make?"

"I don't know if it was," said Sterny. "The information in the real estate brochures are so vague." 'House for Sale,' it says. That varies from 10,000 francs to 100,000, so that I'm acting a little without a set plan."

"Pardon," Monsieur Gurauflot said to him, "I'm somewhat familiar with Saint-Germain. Where is the house you're going to see?"

"Let's see," Sterny said, showing him the brochure.

"But that's a charming house. I know it. It backs on the forest. It's very large. And the interior is said to be very beautiful."

"Ah! So much the better."

"Then you don't know it at all?"

"I've never been inside it. What I'd like to know most of all is if the house is solidly constructed. And I'll admit I know nothing about that."

"That's something that's not so difficult as you might think."

"For a person such as you, Monsieur, who seems to be knowledgeable about practicable things. But Me!"

"It's true, I wouldn't let myself be easily deceived," Gurauflot said, with an egotistical expression.

"You're very fortunate. But when you don't know anything and have the clumsiness not to bring along a man who knows the business, you're wrong. But to tell you the truth, Monsieur, I don't have much confidence in the good faith of architects."

"I can truly believe that, Monsieur."

"And therefore I would prefer to take the advice of a disinterested connoisseur of a man like you, Monsieur, for example."

"Ah! Monsieur…."

It's not necessary to carry this dialogue any further. They hadn't arrived a Saint-Germain before it was agreed that Monsieur Gurauflot would accompany Sterny to the house. The sugarcane merchant announced that important news to his wife and daughters, and it was agreed that they would rejoin the group in the forest. Sterny had hoped that they would ask him what he intended to do on leaving the house, and that he would have an opportunity to answer that he had the whole day free. But Madame Laloine said good-bye to him very formally and with very hurried thanks. And there wasn't the shadow of an invitation.

At this point, Sterny was so disappointed that he became angry at himself and was on the point of giving up the silly role he was playing. But he looked at Lise. Lise was looking at her mother as if, just by the power of her eyes, she could inspire her with the thought that was dominating her. Sterny thought he guessed what she was trying to do. He resolved to tempt fortune right to the end. But nothing he tried succeeded and he left the group, walked up the primitive steps, reached the aforementioned house that had been sold the day before, and separated from Monsieur Gurauflot, who thought he could rejoin the group and took a path that led to the lodges. As for Sterny, sad, distressed, and most of all vexed, he found himself in the middle of the laughing, arguing group who were having donkeys and horses harnessed for a ride through the forest.

"Already back, Monsieur?" Monsieur Laloine asked him.

"And my husband, Monsieur, what have you done with my husband?" Madame Gurauflot exclaimed.

"*Mon Dieu*, Madame, we found the house had been sold, and he then took the shortest path to the lodges, thinking that you must already be there."

"Ah! Well, yes," said Monsieur Laloine. "These little girls have been infuriating us for an hour. They all want to ride horses, and they've gone away to get them. We've been waiting here for an hour."

"I'm sorry about Monsieur your husband," said Sterny to Madame Gurauflot. "I was more than indiscreet in accepting his friendly offer. Please apologize to him for me, Madame."

And he was going to leave, seeing that no one asked him to stay, when he heard Madame Laloine cry out with fear, "Lise, Lise, don't go so fast! Lise.... Lise...."

But Lise had just come out of the stable courtyard on a small horse and was making him gallop as fast as he could. She rode this way a hundred or so feet and came back at the same speed to the group, where she saw Sterny, who greeted her with a courteous smile. She became red as a cherry; then she seemed to thank him for coming back. Just then Sterny began suddenly to shout, "Hey! Groom!"

A boorish peasant had the impudence to answer that call, and Sterny said to him,

"You dolt. Why did you let a woman mount a saddle that's no better cinched than that! She could have been killed. You don't know your job, imbecile!"

And without waiting for an answer, he walked to the right side of the horse and tightened the girth himself, with a skill and strength that astounded the man renting horses.

"*Merci*," Lise said to him, but that "thank you" was only for his ears and probably for something other than what he had just done.

He was perhaps going to speak to her, but Madame Gurauflot came up almost to take him by the collar and said to him,

"Monsieur, would you be kind enough to see if my daughters' saddles are well cinched."

"With pleasure," Léonce said.

And there he was, acting the groom for all the women and young ladies with good grace, with such perfectly straightforward attention that Mademe Gurauflot began to say to Monsieur Laloine,

"I feel sure that if he came with us he would show us the most beautiful parts of the forest. You know him. Could you invite him?"

"Ah!" said Monsieur Laloine, "Do you want me to become a laughing stock? That would be a strange outing to suggest to a man like him."

"Bah! Then forget it," said Madame Gurauflot. "I'm going to ask him if he wants to join the picnic."

Monsieur Laloine stopped Madame Gurauflot with irate glances, but she wouldn't admit she was beaten and went at least to ask him the shortest path to the lodges.

"It's rather hard to explain to you, Madame, but once in the forest I could point it out to you."

"Ah! please, Monsieur le Marquis, don't bother," Monsieur Laloine exclaimed. "Really, Madame Gurauflot, you're taking advantage."

"Not in the least," Sterny answered. "It will take just twenty minutes, and I have nothing pressing."

Monsieur Laloine looked distressed, very annoyed by Madame Gurlauflot's indiscretion.

"I'm repaying the debt I owe her husband," Sterny told him. "That's only right."

They started off, the young ladies and young gentlemen on horses, the older relatives and Sterny on foot.

They at first moved slowly, the mamas constantly crying out that they were going to hurt themselves. Little by little, and when Sterny's directions pointed out the pathway, they moved along, picking up speed, going forward, coming back, laughing at the neckerchiefs which flew away, hats which came off. Sterny spoke gravely, following Lise with his eyes, Lise who seemed to have forgotten him and who wasn't the least of the silly girls of that flock of young girls.

Poor Sterny, how much effort to obtain an invitation to a bad luncheon, how much stupidity performed in one day! To what level had he descended little by little! He had girded Madame Gurauflot's donkey, and he still had not attained his goal. Once more he found that he had been duped. Lise was riding along joyously, indifferent to him, paying him no attention. He then definitely decided to leave. He was furious with her.

At this moment a piercing cry came from a side pathway.

"That's Lise," said Madame Leloine.

She hadn't finished speaking before Sterny dashed through the woods toward the pathway. He came to Lise, who was sitting very calmly on her horse while Monsieur Tirlot , standing on the ground, dusted off and rearranged his hat. Lise was afraid. That was all. Sterny, reassured as to her safety, didn't even look at her, and returning to Madame Laloine, he shouted from a distance,

"It was nothing, Madame; it was Monsieur Tirlot who fell off his horse."

Madame Laloine came up almost at the same instant, and completely frightened by that accident, she say to Lise,

"All right, my daughter, get down off the horse. What happened to Monsieur Tirlot can happen to you."

"But, Mama," Lise said, pouting.

"Come now, since your mother's afraid, be reasonable," Monsieur Laloine told her.

Lise said petulantly,

"Ah! Monsieur Tirlot, you're the clumsy one…it's me they're punishing for your clumsiness."

"For my clumsiness, Mademoiselle? I'd like to see you ride that wild beast. He's thrown me off twice. I was already thrown off down there without saying anything."

"Then why did you cry out here?"

"It wasn't me," Tirlot said. "It was you."

"But counting the last time, you fell three times and Mama wasn't afraid for you."

"That was because you were riding beside Captain Simon," Monsieur Laloine told her. "And I have confidence in him."

"Really," said Sterny, "if I dared, and in order not to deprive Mademoiselle Lise of this pleasure, I'll offer to accompany her and I'll be responsible for her safety."

"But you don't have a horse," Monsieur Léonce, she said fretfully.

"Maybe Monsieur Tirlot wouldn't like to get back on his."

"I beg your pardon," Tirlot answered in curt tone. "I will remount."

"As you like, Monsieur," Sterny said.

Tirlot mounted his horse again, and wanting to act the brave man, he decided to give it three or four quirt lashes. The animal reared, kicked, jumped and redeposited Monsieur Tirlot on the pathway.

"That was well done," Lise said.

"Really?" said Tirlot. "Well! I advise Monsieur to get a taste of it. He'll see."

"Gladly," said Sterny.

"I'd bet a hundred sous," Tirlot said to Madame Laloine, "that your Marquis gets thrown off."

The horse was stubborn, but it didn't take a horseman as skilled as Léonce to control him. Monsieur Tirlot had all the shame of his fall and all the anger at Léonce's success.

They hadn't yet congratulated Sterny when Lise, dashing down the pathway where they were, began to gallop.

"Ah! *Mon Dieu*, go after her, Monsieur de Sterny," cried out Madame Laloine.

Léonce didn't have to be told twice, although his anger against Lise was such that he promised himself he would certainly show her his coldness. But it seemed that young girl had a power over him which he couldn't understand, never having experienced it from anyone else. In addition, she had looks, words, silences which deeply moved Sterny. Just at the time when you could believe her a thousand miles removed from you, carried away by youth and childish gaiety, a word came, telling you she was living beside you. That's what happened to Sterny.

"Ah! *Mon Dieu*," she said to him when he was near her. "We've been put to some trouble."

What could you answer to that? You had to be happy about it. But to be happy about it, you had to believe it and that child was so strange. She spoke words which would have appeared a compromising engagement to a woman who understood their meaning. Then she spoke, she reacted as if she had said nothing. Léonce didn't at all understand that manner of behavior, not seeing that he himself was already more than what he had been in the past.

However, they rode side by side. Léonce wanted finally to give a positive meaning to all he had done, that is to say, make Lise understand that it was love of her that had made him do what she had seen. But he didn't know how to bring up that subject with a soul as strange and timid as a deer which shows it pretty head at the edge of a woodland track and which flees, bounding away into the woods at the first sound of a hunter's footsteps.

And so these two young people, who had doubtless come together to say a thousand things to each other, said nothing. And both became thoughtful and remained silent. It was Léonce who first noticed Lise's sadness. He still wanted to understand that soul's secret in respect to him. He posed one of those questions to her which puts oneself at risk.

"You're sad," he said. "Have I displeased you?"

"Ah! No," she answered him with a deep sigh. "I'm sad."

106

"What are you sad about?"

"Do you want me to tell you frankly?"

"Yes, certainly."

"Well, Monsieur Léonce, (That was the second time she had called him Léonce.) What you're doing is not proper."

Sterny's pride was wounded at this word, which, for a man such as he, was the cruelest insult that a woman could give him. He replied in a changed voice,

"I don't think I have acted anyway improperly, at least vis-à-vis you, Mademoiselle."

Lise turned her sweet face toward him and in the saddest and most tender voice, she replied,

"Oh! How you take things the wrong way. I'm not saying you've acted improperly toward me, or toward anybody."

"Then what do you mean?"

"Oh! Don't be angry. It's for you that what you're doing, and what I've let you do, isn't proper."

"For me!" said Sterny, whose heart was moved with unbelievable violence by that childish voice.

"Yes, for you. You don't understand these people you're with. They feel as well as you do that you're not here in your social level. They'll be afraid so long as you're here and they won't say anything. But tomorrow, day after tomorrow, you'll see, they'll laugh about it, they'll talk about it."

"And what does that matter to me?"

"Oh! Don't say that….."

"But what am I doing differently than the others?"

"The others are doing what they do every day," Lise continued, with a slight movement of impatience. "You, instead, ….They certainly see that you're not at home doing that. You're good. Ah! I think so. Since this morning you're good. You do what you can…but look …me…me…I don't like to see you like this."

"It's however…"

"For me that you've done it." Lise said rapidly, stopping immediately, confused for having in this way admitted Léonce's love for her.

"Oh! Yes, Lise," he said to her. "It's for you, I swear it."

She still didn't answer. She was troubled, nervous, and became pale, because all the strong emotions were painted on that young girl's face. Finally, she picked up her courage and began to speak,

"Monsieur Léonce, you must go away."

"Ah! I cannot," he told her.

She smiled her angelic smile and showed him her motto:

What you want to do, you can do.

"That's well and good," he said to her with passion, "and if I had this talisman which carries this pretext for courage, I would will everything that's possible."

"That's not good, what you're asking me," Lise said to him, smiling. "If I gave it to you, I'd have to tell Mama that I'd lost it. It would be necessary to tell a lie."

That was giving and refusing at the same time. Léonce didn't know what to answer. She was so simple that all his knowledge of women's hearts left him when he was near that child.

However, they had slowed their steps so much that they were overtaken by Monsieur and Madame Laloine, who said to her daughter,

"This is good, Lise. You're behaving wisely with Monsieur de Sterny."

Just then, and as they were talking about resting a moment, a loud din was heard in the forest, and almost at the same instant a mass of horsemen and amazons came out of a lateral pathway. It was the famous bet of the trotters which had left from Marly and had come that far. Almost all of them made off like thunder, but Lingart and his female lion, who was only following at a distance, had time to recognize Sterny. Both of them were so astounded that they reined in their horses and looked as if they couldn't believe it. Sterny on a little rented horse. Sterny in the company of a fat lady on a donkey, because Madame Gurauflot was close to them. They were so amazed that they had not yet recovered. Sterny saw their surprise and turned pale with anger and shame at the same time. But in their amazement neither Lingart nor his lioness were continuing on their way. He advanced toward them, determined to block Lingart's view, when the latter said to him,

"Is that really you. I beg your pardon. I didn't recognize you. You won your hundred louis. Algiboch won against Montereau...We waited for you...You won't come to dinner probably......a thousand good-byes."

And he spurred his horse and was off, while his lionne, her lorgnon in her eye, examined Lise from afar, like a merchant looking at a portrait. She was so engrossed in that act that she didn't see Lingart leave, and remained some seconds after he had left.

Sterny was so angry that he slapped the Amazon's horse. Caught unawares she was almost thrown off. She guessed Sterny's action and while getting her horse under control, she said to him,

"You're a dolt, Sterny. I'll get you back."

And she left at a gallop.

The Laloines had seen nothing in that scene. Everything seemed very ordinary to them. But when Sterny returned near Lise, who had left going ahead, he found her in tears.

"I really told you so, Monsieur," she said right off. "How that woman looked at me!…Leave me, Monsieur, leave me. Go join your friends. Please. I want you to."

And as Sterny wanted to answer, she put her horse into a gallop to get away from him. Sterny followed her at first, but as he came closer to her she dashed away faster. He was afraid that she would at last hurt herself and he stopped.

Lise disappeared from sight and he remained in the middle of the road. He was out of sight of everybody, but he heard the voices of Monsieur and Madame Laloine calling to Lise, shouting,

"It's going to rain. Come back."

He could imagine Madame Laloine's alarm if she found him thus all alone. And he wanted at any cost to rejoin Lise. He let his horse the reins for five minutes. Finally, at the corner of a pathway he saw Lise's horse without a rider. He dashed forward, shouting in his turn,

"Mademoiselle Lise! Mademoiselle Lise!"

She came out of the woods saying to him,

"Well! Monsieur, here I am."

"Oh!" he answered, "how you frightened me!"

There was so much truth in his emotion that Lise was almost touched by it. But she had made her decision, and she answered,

"In which direction is my mother?"

"In this direction, but very far away."

"I'm going there."

"Aren't you going to ride?"

"No," she said, in a faltering voice, "no, that ride broke my heart."

And Sterny only then noticed that she was breathing heavily and that her face was covered with terrible pallor.

He jumped down from his horse and ran to her.

"Oh! *Mon Dieu!* I'm the one who caused you this pain. Forgive me, oh! Forgive me, Lise!" he cried out.

"No, it wasn't you. I was wrong. I…."

Saying these words, she fainted and would have fallen on the ground if Léonce hadn't caught her in his arms.

Just then, the storm broke out violently. Lise was trembling as if struck by lightening. But her fainting was only a passing weakness. She came to herself and heard her mother's voice calling to her.

"Let's go join her."

"But you can scarcely walk."

"Oh! Come on, come on!" she said to him, as her teeth were chattering. "I can walk. I can do it. I will do it."

And she went down a path answering with a shrill voice,

"Here I am, Mama. Here I am."

But before they had reached her, she said to Sterny,

"You will leave us, won't you? I wish it."

"I'll obey you." Sterny said.

That said, there was not a word pronounced and when they arrived near the older parents, she was calm and recovered in appearance. But during their absence the great resolution to invite Sterny had been taken, and he was solemnly addressed by Monsieur Laloine. He at first refused, but with sad embarrassment like that of child who is afraid. He vainly searched encouragement by a look from Lise. But she turned her head away.

"Ah! I understand," said Laloine. "Those gentlemen and ladies who've just passed by are waiting for you."

"No, no, Monsieur," Sterny said quickly, "I have nothing to do with those people there."

"Those people there!" His usual group. Oh! Poor Sterny!

"But then why not accept?" asked Madame Gurauflot, who was taken with the handsome Léonce.

"My presence wouldn't perhaps please everybody, Madame," replied Sterny, bowing. "Allow me Madame to leave."

"But it's beginning to rain," said Madame Gurauflot. "You'll at least accept an umbrella!"

"Thank you, Madame, thank you," Sterny said in a sad voice. "Goodbye, Monsieur Laloine, goodbye Madame. I have the honor to take leave of you, Mademoiselle, he said last of all, turning toward Lise."

She let him leave, but he wasn't twenty feet away when she made a pretext of going a little apart. She wept warm tears. As for Sterny, he left quickly, reached the railway, and returned to Paris. He hastened to shut himself up in his apartment. He was desperate. He was angry. He blamed himself and he blamed Lise. Nevertheless, he couldn't think about her without feeling a trembling of love which made him drunk.

Chapter XVII

However, when some hours of rest had calmed that unaccustomed agitation, Léonce thought more seriously than he had perhaps ever done in his life.

He was in love. He felt it. He wasn't ashamed of it, but he was afraid of it.

Seduce Lise! That would be a shameful and cowardly act.

Because, he told himself, she would love me if I wished it. She would love me, I'm sure of it. And she would blindly give her whole heart that is so easy to break to that love sweeping her away. And what else could I do but break it? Because to marry her is impossible madness. Well! he added, I remember when I was a child, one day when I was very sick, my mother carried me to the church. Making me kneel on her knees, she face me toward the Virgin and made me repeat after her:

"Holy Virgin Mary, who saw your son die, save me for my mother!"

That image that I prayed to has remained in my memory as something sacred and ineffable. I have never told this secret to anyone for fear that a joke might insult it. Well! Lise will be for me a similar memory, a heavenly image seen for a moment which I'll keep in the sanctuary of my soul to serve as a shelter for my life. Because I don't mix my heart up with my life.

Eh! No! That youth, that strength for which our century no longer has a goal to strive for, I give to dissipation to ridicule. But if I had lived in some other time, I wouldn't be like this, because it's shameful to be what I am. Ah! If Lise were not what she is, if she were a queen, I would attempt everything in order to merit her. In thinking of those words she carries over her heart, I would dare it.

What you want to do, you can do.

But she is nothing. I can only go down to her level. Let's not think about it any more! Let's not think about it any more!

To achieve that end, Sterny looked for ways to occupy at the same time what he still believed was his mind and his heart.

The next day, when he appeared at the club, he was expecting some allusion from his friends. But a conspiracy was organized against him. No one said a word to him on this subject. Only Eugène said to him gravely,

"I'm betting twenty francs against you, Sterny."

These gentlemen's ladies greeted him, when meeting him in the opera corridors, with rosary bows and lowered eyes. Sterny understood the joke and wanted to reply victoriously. He gambled like a mad man and by his audacity, which threw off all calculations, almost scared Lingart.

He pursued that beautiful girl from the opera they said was so perfect who had made her debut with enormous success. He put so much desperate ardor into doing it that neither Lingart, nor Eugène, nor any of the others could come close.

At the end of a week, she belonged to Sterny, who had treated her with the most cavalier insolence

But—two weeks after the party at Saint-Germain—one evening when he was with his lioness in a box at the Français, he recognized two women in front of him who were staring at him.

One was Prosper's wife; the other was Lise.

"How they're looking at you from that box," said the dancer. "Do they know you?"

"No," said Sterny, who blushed in spite of himself because of his lie.

"Then why did you move to the back of the box. One would say that you're afraid!"

"Ah! Enough of your jealousy!"

"But if they don't know you, there's no jealousy involved."

Sterny leaned across the front of the box and saw Lise, who was listening to two young men who were chatting and seemed to be talking about him.

Suddenly Lise raised her head abruptly and looked at Sterny with unspeakable terror, as if someone had just said to her,

"That man is the executioner."

Léonce leaned back into the box without daring to greet her in order not to expose her to the insulting looks of his mistress. However, he wanted to leave.

"If you leave my box, his mistress told him, I'll create a scandal. Do you know that woman?"

By an unusual instinct, Sterny had guessed what had just taken place some feet from him.

"Who is Mademoiselle N....with?" one of the young men asked.

"Oh! With her lover, the Marquis de Sterny."

"Has he been her lover a long time?"

"For a week at the most."

Sterny hadn't heard a word of all that, but he'd read it in the look Lise had thrown at him.

He would have liked to go to her, but he was held by an infamous chain. He still wanted to leave.

"If you go to that woman's box," his mistress said to him, "I'm going to slap her in front of you." Then she continued with a look of disdain, "That must be the common little coquette from Saint-Germain."

At that moment, Sterny could have stabbed the dancer. But he had to hold his temper; he could only lead his lioness away. And in an excess of rage, he broke everything at her apartment, glass, porcelain, furniture. Since he couldn't beat the woman, he did all the damage possible by taking from her everything he had given her.

Léonce returned home furious.

The next day he went to Monsieur Laloine's. He was told that he was in the country with all his family.

All right, Sterny said to himself, *I'm an idiot. There was another scene of palpitations, and the beautiful one went for a stroll the next day, whereas for me... Truly, I'm becoming a brute.*

That said, he thought that he hadn't done enough to forget that little girl with whom he had so stupidly compromised himself.

Two weeks later, thanks to follies greater than ever, thanks to a race where he was hurt, and which the newspapers wrote about, thanks to a bet of a thousand louis that he lost, thanks to a series of orgies with the most shameless prostitutes, he had managed to no longer think about Lise. But nevertheless, several times that sweet, pale face seemed to appear to him, paler, dying, sad, looking at him in despair, as if reproaching him for losing himself and for having lost her.

That image came to him even in his sleep, and as he was still dreaming it in the morning, wide awake, they announced Prosper Gobillou, who came in with a sad and sorrowful look

"But you look very sad for a newly married man, Prosper," Léonce said to him.

"That's because there's sorrow in the household," Prosper said to him. "You understand, that poor Lise?"

"What! Lise?" Léonce asked, terrified.

Prosper pointed to the black crepe on his hat.

"Dead!" said Léonce with a terrible cry.

"Dead!" said Prosper. "She died like a saint!"

"Oh! *Mon Dieu! Mon Dieu!*" Léonce cried out with a despair that frightened Prosper. "That's not possible…Dead! Without my seeing her again! Dead…"

"Alas! Yes," said Prosper, "I've come from her burial and I've come to bring you her last wish."

"Her last wish!" said Léonce.

"Listen to me, Monsieur le Marquis. You must not hold it against that poor child. She had a fiery disposition and a too excitable heart. But here's what happened:

"The night she died, I was sitting up near her with my wife. She called to her and told her to take off the little hair chain she wore around her neck. Then she motioned me to her.

"Prosper, she said to me, You'll give this to Monsieur de Sterny. Tell him not to be as careless and cruel toward others as he was toward me. I'm sending him this motto. Let it become his, and he will one day be a worthy and good man. I'm sure of it.

"Then she gave me this medallion, this hair and this pin. And an hour later she expired, murmuring: 'What you want to do, you can do, except be loved… Loved!…Loved!,' she said again. Then everything was over.…

Léonce fell on his knees, and received on his knees that pledge, so pure and so unexpected. His tears flowed abundantly for two hours. When he was calmer, Prosper left him.

From that day, Léonce shut himself up at home and was seen nowhere.

Everyone was very astonished at this retreat, even more astonished to learn that he was making ready to leave France for a long stay. And perhaps his friends would have thought he had gone mad if they had seen him the evening before his departure, praying on his knees near a tomb. They wouldn't have been mistaken, because a week afterwards he was in Doctor Metrasipot's sanitorium.

THE END

Unseen Dramas

On the seventh floor of a magnificent house in the Chaussée d'Antin neighborhood, there lodged, several years ago, a young man named Marc-Antoine Riponneau. He was a stocky twenty-five-year-old boy with a round, reddish face, bulging blue eyes, a slightly turned-up nose with wide nostrils, and full cherry-colored lips. It would have been a true face of happiness and contentment if it were not for a low forehead and hair so bushy that it could only be worn in a short military cut that gave his face a sordid and envious expression, denoting stubbornness more than intelligence.

Marc-Antoine was a clerk in the Ministry of Finance and earned 1,800 francs a year. He could get by with that, but he wasn't happy with it. An employee of the State Budget Office, he had picked up all its illusions and taken them into his own private life. So, no debt entered into with interest due every six months; no fluctuating debt that you never paid, because you always owed it (because you borrowed to pay interest on what you had already borrowed). What he had already cut out of his budget as one of those most deceptive dreams of finances was the chapter on unexpected resources. Marc-Antoine had 1,800 francs; he counted on only 1,800. Although still counting on them, he estimated them only as 1,700 francs, seeing that the up-coming law governing pensions could force him to set aside something or force him to enroll in some kind of insurance program.

Every expense was invariably assessed, foreseen, and covered. Thanks to a great deal of strict budgeting, he ate moderately so as to be well clothed. And thanks to being very careful in moving about, he kept his suits in still decent condition, even though they would have been worn thin a long time ago on the shoulders of a very active person. Riponneau didn't allow himself to stretch out his arms or legs any great distance or to relax completely except at the hour when he had taken off all clothing that could be damaged by too much freedom of movement. It must be said that at that hour he amply compensated for it. And it was with the most disorderly pantomime that he accompanied the following exclamations:

"To have only 1,800 francs and to have in oneself the germ of all great ideas!"

The germ of the so-called "all great ideas," accurately speaking, meant a desire for all the luxurious pleasures of life.

"Ah!" Marc-Antoine continued, "Ah! To be poor and to see across from you *on* the second floor of that big house, a Monsieur de Crivelin and a Madame Crivelin! They're rich and everything goes great for them; everyone in society flatters them; they're happy!"

At this point Master Riponneau stomped his foot.

"If I were only like Monsieur Domen, who occupies the whole second floor of our building, he continued, what a different use I'd make of my fortune than he does of his! But what does that matter? He's happy in his fashion, since being able to live anywhere, he lives only at home. As for me, I have to deprive myself of everything. In addition, it's not only wealth; he has glory, reputation. Thunderation and thunderation! He's happy!"

At this point in his complaints, Riponneau was trembling.

And then there began new exclamations both against the hosier who occupied the shop on the right of the carriage entry, and against the confectioner who occupied the store on the left, and against all the inhabitants of the house, one after the other, because, without exception, that house had splendid residents. Lackeys, dogs and horses swarmed in the courtyard, the kitchen chimneys sent off odors of truffles and pheasants. In the stairway when he went to pick up his milk each morning. Marc-Antoine encountered svelte chambermaids wearing aprons white as snow, smelling of their mistresses' perfume. Then he bumped into the plump faces of the cooks. His boots, polished with a great deal of trouble, looked dull when compared to the glistening shine on the varnished shoes of the valets. The masters insulted him by way of the menials.

Then, in the evening, the delightful voices of the concerts, the murmurs and the soft noise of the dance, and sometimes, through an open window, a beautiful blonde or brunette head crowned with flowers, a supple and graceful body shining with the reflections of silk, or veiled with the mist of muslin; sometimes the sweet nonchalance of idle happiness, sometimes the ardent fever of pleasure. All that surrounded Marc-Antoine with an atmosphere burning with desires, in which he moved about, opening his lungs to that perfumed air, his lips to those divine phantoms, without being able to hold onto anything, grasping empty air, embracing shadows and becoming transported by degrees to rage which made him beat the floor with his feet and the walls with his fists.

Now, one evening as Riponneau's exasperation reached a terribly turbulent height, he heard a knock at his door, and almost immediately there entered a man about sixty-years-old with a wide and bald forehead, wrapped in a house gown of Indian cotton piqué like those old down quilts of our grandmothers. That man had a lively, piercing eye, a clever, laughing expression, which was, nevertheless, full of goodwill.

In a soft and composed voice, he said to Riponneau: "Neighbor, everyone is master in his own house. I wasn't present at the taking of the Bastille, nor a participant in the July Revolution, not to recognize this great political principle. But all liberty has limits, because without that it would encroach on the rights of others. You have the right to shout, but only to a certain level, because I have the liberty to sleep. And if your liberty destroys mine, it becomes tyranny and mine is a slave. This is contrary to the two Revolutions that I've just told you about."

Marc-Antoine was about to get angry. The neighbor didn't give him time. He continued:

"What's more, it isn't for myself that I'm objecting. I can willingly live in silence or with noise. But I'm speaking to you on behalf of your little neighbor, Mademoiselle Juana, the seamstress. I saw her come home very pale this evening, very much in pain, and with her eyes all red with tears and the fatigue of her work. She went to bed, the poor child, hoping to sleep, she told me. Well! My dear neighbor, for that poor dear little one, practice your melodramtic roles a little quieter."

"Hein!" Marc-Antoine said.

"What's more," the neighbor continued with a knowing expression, "I've seen *Talma,* Monsieur, and believe me, it wasn't at all with grand gestures that he got his most beautiful effects. Look, in *Manlius* he did nothing but lift his thumb and glance to one side when he said these two verses:

> *C'est moi qui, prévenant leur attente frivole,*
> *Renversai les Gaulois du haut du capitole.*
>
> *It was I who, foreseeing their trivial assault,*
> *Repulsed the Gauls from the height of the capitol.*

"And the audience brought down the house with applause. Believe me, Monsieur, good delivery…"

"But, Monsieur, I'm not an actor."

"Ah! Bah! Then you're a lawyer?" asked the old neighbor.

"Of course not."

"You're too young to be a Deputy. Who are you then to shout this way about nothing?"

Marc-Antoine hesitated and then answered:

"I'm poor, Monsieur and I'm tired of the good fortune of the rich. I amuse myself in my own way."

The neighbor looked at Riponneau with interest. The old man's face showed a battle between a first movement of malice and a second of kindness. Kindness carried the day. He took a seat, and with that gentle authority which age and indulgence give, he said to Riponneau:

"Ah! You're poor and as a consequence you're unhappy. Let's talk a little bit, neighbor. You know that it's among the poor that there's generosity. And I, who am fortunate, I'm going to give you a little of what you lack. I'm going go make you part of my happiness."

"And how do you think you can do that, neighbor? Because, if I have observed your habits correctly, you live alone."

"Yes."

"You work from morning till night."

"Yes."

"You rarely go out."

"Yes."

"Then where is your good luck and what can you give me?"

"Nothing, but I would have done a great deal if I lift something from your heart: that's envy, which eats away at and blights all your youthful joys, like a worm in the heart of a tree."

"Me, envious!" Marc-Antoine exclaimed, blushing.

"Look, young man, are you married?"

"No."

"Do you have a mistress?"

"No."

"Do you have a family that…"

"I'm an orphan."

"Do you have any debts?"

"No."

"No wife, therefore no children; no mistress, therefore no rivals at all; no family, therefore no ties; no debts at all, therefore no creditors knocking at your door. In short you are exempt from all the plagues of humanity. So, if you're unhappy, that doesn't come from causes outside and independent of yourself. Your lack of happiness comes from an interior cause inherent in your personality. That cause, that's envy."

"And even if that were so," Riponneau said, "if I envied the happiness of everyone around me, what would be the harm in that?"

"The harm is in suffering from what is foreign to you, which is profoundly irrational."

"Bah!" Riponneau replied, T"here's nothing unreasonable about wishing for good luck."

"It's not reasonable to wish for sorrow, despair, constant torment, the perpetual worries which come with it."

"All that is commonplace, my dear neighbor, banal commonplaces that the poor tell their brothers; overbearing derision of the rich when they're the ones using that language."

The neighbor reflected and after a rather long silence he said to Marc-Antoine:

"Well! Answer frankly. Which one among those around you do you envy? In whose place would you like to be?"

"In whose place?" Marc-Antoine answered. "But there's not one who isn't more fortunate than I am. And there's an open field if you want to talk about desires. And you aren't robbing anyone when dreaming about the wealth of others. Don't you think I would prefer to be in the position of the Crivelin couple rather than in mine?"

"Really?"

"But damn! Last week, I didn't sleep all night because of the noise from the party they gave. The most magnificent carriages crowded the street; the names of the most important people were announced in a stentorian voice at the door of their drawing rooms. Those who entered were excited about coming; those who left regretted having to leave. And on the stairway when I left my apartment, going up and down ten times to get away from the shrill noise of the party, I heard on all the steps."

"What nice people!! What gaiety! You can certainly see they're happy!"

And other said:

"They're marrying their daughter to Count Formont! A beautiful marriage! Youth, beauty, fortune, social connections on both sides. They're fortunate, but they certainly deserve to be!"

"Ah!" said the neighbor. "You heard all that on the stairway?"

"Yeah!"

"Well! If you had been in the drawing room, it would have been even better. There was joy, laughter, congratulations everywhere, and on the faces of the masters of the house, satisfaction which comes from bringing about the happiness onehas given. And there was on all sides, assurances of friendship, and the drunkenness of the Count de Fromont, and the joy of Adèle de Crivelin, and their furtive exchanged looks, and the soft, kindly smiles of the old people who intercepted those looks and dreamed of their past. And there was the pride of the father, the love of the mother, who were triumphant and delighted with the success of their daughter. It was a charming picture at midnight, at one o'clock in the morning, at three o'clock, and still at five o'clock. But at daybreak, the curtain was lowered; the comedy was over; and the drama began."

"Ah! Bah!" answered Marc-Antoine. "Was Monsieur de Crivelin's fortune compromised, and did he, like so many others, hide his ruin in festivities?"

"No."

"Is it because his wife wasn't what she should be?"

"She is the best of women."

"A mistake of his daughter's."

"She is an angel of purity."

"Well, then, what is it?"

"A good deed, nothing but a good deed, forgotten for fifteen years, which has suddenly come back to them in the form of a hideous scoundrel with a yellow, bilious face and a filthy mouth, who rolled his filthy rags around on the silk upholstery of the gilded furniture, which had been touched an hour before by the finery of the young and beautiful dancers."

"I don't understand you."

"Then hear me out. That man, clothed in filthy livery, stayed all night in the antechamber. In such a crowd of lackeys, that one had escaped being noticed by the servants of the house. But as the rooms, and the antechambers after them, began to be emptied, they noticed him and looked at him with a disapproving eye. But the fellow only acted more at home and stretched out more insolently on the benches. The moment finally arrived when the last guest left. The filthy lackey stayed at his post. They finally asked him why he was staying."

"I'm waiting for my master, Monsieur Eugène Ligny."

"There's no one left here," they told him.

"I told you that he's here. Go ask your master for him. He'll find him."

The servants were beginning to get angry. The boor raised his voice and Monsieur de Crivelin appeared at the door of the antechamber, asking the reason for the noise.

"This man refuses to leave," answered the valet de chambre. "He claims he's waiting for his master."

"And what is his master"s name?"

"The one I'm looking for," said the unknown lackey, "is named Eugène Ligny and I won't leave without seeing him."

He had scarcely said these words than Monsieur Crivelin fixed his terrified eyes on him. He turned pale, he trembled, and, hardly containing the terror and trouble he was experiencing, he ordered the domestics to leave and invited that man to follow him.

Usually, small misfortunes come as part of great catastrophes. A household which has just given a dance for five hundred people is in general very little orderly. The French doors pulled back leave the apartments open to full view. Monsieur and Madame de Grivelin, had kept sheltered from the invasion only their daughter's bedroom and their own bedroom. All the other rooms were fully open. Madame de Crivelin was in her maid's hands when her husband came in to ask her to go to her daughter's bedroom and leave him their bedroom a moment for an interview of the greatest importance.

"Ah!" She said, laughing, "I'll bet it's Monsieur de Formont, who's following you. But, really, it's good for lovers not to sleep. Send him away until later."

"No, it's not that…it's…Please, leave until I come ask you to return."

"But what's wrong with you/" exclaimed Madame de Crivelin. "You're pale; your face is all…What's wrong?"

"Nothing, my dear love, nothing. But, please, leave us."

Madame Crivelin gave in, but carried with her worry which soon reached her daughter. Adèle wasn't yet asleep, and, seeing her mother come into her bedroom, she questioned her. Seeing Madame Crivelin's fright, her worry, she trembled in her turn. So there those two poor women, put out, shut up in the narrowest corner of their splendid apartment, anxiously waiting the outcome of so unexpected, so bizarre an appointment which had greatly troubled Monsieur Crivelin. Who was he with? What was he saying? What such powerful interest dominated him to make him give such an interview at such an hour?

Adèle saw Jules de Formont dead; Madame de Crivelin's mind wandered about in a maze of impossible suppositions.

During that time, here's what was happening in the bedroom where Monsieur Crivelin had shut himself up with the filthy lackey

"Then you recognized me, Eugène?" that man said to him.

"You're here," Monsieur de Crevelin said to him, "you're alive?"

"When you thought me dead! That's a joke, isn't it? Have me brought a glass of wine and a slice of ham and you'll see I'm not a ghost."

"Now, see here, Jules, you didn't come here for that! Speak! Then speak, wretched man!"

"During the six hours I spent in your antechamber I was dying of thirst and hunger. I want something to drink and eat."

"What do you have to say?"

"I want to drink and eat. Go get it yourself if you're afraid it will soil your servants' hands to serve me."

Crevelin bowed and left. A moment later he reappeared with a platter that he placed in front of the filthy blackguard.

"Now, speak! What do you want?"

The man named Jules got down to the business of eating and began thus:

"Listen Eugène, this is what you wrote me seventeen years ago:

"*You see, Jules, your foolish behavior has had the result I predicted. From bad behavior you went to sins, from sins to crimes, and now an infamous conviction is hanging over your head. Since you've been able to escape from your prison, take advantage of your freedom to flee and to flee alone. Don't drag along into the wandering existence you're facing in a new world, a child who has come with difficulty into life. Leave me your daughter. At the time the law struck you down, misfortune struck me also. My daughter is dying. If God lets me keep her, your own will have a sister. If God takes*

121

her from me, your Marie will take her place here with us. Here is enough gold that you can take with you in your flight to give you the means later to reconstitute an honorable fortune.

"Isn't that what you wrote me?"

"That's true," said Monsieur de Crivelin.

"A week later," that man said, "you left, carrying the two enfants to Italy, both barely two years old. You went to join your wife, who had been forced to leave you to go receive the last good-byes and the pardon of her mother, who was dying in Naples. You had married her against the wishes of her family, and that noble had forbidden you to be present at that reconciliation. Your mother-in-law having died, you returned near your wife.

"As for me, to better insure my flight, I placed at the bank of a river a letter in which I said I didn't want to survive my shame. And, a month after your departure, you received news of my death. At the same time, your daughter died at Ancône, and you got her a birth certificate under the name you then used. Then you continued your travels, letting all the strangers you met call the child with you by the name of your daughter.

"You yourself, charmed by her grace, her beauty, by her tenderness for you, you called her by the name of your child. You were traveling slowly, foreseeing with terror the moment when you'd have to tell your wife her child was dead. Suddenly, an idea came into your head. Your wife, taken by her brother, Monsieur de Crivelin, to be near her dying mother, had left your Adèle three months after her birth, at that age when children's faces change with each succeeding year. Marie, the daughter of Jules Marsilly, dead, or so you thought, couldn't she, in a mother's eyes, replace that lost Adèle? Your wife had fallen sick in her turn. The news of her daughter's death might kill her. You decided on the deception. Marie Marsilly became Adèle Ligny."

"Since you know so well the feelings which dictated my conduct," said Monsieur de Crivelin, "can you say it was my crime?"

"I'm not casting any blame," said the drunken man. "I'm just recounting."

He drank two glasses of wine and continued thus:

"Your ruse succeeded marvelously. It even succeeded beyond your hopes. It was not only your wife who was delighted with that very beautiful and charming daughter. Her uncle, Monsieur de Crivelin, who couldn't forgive you for becoming his brother-in-law, became enamored with that child, and eight years later he left her all his fortune, naming you her guardian, on condition that you add his name to yours. That's why you returned to France under the name of Eugène Ligny de Crivelin."

"But I deceived no one. I didn't even deny my name."

"You're not capable of that. But, you picked up the habit of leaving out the

Ligny and calling yourself Monsieur de Crivelin. And as I had seldom heard this name pronounced in my youth, I would never have thought that the rich Monsieur de Crivelin was my old school comrade, Eugène Ligny, if in recent days I hadn't seen tacked up on the door of the office of the mayor or my neighborhood, the marriage bans of *Mademoiselle Adèle Ligny de Crivelin avec the Count Bertrand de Formont.* On seeing that was when I asked myself how Adèle, dead a Ancône, was living in Paris."

"That was a lie," said Monsieur de Crivelin, who saw there a hope of getting out of that horribly difficult situation.

"My good man," the brigand said to him, "Don't try to play a role you don't know. I passed through Ancône the day after the death of your daughter, and everybody there was talking about your despair. Besides, if need be, the records can be recovered. So listen to me gently."

The fellow finished off a second bottle and began again.

"You understand that, once started on that road, the story of your novel was very easy to write. You put my daughter in the place of yours, and now you have perhaps come to persuade yourself in good faith that she's your daughter."

"Oh! Yes!" said Monsieur de Crivelin. "She's my child, my daughter, my hope, my happiness…So, see, what do you want? What are you asking for?"

"Let's pose the question clearly, so that we understand each other. First of all, you stole my child, a crime punishable by law! Following that, to collect the inheritance of the uncle, you produced a birth certificate under which you registered my daughter, when the proof of the death of your daughter is at Ancône. Secondly, to have the marriage bans of Mademoiselle Ligny de Crivelin published, you used a title equally false. That is incontestable. Now, let's reason together.

"For having put a signature other than mine at the bottom of a notarized paper, I was condemned to fifteen years of hard labor. I am poor and dishonored and I'm not in prison only because I'm believed dead. You, on the contrary, for having falsely used a legal document, for having taken away from other heirs an immense fortune by means of that act, you are rich, honored, you swim in opulence and festivities. That's not right."

"But what are you claiming, wretched man? Would you take Adèle from me? Ah! Scoundrel! But her mother, because my poor wife is her true mother, would you kill her? Oh! I would prefer to tell the truth, and the courts would let me keep her, I'm sure of it."

"That remains to be seen. But that's not all the question. And here's an important point: Monsieur de Crivelin's will is made in favor of Mademoiselle Adèle Ligny. If I prove that the heiress is not the Demoiselle Ligny, I'll ruin her. If I ruin her, I ruin you. That's something stupid I don't want to do. Besides, I'll too good a father to commit such a cruelty for nothing.

"But you know what they say, in the morality of honest people, that a good deed is never wasted. As a consequence of that maxim, I'm going to make myself your benefactor. That fortune that I can snatch away from all of you, I'm letting you keep it. It's as if gave it to you. That happiness that I could destroy with a word, I respect it. It's as if I created it. Your wife, who would die because of that discovery, I let her live. It's as if I saved her from drowning or a burning building. That dear daughter whose hopes I would ruin forever, I will allow her to marry her fiancé. Then what am I doing? I make you rich and happy. I save your wife's life; I marry my daughter to a man with an honorable name, from a noble family. In truth, you couldn't be more virtuous, more of a benefactor than that; you couldn't be more Monthyou than that. Good deeds abound, and as it's said that a good deed is never wasted, you're going to give me a million."

"A million! Great Heavesn! "exclaimed Monsieur Crivelin.

"A good deed can't be thrown away," said the scoundrel.

"But you're forgetting," Monsieru de Crivelin retorted, "that I can send you to prison."

The scoundrel got up, his eyes deadly, frothing at the mouth.

"No threats like that, or I'll make you ask me for forgiveness on you knees, or I'll force your wife and my daughter to come here flat on their stomachs to kiss dung off my shoes. I'm giving you two hours to give me your answer. I'll be back in two hours."

And that man immediately left.

"That's a sad story," said Riponneau.

"Oh!" said the neighbor, "That's only the beginning, because the wife and daughter were next door to that bedroom. There, one of their good, devoted servants, who never fail to tell you anything which is disagreeable to you, had warned them that Monsieur de Crivelin was shut up with a man who looked like a murderer and that caused fear in the good people of the antechamber.

"This charitable advice, added to the trouble that Madame Crivelin had noticed in her husband, caused her to eavesdrop on the conversation next door. At the cruel trembling, at the stifled cries that escaped from Madame de Crivelin, Adèle started to eavesdrop also, and both of them learned at the same time the horrible secret which struck them both down, the secret that told the mother: 'This is not your daughter; the secret which told the daughter: 'This is not your mother.'

"That's why, when Monsieur de Crivelin went back into that bedroom, he found them both on their knees, both crying, sobbing, and hugging each other convulsively. Madame Crivelin was no longer weeping for the dead child that she had scarcely known, she was weeping for the child she had raised, which, in her divine maternal power she had made in her own image, the child she had passionately loved, and who had loved her with a saintly love.

"It was then most of all that the drama began, with its tears, its heartrending, its delirium. And that went on for a week, Monsieur. All was despair, tears, terror in that household. And, nevertheless, the next day they had to go to a magnificent dinner at the home of the mother of Monsieur de Fromont. And in order for the secret of this misfortune not get outside, the three hours you envied transpired like that. And, as all three of them were more serious than usual and somewhat pale, people insisted on congratulating them on their splendid party. They drank to their health, to the future happiness of the two spouses. They had to smile, tears under their eyelids, sobs in their throats, in the utmost despair."

"But what did they do? What are they going to do?" asked Riponneau.

"A large sum of money made the scoundrel go away. But he can come back. But in a few years his prison sentence will have expired. That is to say, since he escaped prison for twenty years, the length of his sentence, he would be as even with society as someone who had stayed the whole time tied to his chains. And then he wouldn't be talking like a man who was afraid for his life. He would be the absolute master of that family.

"While waiting, governed by the fatality of their previous existence, they lived every day as they had to live in order for no one to suspect anything, but they wept at night. It was there, by the fireside, where they all three stayed awake, that they spent long tearful conferences, sorrowful oaths never to leave each other.

"That wasn't all. Monsieur. Adèle loves Monsieur de Fromont. She loves him because he is brave, generous, full of lofty sentiments, because she is proud of being loved by him. And precisely because she loves him with this noble and chaste love, she doesn't want to deceive him. She doesn't want such a pure man, from such an honorable family, in the middle of his happiness, to be lashed out by this scoundrel who says he is his wife's father.

"Adèle doesn't want to marry the Count de Fromont.

"But what can be done? What can be said? These are the cries of Monsieur and Madame Crivelin.

"And that child, admirable in every way, answered them.

"'As it's because of me you're suffering like this, it's up to me to take the blame for this rupture.'"

"She kept her word, Monsieur, and for a week that delightful and good creature made herself impertinent, cold, capricious. She used sharp words to stir up the anger she brought about by coldness; she laughed at the tears she caused to flow, laughed at the desperate torments of her lover. But as I told you, the time came when the comedy ended and the drama began. And then there wasn't one of the torments she caused that didn't come back to her more bitter and tearing her heart apart. How many sad tears for the tears she had made flow; how many sad cries because of the complaints people had made to her. In the daytime she suffered by causing hurt; at night she suffered from the hurt that had been caused.

"And that wasn't all. Monsieur and Mademe Crivelin each day their daughter loses strength in the battle she is waging against herself, against her love, against the sadness she was giving and that she was experiencing. This morning the doctor found her devoured by a burning fever, and now she's sick. That is nothing in the eyes of society, an indisposition that will calm itself. And the Crivelin family is none the less a happy family

"And you're the first, you pound the walls because the joy of these happy people is troublesome to you and it sits heavy on you. Do you want their joy, young man? Oh! How right now they would gladly exchange their elaborate apartments, their carriages, and their millions for your attic room, your umbrella and your 1,800 francs."

I told you that I thought Riponneau had a low forehead and a military hair cut, and I added that gave him an obstinate look and the appearance of not being a liar. Not being able to deny the misfortune, he wanted to justify it. Here's how:

"Ma foi," he said, "if they're unhappy, they certainly deserve to be."

"Bah!" said the neighbor.

"When you commit such acts and get punished for them, that's logical. I'm sorry for them, that's all, and I certainly wouldn't want to be in their place. Besides, their misfortune depended on an accident that might not have happened. In which case, nothing would have happen to trouble their happiness. Take, for example, someone like Monsieur Domen. Certainly that man has committed more than one sin in his life, and kinds that society wouldn't usually pardon. Well. Because he's rich, because he has a reputation, and talent, everything is accepted. People admire him, he's even celebrated for what would be the shame and despair of anyone else. He's happy, and I don't see what could come to trouble his happiness. It certainly couldn't be the discovery of his equivocal position, because he glorifies in it. He wears it with so much pride that I find it insolence."

"Ah!" said the neighbor. "You envy that, and you're not the only one. In fact, he looked for fortune and glory in the arts, and he found fortune and glory. He loved a married woman. He audaciously took her away from her husband, and more audaciously still he silenced the husband by threatening to reveal all the hideous, dirty things because of which the husband caused a good, noble, charming woman to give herself to another. He didn't stop there. He took that woman under his protection. He made public his love, his adoration his respect for her. And that woman, people respected her because of the respect he showed her. They said about her, that she couldn't inspire such respect without deserving it. And little by little, everyone tolerated, often agreed with that life style. And, as it was accompanied by wealth, if it pleased Domen to open his house to all the great artists in Paris, every one who was less famous, crowded into his drawing rooms. If he traveled, he was treated like a king. He was entertained, he was praised, and that woman took half of that celebrity, of all that happiness."

"Well, Monsieur," Riponneau retorted. "Those two were happy, I hope. And you have just painted their happiness in ways that surely aren't exaggerated, and against which you probably have nothing to say."

"Their happiness!" said the neighbor in a bitter voice full of bitterness. "Their happiness!" he repeated. "Oh! Yes! On the surface it was full of laughter, golden, blooming, and resplendent. But tear aside that veil, go beyond what you're shown, and you'll find the wound, the open wound, painful, gangrened and incurable. You envy that existence. Ask instead for hell, poverty, famine."

"How can that be? How can that be?" asked Riponneau, making himself seem important.

"You said a while ago that it was chance that brought about Monsieur and Madame Crivelin's misfortune, and if that chance hadn't occurred, they would have been happy despite the fault. If that accident disappeared, if that Marsilly died, all the happiness would return. That's possible. But in this happiness you're envying, in the happiness of Monsieur Domen and his beautiful mistress, Madame de Montès, is a constant guest who has never left them one moment, and who will never leave them. He sits at their table, he rides in their carriage, he keeps watch beside their bed. He's there every hour and every moment of their lives. Pride covers with its purple cloak the wound of the two victims, but it always bleeds."

"Come now! Come now!" said Marc-Antoine. "These are certainly beautiful phrases. But without knowing personally Monsieur Domen, I see people who are almost always with him, and they would be hard put to say what bad luck he'd had. On the contrary, there are exclamations every instant about how unbelievably lucky he is with everything he touches. How is he unfortunate?"

"In everything. He hasn't had one misfortune as you understand it, but everything is a misfortune for him."

"You don't say!"

"Everything, and what is most terrible, grief comes to him from every direction."

"Ah! Bah!"

"Listen! One day he was invited to a dance with Madame de Montès at the house of friends who, being aware of the secret of their liaison, had forgiven them and had the courage to protect it from the eyes of the world. Madame de Montès enters, sits down without anything indicating the least disapproval by anyone. They dance, but when the contradance is finished, the two women who had been seated on either side of Madame Montès did not return to their seats and she remained surrounded by the empty seats, exposed in this pillory of silk. The dance continued. Nobody asked her to dance. Domen didn't accept the lesson, either for himself or for Madame Montès, and he led her into the next dance. No one seemed irritated, but the person across from him pretended to have made a mistake about his place and slid gently aside. That insolence originated with a woman who had had thirty lovers, but whose husband was there. Finally, if it hadn't been for an eighteen-year-old young man who was holding a child of fifteen by the hand, both of them seeing only two dancers, if it hadn't been for those two innocents, Doman and Madame de Montès would have remained there, abandoned and repudiated. Don't you think that this dance, which to you seemed a triumph, had been paid for cruelly dearly?"

"And it was always like that?"

"No, assuredly not, neighbor. Neither of them would have endured that affront twice. But wouldn't it have been enough to have undergone it to be constantly afraid of it? It was then that Madame Montès started having a taste for not going out, which was only a self-imposed exile. Domen loved her. He wanted her to have a charming house. Crowds of men came there; women stayed away. Some husbands had the courage to bring their wives, because they had been able to appreciate what there was of true honor and devotion in that guilty couple. They dared it once; they didn't dare it twice. After the insult by rejection came the insult by desertion.

"And now, Monsieur, once that leaven has been thrown into that existence, everything is soured, everything. If, when taking a walk, a friend passes by without seeing them, it isn't that he didn't see them, it's because he's ashamed to greet them. If there's an insolent servant in the house, he's only that way because he thinks he has the right to insult a woman who doesn't wear the name of his master. And in those travels I told you about, a man came up to Monsieur Domen, who had Madame Montès on his arm. He told Monsieur Domen that he was happy to have met such a famous sculptor, a rival of Torwaldsen and Canova. And as he only knew Domen's life as an artist, he bowed, smiling at the woman who was on the arm of the great artist, congratulating her on bearing such an illustrious name.

"What did they answer? Did they have to confess their position, their history, and their entire life to that stranger? Should they say nothing? But the next day that man proudly recounted that he had met Monsieur and Madame

128

Domen. He wanted to invite them; he wanted to give a party for them until one of those parasites who live off tales about everyone's life, told him he was mistaken, or rather that they had deceived him. With this additional accusation that they lied, that would be a new banishment. And, nevertheless, they had done everything to at least be open about their sin so no one could be mistaken. Do you think that's any way to live?"

"Hum! It's annoying, but there are compensations. First of all for Domen, who's invited everywhere."

"And who is exiled everywhere. Do you know that he's ordered his servants to secretly give him all the letters, since he might be able to find, in their number, an invitation addressed just to him alone and Madame Montès would suffer injure and sadness by that exclusion. And if she learns about her husband's orders, if she learns that the letters he receives are hidden from her, do you think she would, first of all, discover the devoted attention that tried to spare her pain? She would see a mystery there, an intrigue, a new lover. She would be jealous.

"Doesn't she have the right to think that? Not because Domen is flighty, inconstant, but because she knows that he's suffering, that he's unhappy; because she knows she's taken him away from life in society which should be his; because she knows that, finding at his home only solitude, sadness, complaints, he must go look somewhere else for joy, laughter, pleasure. This is necessary for the life of someone whose labor is hard and incessant, since he works constantly to at least cover with luxury the miserable existence he leads.

"After the leaven that has spoiled everything in that existence, let's look into jealousy. That's no longer a constant sadness. It's cries, despair, threats of suicide, hatred of life. They love each other, Monsieur, and they forgive each other. And they swear that neither of them will give in to that society which crushes them with so much indifference. Domen will reappear in some evening parties. He agrees; she wishes him to.

"And while they're welcoming him, like a traveler no one expected to see again, thus making him aware of what he left and what he's found again, what is the poor woman doing? She waits; she suffers; she walks up and down in that apartment, so much more empty because it is immense. Ask her if, at such an hour, she wouldn't prefer your attic room, without a sou, but with a needle with which to earn her living. If he comes back early, he finds her in tears, which she hasn't had time to wipe away. If he comes in late, he finds her angry, because this is no longer a duty he's accomplishing, it's a pleasure, causing him to lose track of time. I've told you. Of all the misfortunes, this misfortune is the most terrible. This one has no history because nothing has happened. This isn't a bankruptcy which wipes out a whole fortune. This isn't a child who dies. This isn't a disaster which strikes, crushes and passes on. It's suffering all hours, all minutes. I'm not telling you about what's called one misfortune. It's eternal misfortune that must be told. That existence isn't troubled by one of those violent, known maladies which strikes down and kills or is cured. It's eaten up by a hidden suffering that can't be identified, without a name, which nothing can remedy. I tell you that is hell and damnation on earth."

"Well!" said Marc-Antoine, "I can certainly admit they're unhappy. But let me make use of your comparison. You have likened their unhappiness to one of those secret and cruel maladies which medicine can't cure. Who do these maladies strike? Nervous, delicate, susceptible people. These two people have a sickness of their moral nerves, that's all. But I feel that comes as much from their constitution as from their situation. Suppose this was a question of vigorous natures, rugged, physically and morally cold. They wouldn't feel all these pin pricks. You can take, for example, Mademoiselle Débora. What an astonishing story that girl has! Yes, certainly, she has been very unhappy, and she has suffered, and she has paid in advance for the happiness that's come to her. But after all, it came in abundance.

"Who was she? A poor beggar girl who sang on street corners, who held out her hand for the sou that was thrown to her, more often to make her shut up than to make her sing. She was beaten in the evening when she didn't bring the sum demanded by the mountebank who said he was her father. No clothing, poverty, famine, excessive work, constant terror, such was her life up until the day chance allowed her to show that proud intelligence which had mutinied in her.

"On that day, she entered the theater. She let that voice that was despised on the street corner be heard. That voice stirred with admiration all those to whom she sang the magnificent music of Glück, Rossini, Mozart. Fame came in a few years. Fortune came, and so that nothing was lacking in the triumph of vanity of that ambitious girl, the handsomest and the most elegant men of the period came to lay down their love at her feet.

"She took a taste before choosing, they say. She chose the one that the most beautiful and noble women fought over. That man adored her. He was her slave. And it wasn't at all like Monsieur Domen. There was no fear in his love; he dressed it up; he showed it off. And as I don't think Débora had in her childhood learned the delicacy which caused Madame Montès' unhappiness, since, in her situation, love is almost a right, and as I don't suppose she had any remorse because of her weaknesses, I can't see what could disturb such a perfect happiness. But it wasn't only happiness, it was triumph, it was victory. Madame de Montès is less than she should be. She suffers because of that; I understand that. But that Dèbora is more than she has ever dreamed of being, and if she isn't fortunate, who could be?"

"No one, probably," the neighbor answered, "because you yourself aren't. But Dèbora has her hell just as Madame Montès."

"She is jealous of her lover?"

"No."

"She is jealous of her rivals at the Opéra?"

"No."

"She's not very satisfied with the public?"

"No, it's not that."

"Then what's wrong with her?"

"Ah!" said the old neighbor, scratching his nose. "That's difficult to make you understand."

Then he continued. "Do you have any sort of artistic bent?"

"No."

"Have you ever been anything other than a clerk?"

"No."

"Have you ever bought anything extravagant?"

"Never."

"Let's see. Do you have some friend who's rich or who throws away money as if he were rich?

"Ah! That's good. Maybe I'm going to find in that direction the door through which I can lead you into the unhappiness that eats away at that life you find so happy. Tell me, have you ever eaten with that friend who squanders money a dinner given for a coquettish working class girl?"

"Certainly, more than one."

"There I have it, because it's impossible that you've never done that. The shop girl you took to the Rocher de Cancalae or to the Douix ordered dinner. She looked at the menu on the right-hand side, that is, on the side with the prices and she ordered, not because she liked it, but because it seemed to her that it must be the best because it was the most expensive."

"Undoubtedly, that's happened to me. I'll never in my life forget a dinner this winter made up of fifteen francs worth of radishes, sixty francs worth of asparagus, and forty-five francs of strawberries with pheasant and lobster."

"That was all?"

"Ah! *Ma foi!* I don't remember all the side dishes and the wines and the liqueurs. Finally, that amounted to a hundred ecus for four people."

"In this sumptuous dinner, why wasn't there found a small bizarre something that didn't fit the rest?"

"Oh! Yes there was. pardieu! And it was even something rather funny. Can you imagine that our two shop girls, after having tasted all these excellent things, at the end of the meal asked for a piece of pickled port with cabbage."

"All right! See there! Now you have it! Well, my dear neighbor, that beautiful and famous Débora is in the position of your shop girls. Fame, fortune, her lover, those are asparagus, strawberries, and lobster of your two shop girls. With these dishes they would die of hunger. With your magnificent advantages, she's dying of boredom."

"Ah! Bah!" said Marc-Antoine.

Then he added, laughing in advance about the witticism he was going to make:

"But couldn't she, like the shop girls, give herself some salt pork and cabbage?"

"Ah! That's where the difference comes in. It's here you find a bizarre, strange, unexplainable, and, nevertheless a profound nuance between Débora and the woman I talked to about. There isn't, as there in with Madame Montès, a battle between herself and society. It's a battle between intelligence and habit, a combat between primitive nature and acquired nature."

"The Devil! That's something that's devilish subtle."

"Listen to me carefully. You don't arrive at the talent, power, and success of Dèbora without possessing great intelligence, fertile imagination, capable of assimilating every great idea."

"That can't be denied."

"But you don't live in misery, poverty, most of all in a state of beggary, without picking up the habits of hypocrisy which, when the beggar stops putting on his act, turns into petulant joy, coarse language, and jokes. These spit on the benefactor who's been taken in by the con artist."

"That could happen."

"Well! My dear friend, while Débora is on stage, the loftiness of her ideas are on a equal to ideas she's expressing. She's pleased with this play-acting, because its clearly play-acting and she's giving the public what the public asks her for. But when she's taken off the silk dress and when she's taken off the crown of a queen, she doesn't return to the freedom of a street-corner huckster, to her shouts, to her loud laughter. Unfortunately for her, she enters another comedy. Her drawing room is open; elegant men fill it; women with well-learned manners are there. Débora is proud. Débora herself is worth all those women and she wants to show them that. After having appeared in the theatre as a queen, she acts the great lady in her drawing room. She chats, she flatters, she jokes… right up to the time when, tired of that new scene, of that new public, she runs away, escaping into a small hidden room, where the sovereign, respected by all of society, begins to scream at her lover:

"This bores me!

"He tries to plead with her.

"She becomes furious, but it's not one of those polite furies that upbringing teaches us. She sends her lover packing; she swears, she behaves in an unmannerly and common fashion; she smashes furniture; and if a nuisance of a foot-man comes in, she kicks him out. She calls the most elegant man in France an idiot with the same voice that sang about gold and diamonds. He is devastated. She kicks him out and if she is still out of control, she eats with her coachman and hobnobs with her maids."

"Impossible!"

"Then the next day comes, bringing remorse and repentance, because she loves him. She, or rather the intellectual part of Débora esteems and loves the love of that man. She knows very well his worth, she who learned at the lowest school how little others are worth. And she thinks herself vile, unworthy, to have these memories, these regrets, and these returns to her vile past. She feels herself to be all that her lover wants her to become. She calls him back; she asks his forgiveness; and she begins her comedy again.

"She makes herself again the charming and distinguished woman he loves. She puts all her love, all her strength into it. She again wears herself out doing it. The thread breaks and the scenes start again.

"Then she runs away.

"She leaves everything and gets into a carriage. She wanders around aimless-ly, and she sees a huckster winking at his crony, signaling the theft he has just pulled off, holding up the money he's just filched from the victim with which they'll drink and laugh at his expense. When Débora sees that she's overcome with wild regrets, and if she had ever wanted to cry, it was at that moment.

"What would she cry about? About her present wealth? Sometimes. What does she weep for? Her poverty? Yes and no. Ambition, intelligence, lofty de-sires are on one side. It was to satisfy them that she played this double comedy. Habits, turbulent memories, gypsy blood, the irresponsibility of poverty, the delirium of joy in rags are on the other side. And that's what made her detest both the wealth she has acquired, the fame she merits, and the love she expe-riences."

"You'll allow me to point out to you, neighbor, that these are completely imaginary pains."

"You'll allow me to point out to you, dear neighbor, that you've just said something enormously stupid. Except for colic, fever, broken arms and legs and neurology, everything about this story is hardly imaginary. Understand one thing. You don't really suffer except through your ideas. Put a silly girl from the street corner in the place of Madame Mont and she wouldn't suffer from any of the troubles that are killing that poor woman. Put a girl who's a doorkeeper in Débora's place, cool down that devouring personality, and she wouldn't experience any of the sudden changes that torment her. Or, lower the level of her intelligence, and she would return to her past without remorse, without regrets, without cruel judgments against herself. The misfortune is in the battle and it is so poignant, so active, that it burns away and dries up that life, that it threatens it, that it kills it."

"Well!" retorted Ripanneau, "if, in my case, I didn't understand the misfortune, it seems to me that in yours there's no happiness on earth."

"Very much to the contrary. There are people who feel nothing; who experience nothing; who love nothing...."

"And who are they?"

The neighbor's face took on a sinister expression and he gave an evil laugh.

"There are the dead."

Marc-Antoine was afraid and there was an almost solemn moment of silence. Across the room's partition, they heard something like a fall and then long stifled moans.

"It's our neighbor," Marc-Antoine exclaimed.

"Yes," said the neighbor. "She's moaning."

"But something unusual is happening", said Marc-Antoine. "Don't you smell that odor of burning charcoal?"

"I'm familiar with it," said the neighbor, without getting up.

"There's some misfortune over there."

"That's not my opinion."

"It's a suicide."

"You're right."

"Ah! Let's hurry over there."

"Leave her alone. To act that way, she probably has reasons we don't know anything about."

Riponneau threw the old neighbor a furious look of indignation. The old neighbor again shrugged and laughed in Riponneau's face. As for Riponneau, he ran to Jauna's door (the neighbor was named Juana) and kicked at the door. The door, since it was an attic room door, broke apart at the first kick. Ripponneau went in to an asphyxiating, suffocating atmosphere. He saw a white body lying on the tile floor. He stooped down, picked it up in his arms, carried it to his bedroom and put it on his bed.

Oh! How beautiful Juana was like that, although her lips were already almost violet and slight foam ran along the edge of her mouth!

The young girl had gone to bed after she came out of the bath, after having lit the fatal stove, with her best night cap on her head, dressed in her finest and whitest linen. She had acted like a coquette for death, a pretty coquette, and death had avidly come for her to place his icy hand on the naked breast of his fiancée. But fortunately Marc-Antoine had arrived in time and he saw that pure white forehead come alive again, those eyes with velvety lights open and close again in astonishment. He saw those lips come apart to draw in the pure air he was filling the room with through the door and windows. He saw her bosom rise, filled with the long breaths that brought her back to life.

How beautiful she was! But we must say at this first moment Riponneau wasn't at all thinking about looking at all that, except to watch with anxiety the resurrection of the unfortunate girl.

Finally the moment came when life had completely gone back into that beautiful body. Juana tried to speak; Juana tried to ask questions. She was told to lie quiet, that she must rest. She wanted to get up and flee. It was then that she became aware of how she was dressed when she was found. And she herself was embarrassed, and even more beautiful. She hid herself in the covers of that bed on which she had been placed.

Then tears came.

Tears, that dew which fall from the heart and which leaves it for a moment calm and rested, like the waves of rain which fall from a storm cloud and which, for an instant, give heaven back its calm and transparency, until the moment when the sun takes back that rain to make a new storm and the heart takes back its tears to create new despair.

That was the neighbor's poetry as he watched Juana fall asleep, exhausted by fatigue and tears. Riponneau was also seeing her, but not as he saw her now, in her night cap, wrapped up in his sheets, but at the moment when he wasn't looking at her, when she was stretched out on his bed, "in the simple dress…" (You know the other verse), and this memory came back to him so strong, so charming, so delightful, that despite how much he had been bored listening to his neighbor's stories, he wanted to ask him about that of the poor girl.

"You who know all the people in this house," he said to him, "you must know who this Juana is, and you must know most of all what pushed her to this desperate act."

"What she is," said the neighbor, again looking disdainful, "what pushed her to kill herself…what's the good in telling you that?

"Wasn't she still singing yesterday like a warbler, spreading her joyous wings, and going down these six flights of stairs like a bird coming down from heaven, light on her feet, bubbling over, smiling, completely spick and span and happy? What is she? What led her to kill herself? That's yet another of those unseen dramas which takes place covered by the public existence of everyone. It has the same shooting pain as a tooth ache, which can't be seen and which murders you. You wouldn't believe it."

"Ah!" said Riponneau, "the result is there to make me believe it."

"Bah! You'd say that she is insane."

"Do you take me for an imbecile or for a cold egoist like you? Because you said these words to me a while ago: "Let her alone." But you thought those groans we heard were a joke, didn't you?"

"Not the least in the world. But I was wise for her…and perhaps for you."

"For me!" exclaimed Riponneau. "What do you mean?"

The neighbor's eyes lit up with a flame which seemed to travel throughout the bedroom, the wall, and lose itself far away in space. And he coldly began again.

"The future will answer you for me. Now, here are some of the words you wanted to know.

"That Juana is the daughter of a worker, a printer of colored cloth. She's the seventh child of a numerous family, the seventh child who arrived almost ten years after all the others, as a consequence the seventh child poorly received by the older ones and the younger ones, the father and the mother.

"My young friend, nothing is as saintly, sacred, beautiful, and respectable as maternal love, paternal love, fraternal love. But it's precisely because these feelings are the most powerful in nature that, when they are broken, they become totally cruel and wicked. It's like the ship moored by a triple steel cable. When the strength of the wind is violent enough to break the cable, the ship is swept away beyond any known path.

"It would make your heart bleed to see what that child has had to suffer from the harshness of her family: withholding food and clothing, cold, hunger, they inflicted all that on her. You see her beautiful and full blown with all that ample beauty that comes with the full development of the strength of youth. Well! All that was skinny, stunted growth, stooped shoulders, small stomach, a gasping voice. Ten years went by before she was able to remove from her family the useless burden that had entered it.

"Finally, a sister of her mother took pity on that child and undertook her up-keep. She was the wife of a rich, fat, screaming butcher, much given to coarse language. In that new existence, Juana drew all that you can from fillet of beef, and good mutton cutlets. That meant the development of a rich physical nature. But as for nourishment for the soul, that was more lacking to her there than in her own family. They had no other words for her except those which reproached her, I won't say the bread, but the flesh she ate. And note this, neighbor, that girl was born with all the good qualities to be grateful. But they did it so well they killed this very rare sentiment in her. She began to hate everything that surrounded her. And she reached fifteen years of age having only one desire, that was how to get revenge on everybody. That was a year ago. She was then eighteen-years-old, when her aunt's death gave her freedom.

"Among the bad lessons she learned while in her aunt's house Juana had profited by the one that revealed to her the deplorable situation of her uncle. Do you want to know what it was? Do you want to know why that man (there are a thousand in Paris like him) having all the appearances of commercial prosperity and happiness in his household, was the most miserable of men? Either through lack of caution or rather prodigality to satisfy his wife's desire for luxury, he had compromised his fortune. He was two steps away from ruin when a friend appeared, an honest merchant of beef. He wanted to come to the aid of Jauna's uncle. He proposed that the uncle buy some bonds. He would lend him cash, the loan backed by a mortgage on his property, and everything the usurer could imagine of useful precautions. Our butcher, whose ruin could be predicted, came out of it successfully and could have backhanded all those who had already given him up as a failed business man. As a consequence, he doubled his expenditures for the adored wife, who had already run him so deeply into debt."

"The lender approved. That was good."

"The maturity date of the loan arrived. Impossible to pay it. And with the certainty of that impossibility, another more horrible certainty. That was that the butcher had bound over everything to the usurer, who generously renewed his loan. Right up to that point he had been cautious, discreet, and submissive. Now he shouted, he jeered, he insulted. In fact the butcher was between imminent ruin and the cold acceptance of his bankruptcy. He preferred ruin, but he had children who would die of hunger, and a daughter who would be dishonored by her mother's dishonor.

"What's more, if he dared file a complaint, the response was predetermined. He was a debtor slandering his creditor. What role should he play? The one which would, at least, save his fortune and appearances at the same time. He became friends with his beef merchant. He made him his guest and pretended confidence, happiness, gaiety. And the neighbors said:

"'He doesn't know anything; therefore there's nothing wrong. He's lucky.'

"Oh! No! Neighbors. It was at first a silent torment, then, when the presumptuousness of the guilty went too far, he broke into the sanctity of his household. He threw temper tantrums. He shouted. But the wife, implacable and sure of her power, answered him coldly:

"'But, *Mon Dieu*, throw him out. I couldn't ask for anything better.'

"To throw out the man who held his existence and his honor in his hands, not only his existence, but that of his children. He couldn't do it and he put back on his shameful chains, rage in his heart.

"But who knew about that? No one on the outside, because the butcher had his vanity. He preferred to be considered an idiot rather than a coward. No one had any idea what he was suffering, except his family, and among his family, Juana.

"What could she learn from that lesson? The idea that with money you have everything, even the right to avoid every obligation, must necessarily have germinated in her heart, so little prepared for life. Thus, when she was free, what did she aspire to? To be rich. Hadn't she lived too long with calculation not to be calculating? She didn't get in a hurry. She waited for a good opportunity. And she didn't listen to any propositions but those that were accompanied by great fortune and backed up by promises of marriage.

"Has she been imprudent enough to trust promises, and now, has she nothing more to give the man who doesn't want to give anything more? Or is it that she hadn't had enough cleverness or enough charm, to shove uncompromisingly the man who loves her as far as marriage? That's something I don't know. But I do know that he's getting married next week."

The old neighbor hadn't finished when an old gentleman, venerably dressed, wearing a wig, and decorated with red ribbons, entered and asked for Juana. What a surprise! He was one of the richest financiers in the French Administration, a Receiver General, worth more than a banker, and he asked for Mademoiselle Juana. They pointed her out to him where she was sleeping, after having told him what she had done.

The financier asked them to wake her and to leave them alone. The neighbor withdrew and Marc-Antoine, thinking he was in his own home wanted to stay. He was afraid the beautiful Juana would fly away during his absence. However, he promised not to listen very much, with the grim intention of hearing everything. The old man drew near the bed and this is exactly what Riponneau picked up.

"You wrote my daughter a letter telling her that her fiancé, Monsieur de Belmont, her future husband had cheated on her; that he loved you; that he had promised to marry you…"

His voice trailed off to a whisper so that Riponneau missed some words. A moment later, the voice became audible.

"You have almost killed my daughter. She's in bed, dying, devastated, and doesn't want to go through with this marriage."

"That's my revenge, Monsieur," Juana said.

"But that revenge strikes people who have done nothing to you, doesn't it? I want this marriage to take place, but my daughter won't consent unless the hand that wrote her that vile letter writes her another one, swearing to her that it was a fabrication intended to harm Monsieur de Belmont…"

"Never!" Juana declared in a resolute voice.

The old man mumbled something.

"Never!" Juana said in a lower voice.

The old man murmured again. Then suddenly, as if inspired all at once by an idea, he looked at Marc-Antoine. And then the mumbling went on, went one, like an unstoppable flood.

138

All this time Juana let out some less and less determined no's. Then she threw a pleasing look at Riponneau, lowered her head and was finally silent. The comedy was over. Here's how it was played.

The gentleman went away, saying to Riponneau:

"Thank you, Monsieur, for the care you've taken of that charming child. All our family, who're interested in her, will be grateful to you for your kind deed. We'll be happy to recompense you by coming to help Jauna's difficulties."

Saying that, the venerable old man left them together.

Now, let's go back over what happened. The play began on a Monday. Let's go forward to **Tuesday**:

"Oh! Juana!" said Marc-Antoine, "do you still want to die?"

"I still wanted to yesterday because I didn't believe in generous and disinterested hearts."

"And you believe in them now?"

"Didn't you save me even though you didn't know me?"

Wednesday:

"What does that mean/ Saving your life wasn't anything. Happiness for me would be to console you."

Thursday:

"There is no consolation for broken hearts except in gentle affection and I have no friends."

"I'll be your friend."

"I have no family."

"I'll be a family to you."

Friday:

"After what I did with someone else, you must despise me."

"I admire and respect you."

"You'll never love me."

"I'm already madly in love with you."

"Like a madman, you're right, since where would that lead you!"

"To devote myself to your happiness."

Saturday:

"My happiness could never be anywhere except in a legitimate union, and you will never want to marry me."

Sunday: (after a night of reflection)

"My name is yours whenever you like."

This dialogue is composed of the last words of eight days of conversations, each four hours long. But when the fatal and supreme words were said, the words: *I'll marry you*, Marc-Antoine was told he would have a rich dowry and the protection of the venerable gentleman he had met.

"Now it's my turn to be happy," Marc-Antoine then shouted. "Fortune, consideration, happiness is mine."

And three weeks afterward he was nominated for the position of assistant director, received a dowry of forty thousand francs and Juana's hand.

Only one thing saddened the happy day. Leaving the house, Riponneau's rented carriage bumped into the white hearse which had come to pick up the corpse of Mademoiselle de Crivelin, and Doctor Funin, who was one of Juana's witnesses, had to leave the wedding dinner to go to the home of Domen, who had failed to kill himself with a pistol shot to the heart.

The wedding guests were told Adèle had died of pulmonary sickness and Domen had tried to kill himself because he hadn't been nominated to the Institute. Only one voice rose to contradict these reports. It was that of the neighbor, that Riponneau had invited to the wedding and who had only this to say:

"*Non*, this was only the inevitable dénouement of those invisible dramas that abound under the epidermis of society."

"What does that mean? What's an invisible drama?" People asked him from all sides.

"You want to know?" asked the neighbor. "Well, look. There's one that beginning even at this instant beside you."

No one understood, not even Riponneau.

But six months' afterward, when his wife gave birth, and when he wanted to clear up some things, and when his wife called him a mean paper-pusher, she proved to him that, without her, he would still be living in his attic dung heap.

A week after that birth, when he got a promotion, he saw chosen a god-father he didn't know, who was the son of the minister who was his protector. Three months after that advancement, after having left, sad and full of care, the bureaucratic green leather throne where his former colleagues had come to humbly greet him, he saw, turning into the *Allées des Veuves,* at the back of a fiacre, badly hidden, his beautiful Juana and the god-father, the son of the minister.

Several hours after that encounter, when he had returned home and wanted to make an issue of it, he was threatened with being thrown out the window.

For a long time after that, during his lifetime, to the extent that his reputation grew by the zeal he put into fulfilling his duties, just so much was his consideration in his own household diminished.

Some years later, his wife, strengthened by knowing the poverty she had pulled him out of and the foolish love that he still had for her, turned the contempt of his servants against him, him ridiculous in his children's eyes, sacrificed the legitimate children to the first-born, stamped under foot all respect. Then Marc-Antoine, at thirty-six, head of his division, Master of Petitions, decorated with the Legion of Honor for his honesty and his ability, cited as one of the happiest men of the century. (Because he put his best efforts into covering up his household scandal.) Riponneau, I say, finally understood what the neighbor had wanted to say to him the day of his marriage about invisible dramas which were beginning.

The most bizarre ideas come to people who are in pain. He was going toward his former house, where he has so much stomped about, so many times struck his fist against the walls. He walked up to the seventh floor where he had lived. He stopped in front of that bedroom door where he had been so unhappy and he began to weep for the misfortune of former times. He didn't look at Juana's, and he came to the old neighbor's door. That was where he was going.

He knocked. Blonde hair and rosy cheeks answered the door.

"What do you want, Monsieur?

"I want to see an old gentleman who lived here some years ago."

"What was his name?"

"I don't know, but he was a copyist, I believe."

A young woman appeared, beautiful and sad. "Oh! I know who you're talking about, Monsieur, a bold old man…"

She described him so that it was impossible not to know he was the one.

"Do you know where I can find him?"

"Wait, Monsieur, I'm going to tell you. He often changes addresses, but he's always sure to leave the last one here."

While the beautiful young woman was looking, a hoarse voice came from the alcove. "What is it, Manon?"

"It's a gentleman come looking for the address of the old renter…"

"Is that your husband?" Riponneau asked with disgust.

"Yes, Monsieur, he's a little sick."

The scoundrel was dead drunk.

"Here is your address, Monsieur."

"But good lady," Riponneau said. "You don't seem happy to me."

And he motioned with his eyes to the husband. "Please let me thank you for your kindness."

Saying that, he handed her two louis.

"Thank you, Monsieur," the young woman said to him. "My husband is a good worker. He works hard…when he's not sick…thank you…"

Riponneau glanced into the room. It showed poverty, the hideous poverty that had come from comfortable circumstances. There remained a bed. It was mahogany; a table, it was elegant; some chairs. These had belonged to a draw-ing room.

He left ten louis in the child's hands, and left, saying:

"Still another of those unseen dramas over which the devotion, the pity, the labor of that poor noble woman throws a veil that perhaps no one but me has lifted."

Leviathan

Julien Green

Julian Green

Julien Green (1900-1998) had the honor of being the only American elected to the *Académie Française*, but to become a member he would have to give up his American citizenship. He therefore declined the honor. Later he was given honorary French citizenship to allow him to accept the honor. He said," A country is also a language and me, I'm French."

Green's mother died when he was 14, and some two years later Green converted to Catholicism. He joined the American Field Service at the beginning of WWI, but, as he was under age, his enlistment was canceled. When he was of age, six months later, he enlisted in the French army, first in the Foreign Legion and then in the regular French army. After the war, in 1919, he enrolled in the University of Virginia and remained there until 1922, when he returned to France.

He began his literary career as a student at the University of Virginia with a first short story, "The Apprentice Psychiatrist," published in *The University of Virginia Magazine* in May of 1920. Although he had been converted to Catholicism, when he returned to Paris from the University of Virginia, he wrote a major manifesto, "Pamphlet Contre les Catholics de France," published under a pseudonym, which launched him into the French literary world. He continued to write short stories, some of them set in Savannah, Virginia, or New England, those about the South drawing on his mother's stories of life before the War of Secession. His first novel, *Mont Cinère*, was published in English as *Avarice House*, and takes place in Virginia on the estate of Kinloch, owned by one of Green's relatives.

Leviathan

He had been waiting for five minutes in front of the *Bonne Espérance,* whose enormous prow hid the entire estuary from him. The dock boys scurried around him between the stacks of coal and the pyramids of casks. There were probably cries and laughter around him, but he seemed to be aware of nothing and kept his head lowered. He was tall, dressed in an overcoat of worn-out cloth with huge pockets, into which he had stuffed his hands. The rim of his hat was pulled over his eyes and hid his face.

When they came to get him, he picked up his valise himself. Its weight made his wrists shake. He followed his guide across the narrow gangplank and onto the vessel's bridge. He was conducted to his cabin.

Once alone, he closed the porthole, turned the handle to lock it, drew the little serge curtain, and took off his hat. He was a man about forty years old, with a sad face, regular features without wrinkles, but his age could be guessed by the defiant and discouraged expression in his eyes and that something in the skin color which was no longer youth. After hoisting his valise onto his bunk, he opened it and took out his belongings with the gestures of someone who is determined not to remain idle a second and who is trying to find a way to distract himself from his thoughts by keeping his hands busy. Toward the end of the day, a sailor came to ask him for the Captain if he would be eating in the dining room. He didn't answer immediately and wanted first to know at what time the *Bonne Espérance* would lift anchor. He was told it was scheduled for eleven p.m. that night.

"All right. I won't have dinner."

And he didn't leave his cabin.

The next day, Captain Suger sent for him to come see him. The Captain had all the mannerisms of a straightforward person, to the point that they seemed fake. He said to him bluntly:

"Monsieur, you know that I almost never take passengers aboard my ship. Probably, my registration authorizes me to do so, but my ship is primarily a cargo vessel. I'm making an exception in your case."

He stopped as if to give his only passenger time to express his appreciation. But the man said nothing. The Captain put his hands in his pockets, and balanced on the tips of his toes, with a somewhat irritated expression.

"I'm going to have to ask to see your identification papers," he finally said.

"Then I'll show them to you, if it's necessary," the passenger said softly.

"Here, what I wish is always necessary," the Captain answered in the same tone.

There was silence during which the man put on his pince-nez, searched the inside pocket of his jacket, and took out and opened his passport. The Captain took that document and examined it with the greatest care. He had a large face. Curiosity put an infinite number of small wrinkles on it. His eyes attached themselves to the passport with a kind of voracity.

"Strange idea you had to travel on a cargo vessel," he finally said, while returning the passport to the passenger. "You know it takes twenty days."

"I know," the man replied and took back his passport.

"Obviously, it's a little less expensive…." the Captain continued, making a little face."That's probably why… ."

He didn't finish and rocked on his tip-toes, seeming to wait to go back on his heels until the passenger had furnished an explanation. But the man said nothing.

"But then," the Captain said, "that's not any of my business…."

He shrugged and turned his back on the passenger, who left.

An important cargo hold full of heavy material assured the *Bonne Espérance* of almost steady ballast despite the stormy sea. She sailed along, heavy and slow, under a threatening sky. Those first days were rather painful for the passenger. He was not at all a sailor; you might even doubt, to see his uncertain walk and his worried expression, that he had ever set foot on a sea-going vessel. The better part of the day he stayed in his room, where he seemed to be content. Some men have the ability to be able to make themselves at home anywhere and in such a way that they seem to have been established there forever. How did they manage that? That was their secret. They just had to move certain objects about, to change the position of a piece of furniture, so that, in some unexplainable way, a hotel bedroom, where they would spend only one night, would seem to have belonged to them for a long time, and to be, for them, a dwelling which they would never leave.

Probably there was something in them opposed to the idea of change which seemed to give what surrounded them an appearance of permanency in some way. It was perhaps an instinctive movement of this kind that motivated the passenger of the *Bonne Espérance* to change the appearance of his cabin as much as possible. He had thrown a beige coverlet which belonged to him, on his berth, thus hiding the blue counterpoint of the Company's logo. He had hidden in the same way the *antimacassar* on the backs of the arm chair, where the same logo was embroidered in bright colors on the backs of the armchairs. Some books stood on a rough shelf which was supposed to hold shoes. Finally, the table was placed in a corner which it dominated, in an obvious way, as if calling attention to the large clear stain that its foot had left in the spot on the rug where it had first been placed. There, where it was now, a roll by the ship

146

a little stronger than the others would be sure to turn it over, but the voyager had only a limited acquaintance with the sea.

Almost from the beginning of the voyage, torrential rains beat down on the *Bonne Espérance* with such violence that it was almost as if they were determined to make the vessel return to its port. But has there ever been an example of a vessel that reversed its course because of rain? The Captain laughed at that terrible weather.

"We owe this to you," he said with impertinence to the voyager when, by chance, he met him in the corridors. At that, the tall thin man readjusted his pince-nez on his nose and managed a mirthless laugh which sounded like a cough. One day, in a blunt and jovial tone, the Captain said to him:

"You know, you're my guest; you're going to have to take your meals at my table."

He put his plump little hands behind his back and continued in a tone calculated to produce laughter:

"That bores you, eh?"

The man shook his head as a sign of protest.

"Then, say," the Captain suddenly said, "Do you ever talk?"

Three days earlier he would not have risked asking such a familiar and insolent question. But he felt himself becoming more and more important as he was reaching the high seas far from the coast of France, he could take these familiarities. The man made a kind of grimace which had to take the place of a smile and withdrew after having taken leave.

After this day, they took their meals at the same table, in a little room forward in the vessel. Large portholes allowed the horizon's stormy view to be seen in its full extent. A strong and harsh light lit the Captain and the passenger seated across from each other.

Leaning back in his chair, Suger said, "Here, you really feel you're at sea: you can't make a movement without knowing that."

And he admitted that of all the vessel's rooms, this was the one he liked best. He was a born sailor, you might say; he didn't like the earth, cities. He loved only the solitude of his vessel.

"You think me happy, probably, because I joke," he said. "Actually, I have the gaiety of those who're depressed."

And, as if that confidence certainly deserved another in return, he suddenly raised his head and exclaimed:

"But you! Tell me about yourself. You don't talk."

That was true. The man said nothing. He ate in silence, looking at the Captain through his pince-nez, nodding his head, but not saying a word. He did not seem timid, however. His eyes had the stare of myopic people who are convinced that everybody had to be aware of their infirmity and of the fact that they had to fix them firmly in their sight in order to really see them. Nevertheless, from time to time something passed across his face, but it was too rapid for the Captain to notice it. Was it caused by a sudden feeling of sickness? Suddenly he frowned and his pupils became misty, seeming to grow larger. Horrible despair spread over his features, stayed there an instant, and then, with a twitch, disappeared almost immediately. That resembled a tic. At those moments, the passenger always took off his pince-nez and lowered his head somewhat.

They were having dessert and the Captain was playing with his knife, making it swing back and forth on his index finger.

"Well, yes," he repeated. "You never say anything. Nevertheless, I'm not giving up hope. A few more days at sea and you'll become more talkative."

The passenger shrugged and took off his pince-nez to wipe its glasses. "We'll see about that," he seemed to say.

The Captain was probably right. A week aboard a merchant vessel, for a passenger, that's almost like being in solitary confinement. That transforms a man. Even those suffering from depression can't resist it. They have to talk; they have to form bonds; they have to make friends, even if it's only to abandon them when they reach port. But isn't it curious that at the end of five or six days of a sea voyage, you think less about the port and you tend to forget it completely the closer you get to it. The monotony of the voyage becomes part of you and, with that, the unusual idea that what has lasted such a great number of hours will never end. If there had at least been a minute's diversion, and if they had passed an island, seen from a distance the extreme limits of a continent. But nothing happened to interrupt the infinite line of the horizon that one saw at daybreak, during meals, during the entire day. For a nervous disposition, this spectacle was affliction, almost torment. It's because of this that those aboard a vessel turn toward those like them, as if toward their salvation, even if they despise them, even if they hate them. Because they must live, they must escape the boredom devouring the days. They must escape the sea, that leviathan stalking them and silently following them.

Did I say that the *Bonne Espérance* was going from France to America? It was sailing the longest route and following a straight line to Savannah. The Captain had adapted. He had long ago become habituated to the sea, by means of conversing with the members of the crew, and with the passengers, when by chance he found he had any. A passenger was a godsend. Like a lot of those with inferior intelligence who have read a few novels, the Captain made pretenses to what he called psychology and amused himself by studying the people around him. He credited himself with insight and was certain that after some days he would be able to find, to use an expression he was fond of, the right *method* to get at those he was examining. I won't go so far as to say he committed his observations to writing, but that was certainly in his character. After he had issued his orders to everyone, overseen the ship's operations, there remained before him a long day that he had to fill. So, the passenger furnished him a precious distraction. He congratulated himself on having him on board, as a mathematician rubs his hands together when confronted by a difficult problem. After thinking about it, he liked his cold mannerisms, that silence that had at first irritated him, and that reserve that, everything considered, made the game last longer and made him more interesting.

Nonetheless, the passenger seemed determined to remain silent. It was clear that the Captain's inquisitive looks bothered him and that he considered the hours spent at meals as extremely disagreeable. But he tried not to show anything of his feelings, and what did appear, was shown despite his efforts. If the Captain had been as observant as he thought he was, he would surely have guessed that the passenger was afraid of him. But he was following another tack and believed he was just dealing with a proud misanthrope. Happy with his discovery, he now tried contriving some clever questions which must at the same time flatter the traveler's vanity and direct him to confidences about himself. That tactic failed, however, as had the Captain's blunt manners and pointed questions before it. The traveler didn't say anything; only, when the Captain became too insistent, he lowered his head, a little like you lower your head in the gusts of a squall.

Now the sky was clear and the *Bonne Espérance* seemed to sail more quickly. The wind was gentle. Silence reigned, scarcely interrupted by the murmur of the waves spreading out before the prow of the ship. But the traveler didn't leave his stateroom. There, alone, he seemed at rest. You would have thought that he feared everything outside that little room and that, on the other side of the door, his life was in danger. Sometimes the sailors who were walking on the bridge saw through a porthole opening a white face with a vague expression, which at once disappeared, suddenly frightened.

Confronted with the passenger's silence, the Captain at first remained disconcerted; then it made him ill-tempered. He had invited that man to his table; he had spoken to him openly as to a friend, to an old friend; he had even confided some circumstances of his private life to him, and what had he gotten in exchange? Nothing. It's certainly interesting to delve into the secrets of a man inclined to silence, with just the help of observation and intelligence, but at the end of the third week, the Captain had had enough. There was something repellent in the morose face of the passenger and his silence was no longer interesting.

The voyage was drawing to an end. A seagull, announcing the approach of land, had settled on the prow of the ship, only to take heavy flight again at once with a snap of his long wings. One day, as he was rising from the table, the Captain planted himself in front of his guest, who had said nothing since the beginning of the meal. He raised himself on his tip toes and fell back on his heels.

"You understand, we arrive day after tomorrow," he said.

The man lifted his head. The Captain's severe expression probably frightened him. He made a sort of grimace, took off his pince-nez and answered in a stifled voice:

"I know."

He seemed so depressed that a movement of compassion took the place of the Captain's irritation.

"Is anything wrong with you?" Suger asked in a moment. "You're not sick?"

The man shook his head.

As he was going back to his cabin, a sudden movement of the ship caused him to leave the wall which he was leaning against and threw him against one of the lifeboats installed on the bridge. He made a convulsive movement and, clinging to some ropes, he looked at the sea with the expression of horror of a man suddenly put in the presence of death.

"Don't be afraid," cried out the Captain, who was following him at a distance.

And he came to help him get back to his stateroom.

That day passed as had the others, except that the Captain asked fewer question than usual. He had evidently come to terms with a silence that he couldn't win over, and even, by a movement of good will which did him honor, he seemed to want to be more likable than he had been up to that point. Was it that the voyager's truly overwhelmed expression had made him feel pity? From time to time he looked at him on the sly and shook his head gloomily.

The traveler ate but very little and most of the time remained leaning over his plate, constantly rubbing his knees with the palm of his hand. At the careful and poor get up of his high buttoned frock coat, he could be taken for a teacher.

The last day rose on a cloudy but calm sea, and when the two men sat down at the table together for the last time, the sky was radiant. The cool air wafted breaths of perfumes in which it seemed the delicious odors of the earth and trees could already be recognized.

"Eh, well," said the Captain, while pouring his guest some wine, "let's leave each other as good friends. Let's drink to one another's health."

The man looked stupid and sad. He raised his glass, held it in the air a moment, and suddenly let it fall on his napkin and the rug.

"I have something to tell you," he murmured.

He turned pale and repeated the sentence louder as if afraid the Captain had not heard it. The Captain seemed carried away by surprise and pleasure.

"So," he said, laughing, "didn't I tell you so? I knew very well that you would finally come around to talking to me. I understand the sea!"

And he let out a resounding laugh, mingled with some restraint.

"Get control of yourself," he continued, seeing that the traveler was trembling.

"You can tell me everything. I'm a model confessor."

At that, the voyager placed his two hands on the table and lowered his head in the attitude of someone gathering his strength. And he told his story.

When he had heard him out, the Captain put down his glass and said:

"Eh, so?"

"Well, so, that's all," answered the passenger.

"What!" exclaimed Suger. "You took ship because of that? You were living peacefully in France."

"I wasn't at peace."

"But you could have been. Nobody suspected you."

The traveler shook his head.

"Then," the Captain continued, "there's surely something else. That hardly constitutes a crime!"

At these words, the traveler quickly raised his eyes and looked at the Captain. His forehead was beaded with a little sweat. Suddenly he struck the table with his fist and exclaimed:

"Everything I've just told you is false. I'm not a criminal."

"Then why the devil did you tell me all that?" demanded the Captain.

"Because you forced me to. You stared at me constantly; you asked me all sorts of questions; you were like a policeman looking for a murderer. I said just anything."

He struck his fist on the table again and cried out in a strangled voice:

"I was afraid. You scared me. I'm going to America on business. I'm not at all a murderer."

The Captain shrugged carelessly and smiled.

"Oh, yes, you are, but you have nothing to fear from me. I won't talk."

The passenger lowered his head and his pince-nez fell on the table. At that moment, the air was split with the piercing cry of a siren, then someone on the prow of the vessel shouted: "Land!" The Captain jumped up and glanced rapidly through a porthole.

"Land!" he said in his turn.

He added: "Thanks very much! I saw it ten minutes ago."

And he left looking important.

He descended the little stairway that led to the bridge and gave orders to some passing men. Birds giving savage cries swirled around the smokestacks. On the horizon, a darker line indicated America.

Then, the Captain returned to the dining room which gave a view from the six portholes. Putting his hands on either side of his face, he shouted joyously:

"Hey! There! Traveler! We've arrived."

But the traveler had already been dead for several minutes.

The Rival of Sherlock Holmes

Hector Fleischmann

Hector Fleishmann

Hector Fransiscus Joannes Fleishmann, (1882–1914) was a Belgian essayist, novelist and historian. Although Belgian, he passed his entire career in Paris. He published his first poems in 1898, including *Cantilenes sentimentales* and *Six Elegies* of a melancholy young man. He notably wrote about the personal lives of those involved in the French revolution of 1789. He contributed to various reviews in Lille, France that often were published in booklets: *The Belfry* (from September 1901), *The Illustrated Contemporary Review* (1902), *The Hemicycle* (1902). In November 1901, with the poet Léon Deubel, he founded the *Revue Verlainienne*, a magazine of art, aesthetics and Verlainian piety, which published three issues. He was editor of the newspaper, *L'Événement* in 1904–1905.

Preamble

There is no one today who does not know Mr. Sherlock Holmes and is not up to date about the least adventures of that extraordinary gentleman. His fame is, one may say, at the least, universal. In all the domains of life, social, political, familial, his activity, his clairvoyance, his rigorous logic is used productively and successfully. Enough is known about the extraordinary results he obtained in cases which seemed impenetrable. Do I need to mention some here: *The Adventure of the Copper Beeches*, *The Adventure of the Six Napoleons*, and a hundred others where his perspicacity so often came to the aide of the Scotland Yard police? Certainly not, because the reader knows those things as well as we. If I speak of them here, it's only to stress Mr. Sherlock Holmes's renown which still today surrounds his name and makes it famous along with the Corentin of Balzac, the Dupin of Edgar Poe, and the Javert of Victor Hugo.

Well, that illustrious, glorious, famous, known; that admired, dreaded, envied, hated; that terror of rogues, the Oedipus of crime, the providence of Scotland Yard, that man had a rival.

The moderation that must be observed in all things makes me write here rival instead of master,although this last title would certainly have been more fitting for him. *Honni soit qui mal y pense!* Far be it from me to think of diminishing the renown of M. Sherlock Holmes to the benefit of M. William Hopkins, because it is William Hopkins who is called the rival of the hero of *The Adventure of the Man with the Turned-up Lip.* That is certainly not my purpose, but should that celebrity prevent me from giving to M. William Hopkins the part of fame that, alas! may perhaps be awarded by posterity?

I think not.

That is the object of this story.

Let there be no mistake: The maxim: "Every man for himself," has not ceased being true in our days. However, M. William Hopkins worked his whole life against that saying, and took for himself the devise "Everyone for all." I will come back to that later.

Today, in this necessary introduction to stories of some mysterious adventures, it will be enough for me to say that I was for thirty years the friend, the confident, of Mr. William Hopkins, as Dr. Watson was the friend and confident of Mr. Sherlock Holmes in the little apartment of the Baker Street bachelor. I obviously speak about them only through hear-say, what I was told and confidences made about them to me, as did Dr. Watson himself. I never knew either of these two friends, since I never traveled in the British Isles, and my calm and placid life was always passed in America, in the shadow of Mr. William Hopkins' somewhat agitated and often eventful life. That is why that resemblance between Dr. Watson and me struck me; however, if I point it out here faithfully, exactly, I do not want to do so by vanity, nor to attach to it any superfluous importance. "Know yourself," the wise man affirms, and the wise man was right. A character naturally given to reflexion, has taught me to know myself, and, in the same way, makes me understand the hero of whom I am today making myself the benevolent historian without pride or vanity.

It is therefore just a simple work of reporting that I deliver this day to the public which still does not know the man to whom some great criminals owe their haven been handed over to the Supreme Court of Baltimore, of New York, of Washington, of Philadelphia.

I dare hope that, thanks to this work, that great unknown figure of the rival of Mr. Sherlock Holmes will come somewhat out of the shadows where modesty and misanthropy have surrounded him. May I be pardoned for putting myself sometimes on stage, but that was sometimes indispensable for an understanding and for clarity of the story. My vanity has nothing to do with it and I sacrifice it with pleasure and willingly to the memory of Mr. William Hopkins, of whom I may say, I think, that since the trouble was his, so should be the honor.

James D. Sanfield, junior
Ex-Engineer
of the Western-Road Aluminum Co. Limited
New York, January 6, 19...

Chapter I

Where I meet Mr. William Hopkins and about the mathematical and methodical mind of that gentleman.

Let's proceed in order. I love order. Every good American loves order. I will not, however, say anything at all about my antecedents, or where I was born, what was my upbringing, what my tastes are, why I chose the career I have followed for thirty-eight years. No, I won't talk about that because this is not at all my biography nor my story that I recount here, but really that of my estimable friend William Hopkins. What's more, if I stopped for that, I would lose precious time, despite my leisure. A good American never wastes his time. Time is money. That maxim, wisely applied during a lifetime of working, has given me an income legitimately acquired that I at present enjoy with a calm and peaceful conscience.

Therefore, we need order, precision, to speak logically: here is how I went about it:

About 1872, I sold Toby Tornwald my engineer office in Arkansas on 328th Avenue. A good business deal, wisely concluded, that insured my old age against the surprises of fate. I was still in good health, whole in body and mind, wanting to consecrate myself in the future peacefully to the study of some mechanical problems for which I had always felt a passion as an engineer.

The business concluded with Tornwald, I got busy with my new quarters. In the Black Road, I found a comfortable and full of light apartment on the ninth floor of a building that had twenty-eight stories. Studio, dining room and bedroom, that was all I wanted. I moved in there, and a week later I undertook the important work on electric turbines and the use of white coal as a source of hydroelectric power, finished since by the National Institute of Applied Mechanics in Saint-Louis.

I led a life methodically calm, dining, eating supper, taking a walk, working, and going to bed at unfailingly regular hours. I employed a clever and devoted house boy. I was living happily. My acquaintance with Mr. William Hopkins dates from that period. One evening as I was finishing one of my chapters devoted to photovoltaic forces, my house boy brought me a vising card. The name was unknown to me. Nevertheless, I said:

"Have the gentleman come in."

The gentleman came in.

He was a tall, robust, and upright fellow shaved with care, with square, firm jaws revealing a man of unusual energy. I like men who show their character in their face. He had broad shoulders, a chest covered by a well cut and comfortable black frock coat, not luxurious, and without excessive elegance. From a broad and flawless collar there emerged a solid neck that supported a handsome, strong and energetic head with hair at the temples beginning to turn grey. He had thin lips, something remarkable in that rugged face.

That was the appearance of the man who came forward confidently, his hat in his hand. If I describe him so minutely with care, that's because the hero of these adventures, William Hopkins, merits being sketched exactly for the eyes of the reader, since he will henceforth occupy all his attention. Therefore, let me be excused because, if Paris is well worth a Mass, as it's claimed, William Hopkins is worth ten lines of description.

Holding the visiting card in my hand, I asked: "You are obviously Mr. William Hopkins?"

"Himself, Sir."

"Very good. Will you please sit down. I am ready to listen to you."

What Mr. William Hopkins said to me is not of major importance for this story, consequently, I will not halt here. For a purpose for which he gave me a reason at least obscure, he asked me, because he knew I was an engineer and we were neighbors, various technical questions about work in mines, well drilling. I had no trouble answering them for him. That conversation revealed to me Mr. William Hopkins' remarkably mathematical mind. Several times he foresaw my words, my comments. I was particularly astonished at that.

"So you can read people's minds?" I asked him, half serious, half joking.

"I couldn't reasonably claim that," he answered. "However, it is certainly less difficult than you think, Sir."

"Really?"

"So, I won't answer you what you're thinking: 'What does this gentleman wish to do with this information he's asking me for?' That would be too easy, and the question, if it does not come from your lips, can be read in your eyes. So there is no difficulty to guess it. As for the rest, it's only a matter of thinking methodically, logically, mathematically, if I may say so."

"I would be very curious to see the result of such an observation based on logic and the figures."

"The numbers? Did I say that?" William Hopkins observed.

"Wasn't it mathematically that you claimed to mind read?"

"Yes, but numbers have nothing to do with that."

"I don't understand."

"Here it is: It no longer takes three lines of writing from someone. It can be more or less. The writing is useless."

"Can you give me an example of that?"

"Gladly. Imagine a crime committed on a New York avenue between three and five o'clock in the afternoon. Imagine that you are accused. You are arrested. What would you do?"

"I would invoke an alibi."

"Exactly. But often fate is against you. Suppose that it is impossible to establish that alibi and you are in a terrible situation, where nothing, if not fate again, can get you out of it."

"That is the exception."

"In life, exceptions have to be taken into account. Things happen, as Shakespeare says, and the crime of which you are innocent, for which no alibi verifiable and recognized as exact can prove you are not guilty, that crime can cost you your life, your honor. However, that impossible to verify alibi, a clever and intelligent judge can furnish it to you."

"How is that?"

"By regarding you carefully."

"Ah! Yes, I could have abrasions, wounds caused by the victim defending himself."

"Yes, but something better still than that absence of wounds can give you the impossible alibi."

"But what means?'

"If the judge asks you: 'Have you changed shoes?'"

"Are you joking?"

"No, Sir. Please pay attention to this: That supposed crime was committed on an avenue between three and four o'clock. An intelligent judge would have looked at your shoes. This is summer. They aren't dusty. Therefore, you aren't guilty."

That extraordinary language silenced me. How can that logic, of which the chain of thought escaped me, what can I say, didn't even occur to me, be answered? William Hopkins, after a slight smile which uncovered his thin lips, enjoyed my surprise and silence and his triumph, continued:

"You are not unaware of the fact that road maintenance orders require avenues to be watered down from two forty-five until three o'clock. That order, as you know, is scrupulously observed. So, if between three o'clock and five o'clock you had passed down the avenue of the crime, you would have had mud on your shoes, the mud taking, in that temperature about two hours to turn to dust again."

"I bounded out of my chair."

"Sir, are you a detective?"

"No," William Hopkins said softly. "I'm an observer…and I have an income."

He bowed to me slightly, saying to me again:

"Thank you, Sir, for the information."

And he left.

I let him leave and began to reflect calmly about the surprises of that conversation.

"Actually," I said to myself, "that was hardly difficult. It was just necessary to think about it, that's all. But why didn't I think about it, that's the question?"

That made me admire the methodical manner even more and I now understand, mathematics, the reasoning of my strange visitor. Based on deduction, constant observation allowed the realization of this extraordinary wonder, making it for the detective more powerful than weapons. Unfortunately, the police pay more attention to what is, without paying attention to what might be. They stop at the possible and neglect the impossible. Because of that, many crimes remain mysterious, unknown, unpunished.

"And this Hopkins is not a detective," I said to myself, "what a pity!"

I admired him, in fact, profoundly. However, that spirit of contradiction, which each of us possesses, that mentality that makes us never take the king in checkers, brought me to think that what William Hopkins had invented, since it was only a story, the solution was easy. It happens differently in life. If he were faced with a real mystery, a real crime, how would he solve it? How would he operate to arrive at the truth? Reasoning is beautiful, assuredly, but action is better. To set up a story by combining the adventures and solving it however he likes, what does that prove?

It was in this way, without knowing it as well as involuntarily, that I diminished my admiration for the merits of William Hopkins at our first encounter about technical information. Later, and the reader will notice it without any trouble, in the course of this narrative, my feelings in regard to my visitor must change considerably.

"Women often change; very foolish is the one who has faith in them," is sometimes said, but the adage can also apply to first impressions, and I give up saying how many times they have varied.

Chapter II

"Several mysterious affairs in the past of Mr. Williams Hopkins, and a rapid glance at that past."

Who, therefore, was this William Hopkins?

The information, just out of curiosity, that I attempted, the day after that visit to gather about him, plunged me still more into the indecision in which he had left me.

He lived in Black Road in the floor below the one into which I had moved. His apartment was located parallel to mine. He must be a widow or a bachelor.

A houseboy, just as for me, fulfilled the office of domestic and cook. It was known that he lived on a retirement income. His life was bizarre. He was many times absent for entire nights, only returning very late the next day. His houseboy was discreet, silent as the tomb, if I can be permitted that expression dear to novelists of Paris—and elsewhere.

Apropos of the search for information, I wrote the words, simple curiosity. That is not completely exact. To that curiosity was still mingled for me a vague and obscure, indefinable feeling that I didn't completely understand until a great deal later when friendship with William Hopkins had made me a discreet but devoted collaborator.

That search for information, however, was not without creating in me some disillusionment. I pressed forward, nevertheless, because in my family we don't back down. At that point, the days rolled forward and my curiosity in regard to my mysterious neighbor hardly diminished.

It's known that time usually makes two individuals who scarcely know each other grow apart. Between Hopkins and me it produced the opposite situation. We sometimes encountered each other in the elevator of the Black Road house. We took advantage of that to exchange some words, banal at the first, which before long had become somewhat more familiar, more personal. We informed each other mutually about our health. Hopkins joked about my good appearance. Little by little, our familiarity became greater. I became bold enough to invite William Hopkins to take a cup of tea and to smoke some Maryland tobacco. He accepted. He visited me; I visited him. After a year, we were perfect friends. Hopkins' apartment was simple and sober. The floors in his apartment didn't have rugs, but were highly varnished. Very few, but, excellent, paintings on the wall. The library was made up of some hundred volumes, from which novels were excluded. There were books of science, medicine, toxicology, things serious and severe which clearly indicated the Hopkins' intellectual tendencies turned toward the exact and positive sciences. In the studio, a table was placed in front of a window, to which Hopkins always turned his back. That allowed him to regard in natural light the face of visitors, following an already old but excellent habit, used by Investigating Magistrates.

In that apartment full of light, unadorned, simple. William Hopkins' house boy moved about silently. It was an environment for a man who was the rival of Sherlock Holmes. It was there that I received the confessions, the confidences of William Hopkins and that's what I'm going to report here with all the precision and meticulous exactness of my memories.

He was born in Topeka, in Kansas, where his father directed an agglomeration of eight buffalo farms. It was a hard job, always on the lookout, tracking the thieving Indian or cowboy pillaging from the herd, a coveted prey. That was not without some danger. There was proof of that the evening when Hopkins father was brought back to his farm both eyes burned from the powder of a pistol shot which had exploded in his face. That misfortune changed young Williams' life from freedom, from the uncivilized, from the unexpected where he roamed through the forests or galloped across the plain; it became that of a prisoner, sad, gloomy. He became the companion of his blind father in the low room of the farm where the man, a statue struck down, looked at the shadows through his great, fixed pupils, thereafter empty.

However, Hopkins the father could talk. His stories were extraordinary. Thanks to him, the child learned all the ruses of the Indian, the precautions of the cowboy. He learned to tell the difference between the step of the Indian and the step of the white man. His faculties, always on the alert, darted over those savage and fearful problems. His mind uncovered the hidden tactics of the enemy, of those Apaches from the great prairies of the Far West who could always smell an enemy and who had not waited for the arrival of the "White Faces" to learn that boldness, still more boldness, always boldness, is the first law of every outlaw.

Those years spent listening to those tragic, mysterious and terrible stories profoundly impressed the soul of the young man whom the child of the past had become. Solitude, reflexion, made logic familiar to him. Caution was combined in him with the logic of mathematics, and when he left the prairie where his father had tracked Leather Stockings, Falcon Eye, Eagle Vision, before smoking a peace pipe with them and burying the tomahawk of war in a great ceremony, the young William Hopkins was ready and capable of tracking, in the great cities of the Union, a game as dangerous, if not more so, than that of the Far West. That free, cautious, ardent and rigorous nature shut itself up in an office where it took on the yoke of accuracy. There it proposed, by reading profound problems in newspapers, to solve them with the help of logic. Still there, after long years, it waited for the day when, free, it could practice, just for his own pleasure the admirable qualities of cold audacity and rigorous logic which chance had given him.

That time came, and William Hopkins' first case was masterly. That was the case of "The Green Tie Band," the terror of Baltimore. Thanks to Hopkins, the leader, a certain Joe Fierling, was caught like a bird in the nest. At the moment of his electrocution, this scoundrel said to Hopkins:

"I would rather be in my place than in yours, because one day you will know what my friends reserve for you."

That promise was to be kept thirty years later. When the time comes, I will tell in what manner. After the success of that first case, William Hopkins voluntarily remained in the shadows, letting the Baltimore police take all the credit for the capture of Joe Fierling. My friend considered that result without bitterness. He wasn't the one who would have cried out faced with that so human ingratitude:

"Ungrateful country, you won't have my bones!"

He returned to New York and waited patiently for the opportunity to bring clarity into the tragedy of some mysteries. It is from that period that date those cases given enormous publicity where the name Hopkins wasn't even pronounced: "The Morton Haunted House," "The Man in the Wax Mask," "The Eight Cadavers in Colonso City," "The Prick Salmon Affair," "The Severed Head in Philadelphia," "The Man With the Steel Claw," "The Union Bank Robbery," "The Attack of the St. Louis Express," and yet so many others that, in their time, left a shiver of horror, of fright and of terror. My complete surprise can then be understood when Hopkins went down the list of the beginning of these tragic cases, in which his perspicacity had managed to find the thread of the muddled intrigues at the point where, for the most part, the police had left them when William Hopkins took it on himself to open them up again and study them simply for the completely personal pleasure of solving them and showing the police the chinks in its armor.

Wouldn't one perhaps think that, because of that, William Hopkins would be loved by the people in the justice system? It would be a gross error to think that. The opposite of that happened. The fortunate results arrived at by the rival of Sherlock Holmes, far from bringing him the respect of those to whom he had made himself an auxiliary by pure dilettantism, he was in their eyes a being who humiliated them profoundly. They held it against that "amateur" (as they willingly called him) for that good luck that was, in him, the fruit of mature reflection, of powerful observation sharpened by habit, the result of rigorous logic. However, despite those discourteous sentiments, if not the lack of gratitude, they never missed an opportunity to call on him for help. They never had reason to regret it, and William Hopkins always gave in to their wishes. He savored a mysterious case as a smoker savors a pure Havana, as a gourmet enjoys a rare dish (honor of a modern Vatel) as a musician enjoys a favorite piece.

The die is cast!

And he went forward.

It was there that the man was transfigured.

It was no longer William Hopkins.

It was no longer an American.

It was no longer an observer.

It was no longer a man.

It was logic.

Yes, really.

Chapter III

The Conspiracy Against the Five Kings of Gold, of Steel, of Railways, of Transatlantic Ships and the Cattle Industry.

At that time we were in Baltimore, where William Hopkins had fortunately just discovered the authors of the theft of the pearls of the Princess of Oldenburg, who was staying at the Cosmopolitan Hotel. That case is still present in everyone's memory, so I won't go back over it here.

We had decided to spend some days in the capital of Maryland and to take a boat excursion in Chesapeake Bay before returning to Black Road and our peaceful apartments. That evening, before sitting down to supper, where there would be particularly tasty quail, Hopkins had gone by the post to pick up his mail. At the entry of the illuminated great hall of the Hotel I saw him return with a worried look, a wrinkled brow and agitated, however, by a sentiment that, in his case, was that of joy and would have demonstrated worry in any other personality.

"Any news?" I asked.

"Yes, certainly, Sanfield, news and need."

"That's something that suits you marvelously, undoubtedly."

"Marvelously, Sanfield, marvelously."

Hopkins' tone of voice didn't cease to surprise me in that circumstance.

"What's wrong with you this evening, Hopkins; I'm really worried about you."

"You're worried, Sanfield, really? And me, am I on a bed of roses? Nevertheless, before talking about this, let's dine first."

We sat down at table. The meal was sad, despite the fact that Hopkins had an excellent appetite. I ate without pleasure the quail that I had promised myself to enjoy. Could I not show myself impatient to learn the new adventure that Sherlock Holmes' rival was going to call on me to share the emotions and the pleasures of danger? Without that, would I be an American? In the middle of the meal, William Hopkins asked to see the timetable of the New York Express Railway.

I saw him look for the time of the next train to New York. At the dessert, he cut up his peaches in an uninterested way, finished his glass of mineral water and, from the letters in his briefcase, he took a letter in a large format written on blue onion peel paper. He handed it to me without saying anything.

That letter contained this:

(Confidential)

STANDARD TRUST Limited New York, May 12, 18..
New York – Washington

Dear Mr. Hopkins,
Something truly strange has happened here that only you can stop before it has produced disastrous results. On this subject I have every power and credit to deal with you. Wherever you are, whatever you are doing, whatever sum you would lose to come to New York, come. We will pay, but there is haste and urgency.

Yours truly,

Sam Harrison, Pres.

The letter read and reread, I gave it back to Hopkins, who looked at me, his head somewhat inclined, through the thin blue spirals of his cigar smoke.

"Well, Sanfield," he asked me, "what do you think about that?"

"These are affluent people," I said, "threatened by some serious danger."

"Yes, that's what they say. But what danger, that's the question."

"A robbery, maybe. For thieves, money is money. Thank God, I don't have that worry. I carry everything with me."

"It's not a matter of you, Sanfield, but of Standard Trust. Did you notice the signature on the letter?"

"Yes, it's that of Sam Harrison."

"Exactly. And do you know who Sam Harrison is?"

"Naturally. Who doesn't know that? Sam Harrison is the King of the railroad systems."

"And a millionaire. He is other things also."

"And what's that, if you please?"

"The letter tells it."

"What does it say?"

"Under the signature of Sam Harrison there is the word pres. That means that he is President of Standard Trust."

"Understood. And so?"

"How can you say that they are afraid theft, the members of the Standard Trust?"

"Why wouldn't they be afraid of a robbery?"

165

"For this reason: that trust is composed of five Kings, that of gold, that of steel, that of the cattle industry, that of transatlantic ships, and finally of Sam Harrison whose kingdom extends over one hundred and ninety-two lines of Union railway. That Trust requires that its members be at least three times a millionaire. Now, when you're a millionaire, you're not afraid of a theft, even if it were of a million. Therefore, it's not a question of theft, since today, despite modern progress, despite automobiles and airplanes armed for the pole (1) thieves don't steal millions."

"Then what are they afraid of?"

"Something they value more than gold."

"Honor?"

"You can't steal a millionaire's honor. Those people fear only for their life."

Once again, the pitiless logic, the rigorous method of William Hopkins confounded and triumphed over me. What that letter from Standard Trust hid, he guessed, even if he forced it to confess, the secret hidden between the lines.

"I foresee that that affair is curious," Hopkins continued. "A millionaire isn't attacked like a plain citizen, and that's an even stronger reason when it's five millionaires."

"Five millionaires," I exclaimed, astonished at my friend's insight, "who told you that it was a matter of five millionaires? Only Sam Harrison signed the letter."

"Yes, Sanfield, but he wrote it in the name of the Trust. Didn't he say that he had complete power and credit to deal with me. A man who is writing in his own name doesn't need to have power and credit to enter into negotiations. Didn't you think about that?"

"No," I admitted.

"That's a mistake," Hopkins said. "You have to know how to read in a letter all that it says and all it doesn't say. That said, let's go pack our bags."

At ten thirty-two, the New York express carried us toward the new adventure. It wasn't without a secret regret that I left Baltimore, that I had scarcely had time to visit, William Hopkins' investigations of Princess Oldenburg's pearls had been so prompt and rapid. The hope of a mystery to solve in New York consoled me for my disappointment.

While arranging his pillows, having put on his night bonnet, and wrapped in his night shirt, Hopkins told me good night. Five minutes later he was deeply and calmly asleep across from me in the railway car. My mind was too preoccupied to distract myself by reading. I drew my traveling cover over my knees, and, having finished my cigar, I imitated William Hopkins. I went to sleep with the monotonous rocking of the train, its gallop traversing the nocturnal plains of Maryland.

Back in Black Road, Hopkins asked me to send a telegram to Sam Harrison announcing his return and visit for the evening at the seat of Standard Trust. The rest of the day was taken up with some urgent errands in Brooklyn and, when the evening came, Hopkins asked me to go with him. A cab carried us toward 8th avenue where the enormous building in white and blue stone, a veritable monument, the location of the offices of that formidable Trust that held in its hands the daily life of all America. On a word from him, in fact, couldn't the railways be stopped, the transatlantic ships remain anchored in Boston ports, in Halifax, in New York, in Philadelphia, in Dover, in Charleston, in Savanna, in Tampa, in Matamoros; the slaughter houses of ten cities couldn't they lack beef, a hundred factories remained deprived of steel, a thousand banks without gold?

Those were the thoughts that overwhelmed me when crossing the brilliantly lit halls, the sumptuous drawing rooms through which an usher in a purple uniform decorated with gold, serious as a judge, splendid as an actor in a middle ages drama. Hopkins admired the magnificence of the building, without, however, showing any great surprise.

An elevator, the silent, soft rise of which tended toward the prodigious, took us to the third floor. Arrived at a vast salon, which must probably take the place of a waiting room, the decorated usher silently disappeared. We looked for a moment at the pictures on the walls, then the usher came back, saying:

"The gentlemen have arrived."

William Hopkins consulted his watch:

"Eight o'clock. These gentlemen are on time."

"Being on time is the courtesy of kings," I whispered in my friend's ear.

He smiled slightly and, decided, followed the majestic usher toward the office of the kings of Standard Trust. A big door suddenly opened in front of us with a flood of electric lights. The usher moved aside. We entered. I was faced with the five most powerful men in the United States. Lightly, like an assistant who knows the value of his help, with a deferential but proper politeness, William Hopkins greeted the kings. At his entrance, Sam Harrison had stood up, his hand extended.

"Welcome, gentlemen."

His questioning look was directed toward me.

William Hopkins understood that look and he anticipated the question of the King of railway lines by introducing me:

"Engineer Sanfield, my collaborator."

"In that case, you are welcome also, Sir," Sam Harrison said.

And we sat down in front of the table. Still standing, Sam Harrison introduced the four personages to us. They acknowledged the introduction by a sharp inclination of their head.

"Mr. Gordon...

"The King of Gold, I believe?" Hopkins asked.

"Himself. Mr. Lemox, of steel; Mr. Stanley of cattle, and Mr. Mortimer."

"Of transatlantics?"

"That's right. And me, I am Sam Harrison, who, with the agreement of these gentlemen wrote you. Thank you, Mr. Hopkins, for having answered our appeal so promptly."

"I couldn't shirk doing so, gentlemen," my friend said. "Here I am; I am therefore at your service. What is it about?"

At that moment I was looking at the five kings of the Trust. Nothing in particular distinguished their faces, if not the expression of energy and of fatigue with which they were imprinted at the same time. These gentlemen truly seemed to have on them the formidable weight of gold of which they were masters and conquerors. The fights, the battles, the efforts of their life could be read in the wrinkles of their foreheads and on their shaved faces. Those feverish faces told of nights without sleep, days of relentless work, weak stomachs, fatigue, *apretes, (pas du tout sure de ce que le mot veut dire ici)* imperious wills. At William Hopkins question, their facial muscles trembled and Sam Harrison who was clearly their delegate and their spokesperson in the business, took charge of answering.

"What's it about? About a matter that is at the same time very mysterious and very serious, because it is threatening our lives and our businesses."

"Well," Hopkins said, "Allow me one statement: do not be offended by the questions I might ask you. You can be sure they are only in the interest of the cause that you are charging me with defending and clarifying. Will you lay out the thing, Mr. Harrison. I'm listening to you with attention."

"Then here it is," began the King of Railroads. "We are washing our family dirty linen and that's why we have preferred to call on your experience, your knowledge, rather than those of the police."

"Thank you," Hopkins said. "Go on, please. I appreciate your praise."

"You are not unaware, Mr. Hopkins, that the trust, The Standard Trust, of whom you have the Committee Director in front of you, is one of the most powerful in the United States. Our power is great, our projects are still more so. Among those is the Trust of Mines. We want to bring together, in our hands, the exploitation of the mines of Colorado, of Kentucky, of Carolina, of Montana, of Dakota, of California, and of New Mexico."

"A powerful and vast project," the rival of Sherlock Holmes observed sententiously and in a low voice.

"We think so," continued Sam Harrison. "But the project hasn't been without arousing the jealousy, the anger, the hatred of our enemies, as soon as it was known."

"What enemies?"

The King of the Railways raise his hands to the ceiling in a desperate gesture.

"We don't know them."

"Do you suspect anyone?"

The King's look consulted that of his four mute, silent, gloomy colleagues.

"No, Mr. Hopkins."

"Really? Frankness is necessary in these mysterious affairs."

"Well, yes, we have some suspicions."

"Who, then?"

"The Trust of some American and Mexican mines."

"Good. Please go on."

"All right, since the day our project was known, we have received daily, each one of us, threatening letters. Here they are!"

From a large briefcase placed on the table in front of him, Sam Harrison took out a bundle of sheets of paper that he gave to William Hopkins, who unfolded the first one, passed it to me, saying:

"Please read aloud, Sanfield. I don't know how to read in the evening."

That sentence was said in a simple and such a natural tone, that I myself thought I was mistaken. That was the first time since I had known Hopkins that such an admission had come out of his mouth. What was he pretending to say with his sentence that seemed mysterious to me: "In the evening I don't know how to read." What obscure design was hidden in it?

Not showing my extreme surprise, however, I took the letter and I read it aloud.

> It is known that the Standard Trust wants to get its hands on the mines of the Union. Let them beware! That's a dangerous game, of which it will be the victim! If within nine days it has not abandoned its project, one of the members of the Directing Committee will be killed. If it persists in its project, the execution of the other four members will follow, two in two days. The mines will only belong to their heirs. Let the Standard Trust choose between life and the mines. It is warned. We will keep our word.

"These letters are typewritten, are they not?" William Hopkins asked.

The five kings looked at him in surprise.

"How did you know that without having opened them?"

"Oh! It's very simple, Sir, today the typewriter is used for death threats. The day they are caught, they have the basis for a denial. But will you tell me the date of that letter?"

"Saturday."

"Therefore two days ago."

"Yes."

"The authors of that letter have therefore two days to wait before keeping their word. That's more than is necessary to find them and stop their projects. I will allow myself to keep the letters for the needs of my investigation."

"Is that really useful?" exclaimed Mortimer, the King of the Transatlantic Lines, coming out of his mutism that he had observed with his three colleagues.

"I dare to think so," Hopkins said calmly, shutting them in his briefcase.

"Then you think you can discover the guilty persons?" Sam Harrison asked.

"I hope to do so," answered my friend. "Criminals always make a mistake, a fortunate mistake, I will say, in their best prepared machinations. A mistake has been committed here also."

"What?" asked the King of the Railroads.

"I will know tomorrow," William Hopkins replied, with a smile that masked his thoughts, not without letting it be guessed that he, even at that moment, already knew the mistake committed by the ones who sent the letters.

"Do you have any more questions?" asked Sam Harrison.

"Yes, with your permission, I will ask you a detail about which I will ask you to respond frankly."

"We agree to that."

"That's useful. What does your fortune amount to, Mr. Harrison?"

At that unexpected question, the King of Railways showed surprise and annoyance. There was a moment of silence.

"You have made a commitment to answer," William Hopkins observed calmly.

"So be it," said Harrison. "I would be ungracious to go back on my word. I am worth four million."

"All right. And you, Mr. Mortimer?

"Two million."

"All right. And you, Mr. Gordon?"

"Seven million."

"All right. And you, Mr. Stanley?"

"I also."

"All right. And you, Mr. Lemox?"

"Three million."

"All right. One last question: Is the share of each of you stipulated equally in the Trust of the mines?"

"Yes," said Mr. Gordon.

"That leads me to pose another question.

"Were all of you in agreement to consider the business as excellent?"

"No," answered Mr. Lemox.

"Who among you had a different opinion?"

"Only me," said Mr. Mortimer.

"You considered the affair bad?"

"Yes, and I still feel it's deplorable."

"Did you invest any capital in it?"

"Yes, obviously, since I had to support the opinion of the majority. The Trust went into it; therefore I went into it."

"Thank you, Mr. Mortimer. Well, gentlemen, I believe that for this evening I won't abuse anymore of your precious time. From now on, accept the letters if any more of them arrive. Let things take their course; let them come in. Before the end of seven days, you will be able to unite the mines of your project to gold, to the cattle industry, to transatlantic ships, to steel, and to railways to the Standard Trust. I have the honor to bid you good evening, gentlemen."

And Hopkins walked toward the door. Just as he reached the threshold of the door, he turned around abruptly:

"If something new comes up, please let me know. I am not leaving New York."

And he left, me walking on his heels.

Chapter IV

"Some thoughts of William Hopkins on the preceding"

When we had reached the avenue, Hopkins asked me:

"Do you feel tired, Sanfield?"

"No."

"Would you walk as far as Black Road?"

"Gladly, especially if that would please you."

"Then, let's go."

We went some steps back up the avenue to take the Western Road. Stopping in the pale light of a tall electric street light, Hopkins abruptly asked me:

"What do you think about all that, Sanfield?"

"I really don't know what to think," I said. "The case seems to me at the same time both simple and complicated."

"Marvelous, Sanfield, you have guessed correctly. The case is simple and complicated. But why is it simple and why is it complicated?"

"I wouldn't be able to say. It's an impression, an intuition, rather. This feeling isn't based on anything formal. I'm judging by how the affair looks."

"Well" Hopkins answered. "I'm going to tell you why it's like that. It's simple because the letters sent to Lemox, Gordon, Stanley, Mortimer and Harrison don't come from the same source as common anonymous letters containing threats of death under certain conditions. It is mysterious because one can guess obscurely, and badly at that, the goal pursued."

"But the goal, it seems to me, on the contrary, is absolutely clear," I said. "They want to prevent Standard Trust from getting the mines it covets. That's the goal."

"To prevent that sale to the benefit of whom?"

"But it seems to me, Hopkins, that they told you."

"To the benefit of the Trust of the American and Mexican mines?"

"That's exactly right."

Hopkins shook his head.

"No," he said. "It's not that. It isn't the Company of the American and Mexican mines that wants to prevent the purchase of the mines of the seven provinces by Standard Trust. It could get that some other way."

"And how is that?"

"By buying them!"

"In buying them? What does that mean?"

"Yes, if the Company of the American and Mexican mines wanted to prevent the sale of the mines coveted by Standard Trust, they would rush to acquire them before Standard Trust had begun its operations. It would be done and the mines would belong to the Company the day the Trust wanted to have them. They then would see that where there was nothing, the king loses his rights, that king whether that of gold or the cattle industry."

"But if the Company doesn't want those mines?"

"Then why would they want to prevent the purchase by the Trust?"

"If it wanted to delay the purchase?"

"A good business deal can't be slowed down."

"If it doesn't have the available capital?"

Hopkins didn't answer that question immediately. We had arrived in front of a bar.

"Let's drink a grog," he said. "That will warm us. The night is cool."

We were served the grogs. Hopkins asked for a business directory and after having leafed through it for a few minutes, he said:

"The Company doesn't lack the necessary capital to buy the mines."

"How do you know that?"

"Here is the business directory of Societies and Companies. That of American and Mexican mines is listed as founded two years ago with a capital of four million. Its stock has tripled in value at t the Stock Exchange during that period of time. Therefore, it is prospering. Therefore, it has the capital. Drink your grog, Sanfield, and let's go."

Hopkins logic had won out over my objections. We started walking again and our dialogue continued.

"That shows that someone other than the Company is interested in preventing the Trust from completing the affair. The path pointed out by Harrison is bad. We won't find anything there. I made a mistake this evening."

"What?"

"Did I ask how the Company could know the projects of the Trust?"

"As a matter of fact, you didn't ask that question."

"I'll see tomorrow if it's useful."

We had come to Weston Park. We walked though in silence the dark little alleys where the night wind bent the branches of the dark trees. Suddenly, after having stopped talking about the conspiracy against the Standard Trust, Hopkins asked me:

"As an engineer, you must often have done work in the other states, Stanfield?"

"Yes, certainly. I traveled a great deal."

"You know California?"

"Yes, I installed three electric factories there."

"And New Mexico?"

"I set up the Santa Fe electric lighting system."

"And Colorado?"

"In Denver, I installed some turbines."

"And Kentucky?"

"I don't know Kentucky."

"And the Carolinas?"

"I was in Columbia for eight months."

"And Montana?"

"At Helena, I supplied plans for the sophisticated exploration of the sources of petroleum."

"And the Dakotas?"

"I went across it in a month, in short day trips."

"Good. Very good. You're familiar then with the country?"

"Yes."

"Well?"

"Rather well."

"You know about the mines that are found there?"

"Some of them."

"What's your opinion? Is it a good business deal that the Trust is making there?"

"Certainly, it's even one of the best and the most brilliant."

"Ah! Ah! Then Mortimer was wrong."

Hopkins said that in a calm, neutral voice, but I understood perfectly that he attached a certain importance to that observation. He continued:

"The man of the anonymous letters doesn't do things by half measures. To murder five persons for the sale of a mine! The fellow isn't joking."

That remark made me laugh. Hopkins seemed particularly struck by my laugh.

"Have I said something stupid?" he asked with a brusque worry, bizarre at the least.

"Certainly not, but that fellow there amuses me with his threats. I have rarely encountered a gentleman more decided."

"When you know his name, you'll admire his business sense," Hopkins said. "But, I believe we're here, Sanfield."

In fact, we were in Black Road. The elevator took us up to our respective floors. As he left me, Hopkins again said to me:

"Today is Monday, Sanfield. Before the end of the week, we will have put our hands on the fellow."

"Do you think so?"

"Yes."

"Have you found something?"

"Yes."

"What is it, Hopkins?"

"The trail."

Chapter V

"The man with the red beard comes to give the first warning and Hopkins begins the investigation."

The day after that visit to the Standard Trust, taken with a sudden violent migraine, I stayed in bed rather late. About ten o'clock the electric doorbell sounded in the antechamber, and I recognized William Hopkins thumb pressure. He soon entered, holding a telegram.

"Good Morning, Sanfield. There is some news."

"Ah! Really?"

I sat up in my bed.

"Read," Hopkins said, holding out to me the crumpled paper. He let himself collapse into an armchair, lit a cigar, and silently, his legs stretched out on the rug, his head leaning on the back of the chair, his eyes raised to the ceiling, calmly waited for me to finish reading.

The very brief telegram was signed by Sam Harrison: *Come. Things are hastening forward. Urgent.*

"It seems that the fellow has a good nose," Hopkins said, taking back the telegram.

"What are you going to do?"

"Go to Standard Trust as they have asked me to and I came to get you. It's annoying, Sanfield, that you aren't ready."

"I have an atrocious migraine."

"Get up, even so; the open air will calm that."

That was an order. Besides, the business of that conspiracy began to interest me too passionately to resist the ardent wish to see the twists and turns unfold before me. So I got up and ten minutes later a cab took us toward 8th Avenue. That time only Mr. Lemos and Mr. Mortimer were with Sam Harrison. In front of them, on the table, was placed a tall, narrow box with the cover open.

"Ah! Here you are, Mr. Hopkins," said the King of the Railways, coming to meet my friend.

"You wanted to see me? What is there new, Sir?"

"That," said Mr. Mortimer, pointing to the box on the oblong table.

William Hopkins picked up the box.

"Be careful," said Mr. Lemos. "That seems dangerous."

Having looked at it from all sides, Hopkins took a black, cylindrical object with a fuse wrapped around it out of the box.

"That's a bomb," he said simply.

"That's what I said," Mr. Mortimer remarked.

"Which of you gentlemen received that object?"

"Me," said the King of the Transatlantic Liners.

"All right. Please tell me how it happened."

Without waiting to be invited, Hopkins sat down, seating himself comfortably, motioning to me to imitate him. I seated myself in my turn and Mr. Mortimer spoke:

"This morning, during my usual walk, a man came to my townhouse at Kensington Park with a carefully wrapped package. He had spoken to the butler and asked him to give the thing to me personally, immediately."

"All right. Did the butler know this man?"

"He assured me that he didn't."

"How did he describe what the man looked like?"

175

"The man was dressed in a large overcoat and had a red beard."

"All right. And his hair?"

"It was red also. That question seems useless."

"Not as useless as you might think, Sir. The man could have a red beard and black hair."

"That happens rarely," said Mr. Mortimer, in a tone not without mockery.

"Never," Hopkins answered, "except that man is wearing a false beard."

"Who told you that?" exclaimed M. Mortimer.

"I guessed it, because a red beard is not an ornament, and when nature gives you one, you gladly get rid of it. The man could have a red beard, but false, because nothing takes more character away from a face than a red beard. If the man were clever, he would have thought about a wig. That man, did he have red hair?"

"I don't know," the King of the Transatlantics said.

"The butler will tell us," continued William Hopkins.

"Is that all the man said to the butler?"

"He added: 'Please tell Mr. Mortimer that it's a matter of the mine business.' From that I concluded that the bomb was the warning anticipated in the anonymous letters received for two days."

"And you are certainly right, Sir."

"What do you plan to do, Mr. Hopkins?" asked Mr. Harrison.

"Begin the investigation. Mr. Mortimer, do you have your car?"

"Yes, I have a car."

"The one I noticed in front of the door to the house, red with black stripes?"

"You are observant, Mr. Hopkins," surprised, the King of the Transatlantic Lines exclaimed.

"That's my job," timidly confessed my friend. "Mr. Mortimer," he continued, "Would you please take us to Kensington Park? There may be information to collect there."

We took leave of Mr. Lemos and Mr. Harrison. In a few minutes, Mr. Mortimer's automobile deposited us in front of the royal steps of the Kensington Park townhouse. The description of that magnificent building can have no place in this story, so it is not proper to stop here very long. The element of curiosity for Hopkins was in interrogating the butler. Called by a footman, he came to the drawing where all three of us awaited him.

He was a tall man, very decorative, very convinced of his role in the domestic life of the townhouse. At Hopkins' first question, he coughed with a look where the most profound disdain could be read. Mr. Mortimer himself had to intervene to make him decided to speak.

"James, answer the gentleman as you would me."

"At what time did the man with the red hair come?" interrogated William Hopkins.

"At eight o'clock."

"How much time after the departure of your master?"

"About an hour."

"He had a red beard?"

"Exactly.

"And his hair?"

"His hair was grey."

"What do you mean grey?" Mr. Mortimer exclaimed.

"Yes, Sir, his hair was grey."

"But, you're crazy, James!"

"What did the man say to you?" Hopkins interrupted.

"He asked me to give the package to Mr. Mortimer in person."

"That's all?"

"Yes, that's all. When the package was delivered, he left."

"Didn't he, however, speak to you about mines?"

"No, not at all."

"Come now, James. Are you losing your mind?" shouted the King of the Transatlantics. "That man said to you: 'Please tell Mr. Mortimer that it's about the business of the mines,' didn't you repeat that to me?"

"Me, Sir?"

"Obviously you, James, who do you think it is? Where is your head?"

"The poor man is obviously upset," Hopkins said. "Don't hold it against him, Sir. What I know about the man is enough for me. You can send the butler away."

"Leave!" Mr. Mortimer said in an angry tone. The man turned around and went back through the door. When he had left, the master of the townhouse asked: "What do you think about that, Mr, Hopkins?"

"Nothing, Sir, while waiting for other events. I think we should let the man with the red beard continue to act. He is, up until now, in control of his movements, since a man is master in his own house. The most clever always let themselves get caught."

"Do you want my car to take you back to your house?"

"No, really, thank you. I still have some errands to run this morning, so I won't need it. I will have, I think, the pleasure of seeing you this evening at the Standard Trust?"

"Yes, certainly."

"In that case, I will perhaps have some news for you."

We left. We walked side by side, Hopkins plunged in the silence of his thoughts. Arrived at the wide avenue that goes through the new quarter of Salt Lake, I felt my friend's hand seize my shoulder. He was pale, his eyes extraordinarily brilliant.

Frightened, I cried out: "What's wrong with you, Hopkins?"

"I have it," he said to me in a low voice.

Chapter VI

"Reappearance of the man with red hair with a red wig, not to bring in, but to carry out."

Having dined on the Brooklyn side in a modest restaurant, Hopkins and I returned to Black Road about three o'clock. A strange spectacle in the apartment of the rival of Sherlock Holmes awaited us. During all the walk back, it had been impossible for me to get a word out of my friend. His mutism was complete, inexorable, absolute.

"Is there some danger, Hopkins?" I finally asked.

He looked at me with his deep and clear eyes, which searches your soul and told me laconically:

"Whoever loves me will follow me!"

"I'm afraid, Hopkins...."

"Let those who are afraid take cover behind me!"

"You know very well I'm not afraid, Hopkins."

"Then let's go on."

It was in this way that we reached Black Road about three o'clock.

"Do you have something to do at your place?" Hopkins asked me.

"No, nothing that I know of."

"Then come smoke a cigar at my place."

On the seventh floor, the elevator stopped. Hopkins pushed the electric button. Some minutes went by. Again he rang. There was heavy silence behind the closed door.

"It's strange that the houseboy has gone out at this hour," Hopkins observed in a low voice, while he took out of his pocket a strange, nickel-plated key. He put it in the lock, turned it and the door opened. We went in. The door to the studio at the end of the corridor served as an antichamber. When he pushed that door, Hopkins let out a cry and rushed in. The houseboy, bound and gagged was stretched out in the middle of the floor.

"I should have suspected this," Hopkins said. "He came during my absence."

"Who was it?" I exclaimed.

"The man with the red beard," said the rival of Sherlock Holmes.

He was leaning over the houseboy and, having examined the knots of the rope restraining the prisoner, cut the ropes without, however, touching those same knots. A dry sponge was stuffed into the mouth of the servant, allowing him to breathe while stifling his voice. When this gag was removed, the houseboy let out a cry where there was mingled, at the same time, terror of the attack and thanks for the salvation.

"Ah! Mister Hopkins!"

"Well, my boy, what's happened here?"

"The man...the man..." stammered the boy.

"A man with a red beard, isn't that right, my boy?"

Astonishment could be read in the houseboy's pupils.

"Mister Hopkins...you...you...know him?"

"Yes, my boy, but tell me what happened here."

While talking, Hopkin's eyes had been searching through the room. The papers on the work table had been rummaged through; the drawers of a low chest were turned out on the floor with their documents, their books, their notebooks, thrown about. Everything was in a disorder where the haste of the thief could be seen at a glance.

The houseboy recounted: "About noon, a man came, a man with a red beard, who said he knew Mister Hopkins. He said an appointment had been set and he had been asked to wait. I took him in here at his request. His fist abruptly hit my neck. I was stunned and fell. That's all I know."

"Marvelous," said Hopkins. "That's what I was thinking. Do you know what the man with the red beard came here to look for, Sanfield?"

"Can I guess, Hopkins?"

"This Sanfield!"

Saying that, my friend took from his pocket the bundle of threatening letters addressed to the members of the Directorate Committee of Standard Trust.

"The letters!"

"That's exactly it. He understood that the mistake was there, the unfortunate mistake that would get him caught. He wanted to correct his error. That's why he came. He didn't find anything. He left here all hope of usefully repairing the mistake; we've got him."

And a triumphant smile illuminated the face of the logician who surpassed at this moment by a hundred leagues the most beautiful imaginations of his fortunate and illustrious rival, Sherlock Holmes. Then abruptly speaking to the houseboy:

"Isn't it true, my boy, that the man had red hair?"

"Yes, Sir."

"That's it," Hopkins said. And he rubbed his hands together.

"Please notice, Sanfield, that the fellow is clever and that he's making progress. But once more that progress is my fault; I tell you so truly. But we're going to hit him with something that he won't recover from that he doesn't expect. Note something else, Sanfield, this morning at eight o'clock when coming to Mr. Mortimer's, the man with the red beard didn't have a wig; in coming back here, at noon, to my apartment, he was wearing a wig. Don't you find that particularly strange?"

Then turning abruptly toward the houseboy he asked:

"My boy, do you know how to use the typewriter?"

"Yes, Sir, I took a course at the school on Long Island."

"Good. It's a matter today of doing honor to the professors on Long Island. Come. I ask you for a minute, Sanfield. There are some cigars and whiskey. I'll be back."

With the houseboy, Hopkins disappeared into the neighboring room. I lit a cigar and poured myself a glass of whiskey, waiting for their return. I was on my last puff and my last swallow when I saw Hopkins enter with a person totally unknown to me. He was a man with temples turning white, somewhat stooped, a drooping lip, dressed in a worn but clean frock coat, white tie, his nose straddled by somewhat cloudy gold-rimmed glasses, behind which his look was sharp and lively.

I rose to greet the new arrival.

"You don't recognize this gentleman?" Hopkins asked me.

"I don't at all recall his face."

"This gentleman is the typist for the Mortimer offices."

"Ah! I greet you, Sir."

William Hopkins burst out laughing.

"Marvelous, Sanfield. I see I have succeeded."

"Succeeded?...How?"

"This is the houseboy!"

I collapsed in the armchair. That person with the gold-rimmed glasses was the houseboy!

"Doesn't the student do me honor?"

"That's extraordinary," I murmured. "Who wouldn't be deceived by that?"

"This is the last card I'm playing. I have everything needed to win the hand and I take my good things where I find them. If what I presume is correct, tomorrow we will have the man with the red beard. I'll be back in an hour, Sanfield. Dip into my cigar box and drink my whiskey. Good bye."

Followed by the so cleverly disguised houseboy, he left. I took a new cigar

180

(they had a truly remarkable savor) and enjoyed the Bourbon.

William Hopkins was on time. An hour later he opened the door to the Black Road apartment.

On entering he said: "It's done, Sanfield. Everything is going as desired. The houseboy is there in place."

And he told me how he had brought it about. He had gone to see Sam Harrison under the pretext that he had come to pickup new information necessary for his investigation. In the course of that conversation, he had asked to place one of his friends, an accomplished typist fallen on hard times, in one of the offices of the Trust, with Mr. Mortimer, for example. Sam Harrison hadn't opposed it. A telephone call from him to the Head of the Personnel Department of the Transatlantic Lines had immediately gained admittance for the typist. Hopkins had thanked him and left.

"There now remains nothing else for us to do but wait for the houseboy to return. I think the houseboy will have followed my instructions. Have a cigar, Sanfield."

Hopkins' conversation during these hours of wait was truly charming. He showed me his closet that was rich with a hundred of the most varied disguises. He was somewhat proud of it.

"There are my jewels," he said, jokingly, pointing to the most ill-assorted collection of second-hand clothes, where the leather coat of the coachman was next to the short jacket and scarf of the civil servant, the frock coat of the clergyman with the leather chaps of the cowboy, with the metal button tunic of the policeman with the heavy vest of the dock worker at the ports. On closing the doors to the armoires, Hopkins sighed with a comic tone that made me laugh.

"Nevertheless, I have something there to outfit an actor!"

About eight o'clock the houseboy returned.

"Success?" the master asked authoritatively.

"Yes," the servant answered concisely and he handed him a bundle of sheets of paper.

"Sanfield," Hopkins said, "it's late and I can't keep you. My night will be filled with work and I'll probably have to work right up until dawn. So, goodnight. I'll come wake you very early in the morning. I have the key to the mystery. It's ended, draw the curtain, the farce is over. I'll see you tomorrow."

We shook hands, and, with his houseboy, Hopkins shut himself up in his studio. He was preparing for the denouement of the comedy.

Chapter VII

"Making important visits in the early morning is agreed on."

"The cab is waiting for us at the door," Hopkins told me as he entered my bedroom the next day."

"In that case, I'll ask you for five minutes and I'll be with you, William," I said, jumping out of bed.

Hopkins had sat down.

"Beautiful day," he said.

I looked at the dull, gloomy, grey sky trailing its clouds of greyish ashes, opaque soot, above New York.

"Are you joking, Hopkins?" It's going to rain, if it's not already raining. What are you talking about…a beautiful day?"

"I mean a beautiful day for our business," answered the modest rival of the famous friend of Doctor Watson.

"Then you've been successful, Hopkins?"

My friend took out his watch and neglecting to answer my question, said: "Three more minutes, Sanfield."

I understood that he didn't want to say any more about it at that time, and long accustomed to Hopkins fantasies, I was careful not to insist. A quarter of an hour later, the cab stopped in front of the monumental steps of Mortimer's townhouse at Kensington Park.

The King of the Transatlantic Liners had left, as every day, to take a morning walk but wouldn't be long in returning. We waited in the vestibule and soon a rapid and staccato step drew us from the silence with which we had been surrounded. It was Mr. Mortimer arriving. In his hand he held a box that the mysterious man with the red beard had brought, similar to that we had seen the evening before on the table of the Conseil of Standard Trust.

"Mr. Hopkins, I am glad to see you," the millionaire shouted on seeing us. "Here is a new object that has just come to me."

"The joke continues," smiled my friend.

"Please come through to my office," said Mr. Mortimer, going ahead of us through his salons where the luxury was well made to astonish eyes even more accustomed to the magnificence of art and wealth. The work room of the King of the Transatlantic Liners, opened at the end of a long gallery ornamented with marbles and bronzes lit by glass windows letting light in from an admirable garden. He entered, threw his hat and overcoat on a chair and made a rapid motion inviting us to sit down.

"On my side," he said, "I looked all day yesterday trying to find a trace of the strange bomb carrier, but I wasted my day. Everything was in vain and again this morning a new bomb was brought."

During this rapid discourse pronounced in a confident voice, William Hopkins' attitude hadn't ceased to surprise me. Imperceptively, he had moved toward the chair holding the hat and coat of the millionaire. With a movement, that at first sight seemed to be clumsiness and involuntary, but that in reality was cleverly calculated, Hopkins had made the hat fall to the magnificent rug on the office floor. The headgear rolled several meters and stopped in one of the corners of the office. My friend hurriedly rushed to pick it up. Having held it in his hand several instants, he turned it over and looked carefully at the inside edge and with his finger detached something that at the distance where I was sitting, I couldn't identify. This done, he put the hat back where it had been and with the most natural tone in the world, he asked the millionaire:

"Don't you find that wigs are poorly made these days, Mr. Mortimer?"

The King of the Transatlantic Liners was startled and asked:

"What do you mean?"

"That I regret a great deal, Sir, not having been at home yesterday, at noon, when you visited!"

"You're crazy, Mr. Hopkins!"

"Not at all, Sir; I know what I'm saying."

At these words, the King of the Transatlantic Liners rummaged in his pocket with the familiar gesture of the man grasping the butt of his revolver. That movement didn't escape William Hopkins who said calmly:

"When you've killed me, I'll need only six feet of earth. But that won't settle the matter. Let's talk, Mr. Mortimer."

Seeing himself caught, the millionaire fell, dejected, into an armchair, and his stifled voice, like a rattle of agony, murmured:

"I am in your hands. Everything is lost…"

"As regards honor!" Hopkins finished. "Everything can still be worked out, Mr. Mortimer."

"I confess," said the King of the Transatlantic liners, "I am the man with the red beard."

Hopkins simply said: "I knew that."

Mr. Mortimer's response was a look of astonishment.

"Yes," continued Sherlock Holmes rival, "I guessed it the first evening. I want to spare you a confession, because that's something that's always painful. And, being a man, understanding human weaknesses, I don't want to strike a man of quality…and of a value like yours. Therefore, I'm going to tell you what happened. If I'm wrong, please tell me so."

Having crossed his legs, joined his hands, William Hopkins continued in these terms:

"You have been a trapper in Arkansas, Mr. Mortimer?"

At these words, the millionaire was jolted.

"Nobody knows that except me," he exclaimed. "Who told you that, Mr. Hopkins?"

"The knots on the rope tied around my houseboy. These knots could only have been made by a trapper and a trapper from Arkansas, since you are not unaware that each group has customs and these customs vary by states. So I continue. When I said, at the reunion of the members of the Standard Trust, that I couldn't read in the evening, I wanted to observe the expression of each member during the reading of the threating letters by my friend, the engineer. Sanfield. At that reading, only yours didn't shudder. That was either that you were stronger than your colleagues or forewarned and perfectly aware of the importance and value of those letters. In any case, it was a clue. That evening I learned that only you opposed the purchase of the mines and that you had depreciated their value. To what end? I don't know, but I count on your informing me when I have finished. That same evening I said that the author of those letters had made a mistake. I saw you had been struck by that remark. When I spoke of carrying the letters away, you were the only one who had exclaimed: 'Is that really useful?' Therefore you knew that the clumsy letters would be dangerous in my hands. You understood the danger the next day; that's why, knowing I was absent from my home, you attempted to get back the letters."

"That's true," the millionaire confessed. "Me, I did that."

"I knew that," Hopkins continued imperturbably. "For that, you again put on the red beard disguise adopted to take the bomb to your butler. That bomb had the sole purpose of terrorizing the members of the Standard Trust and showing them that the authors of the letters were capable of pushing their threats right up to execution. You counted on their giving in after that and giving up purchase of the mines. When I interrogated the butler, you fell into the trap I had set for you, oh! very innocently!

"At the time of the first use of the disguise you had forgotten the red wig, completely indispensable for the red beard. It was the grey hair—and yours is grey, Mr. Mortimer—that the butler remembered. Others might notice that. So you went to Black Road with a red wig. I don't need to learn from your own mouth confirmation of that same detail. There, a moment ago, I found, stuck to the leather interior of the hat, some red hairs. Therefore, you had the wig. Not having found the letters at my apartment, you wanted to speed things up, strike a blow of terror. I would have to wait to know if you would dare to go right to the end of what you promised in the letters; although in the depth of myself, I doubted their sincerity. It was then that I also precipitated things; I took away from you the resource of time, because time and I hold the game in our hands. That resulted in the bomb of this morning. I know the bomb was harmless. It coincided with the discovery of a very interesting thing, knowing that the typewritten letters had been done on one of the machines in your office. The houseboy that you almost suffocated yesterday found that out the same evening. How? That's my business. You see Mr. Mortimer nothing was simple."

"Nothing is left but to kill myself," the millionaire tragically sighed.

"What a great artist is going to die," Hopkins smiled maliciously. "No, dear Mr. Mortimer, you won't kill yourself. You are simply going to say why you wanted to prevent the sale of Kentucky, of Colorado, of Carolina, of Montana and of Dakota by the Standard Trust. After that we are going to find out together a method to reduce that affair to its simplest expression."

"Your words give me confidence, Mr. Hopkins," the millionaire said," and, since you have so cleverly discovered the thing, I don't hesitate to tell you frankly my goal. My two million are inferior to those of other members of the Standard Trust, possessors of greater fortunes. I look for a thousand ways to increase them; but we aren't lucky at our age. While this was going on, the business of the mines came up. I understood immediately how important they were and what a source of enormous profit could ensue on acquiring them. I used my ingenuity to discover the right way to prevent the purchase by the Standard Trust. I opposed with all my strength the realization of the business. My colleagues went ahead and decided to acquire the mines. Then I had recourse to the threatening letters, persuaded that fear would do what I hadn't accomplished, and allow me to take for myself what Standard Trust wanted for it. That's the exact truth."

"The plan was clever," Hopkins said, "and worth being applied in other circumstances. I suspected that without being certain. What you have told me dissipates my last doubts."

"And now," Mr. Mortimer asked, "what's to be done? What's to become of me?"

"Give me your word of honor to renounce your projects," my friend said.

"I give it to you."

"Solemnly?"

"Solemnly."

"Good. I will tell Mr. Sam Harrison that I will be available this evening to the Directorship of the Standard Trust to give an account of the result of my mission. I hope to see you there."

"You're going to tell that I...?" exclaimed the king of the Transatlantics, his throat tight, his hands trembling, pale and worried.

"Do you have confidence in me?"

"Yes, certainly, but…"

"In that case, please have confidence right to the end. I must be first to take leave of you, Mr. Mortimer."

Accompanied right to the door by the lost millionaire, we left the sumptuous office where the rival of Sherlock Holmes had just so cleverly unmasked the former Arkansas trapper who had become king of the transatlantic steamers—the evening before in danger of being brought before the Assize Court, since it is still true the Tarpeian Rock* is near the Capitol.

Chapter VIII

"A short chapter on a brief meeting of the Standard Trust"

"Sanfield," Hopkins said to me, "I am very hungry. The success of our case is well worth an excellent dinner. Let's go to Vaux Hall Garden. The French wine there is worth our interest. Hailing a hansom cab, we started toward that famous restaurant of real quality. On the way, I observed my friend's expression. It was shining. From the cigar in the corner of his mouth, he let out through the window a bluish smoke that the sharp breeze shook out in the distance through the grey streets of that gloomy rainy morning. The lunch was tasty and admirably presented. In the café, in front of a glass of gin, Hopkins recalled the events of the morning and the sequence of the events.

"Everything in that case fit together," he said. "From Sam Harrison's first words, I understood that I had to narrow the circle of my investigation. What I said to you on coming back that evening to Black Road, was the first milestone in my reasoning. What you told me about the mines coveted by the Standard Trust was the second milestone. The trail was laid out; I had only to follow it right to the end. You saw, Sanfield, if we accomplished that. Once we had arrived at the identification of the man in the red beard, I felt I was on the trail and I said to myself: I'm there, I stay there. I stayed there. Was I wrong?"

"Hopkins," I said, "your investigation borders on genius!"

"No, no, good friend, nothing was simpler. Whoever had reasoned it out would have arrived at the same result in more or less time. The essential thing for us, today, is that the business be finished."

---

* Tarpeian Rock is a steep cliff of the southern summit of the Capitoline Hill, overlooking the Roman Forum in Ancient Rome. It was used during the Roman Republic as an execution site

"But we still have your visit to the Trust this evening?"

"Oh! That's only a simple formality!"

"What are you going to do, Hopkins? And how do you hope to terminate all that without there resulting some damage to Mr. Mortimer??"

"Dear friend, it's two o'clock. I'm going to inform Sam Harrison of my visit at eight o'clock this evening. That leaves me six hours to find out what decision I will make. Let's go take a walk in Brooklyn."

At the beginning of Chelsea Road, Hopkins sent a telegram to the king of railways, and having spent a short moment in the apartment on Black Road, we ended the day with a walk along the quays where the European transatlantic ships docked. As eight o'clock struck, we were introduced into the room of the Council of the Standard Trust. Just as the day of our first visit, the five kings were there, seated in a circle around the huge table. My regard looked toward Mr. Mortimer. Only the pallor of his face betrayed his secret anxiety.

"Well, Mr. Hopkins?" inquired Sam Harrison at the entrance of the rival of Sherlock Holmes.

"Gentlemen," said Hopkins, standing in front of the table, his two hands placed on the table covering, "I won't keep you long. Your time is precious and I have none to lose. The author of the anonymous letters has been discovered. He has confessed. His name will tell you nothing more than that he will not recommence or continue. That man is dead, and it is only the dead who do not return. I am bringing you here the formal testimony of his repentance and his regrets. You can in all safety buy the mines of Colorado, of Carolina, of Dakota, of New Mexico, of California, of Kentucky, and of Montana. I like to believe that Mr. Mortimer will no longer oppose it. He will recognize as you do that the business is truly excellent, since it has excited covetousness that was not afraid to confirm it by threats of death in regard to your estimables and honorable persons. What's more, Mr. Mortimer will receive no more bombs. I bring you at the same time a formal commitment for that. That's all I have to say to you, gentlemen. I am at your service."

"Thank you, Sir," said Sam Harrison. "The Standard Trust expresses its gratitude to you."

Saying this, he took out of his pocket a bank book, filled out a check, tore it out and handed it to Hopkins. "The cashier is open from nine o'clock to three o'clock, Sir."

Hopkins took the check, thanked him and left.

Thus ended the mystery of the conspiracy against the king of gold, the king of steel, the king of the cattle industry, the king of the railways, and…it must be said, as unlikely as that might appear…against the king of the transatlantic steamers, poor and ashamed of his two million.

Chapter IX

"The Cadaver of the Trafalgar City Lime Pit"

One day, it was toward the end of July, we were taking a walk, Hopkins and I, in the beautiful Exotic Plants Garden which surrounds the Palace Museum beyond the road to Trenton Metropolitan City. The heat was overwhelming and despite all the frozen liqueurs and the most varied refreshing drinks, an intolerable thirst corroded the throat, drying out the mouth. Sweat ran across the forehead. We were sitting near the cascades from the waters crossing the Palace Museum garden in a foamy and bubbling stream.

What was happening? Was it the heat, the overwhelming atmosphere, the thirst, something else; I don't know: still, I fell asleep on the bench beside Hopkins fanning himself with his Panama straw hat. I was abruptly awakened. It was my friend shaking my arm.

"Sanfield, are you asleep?"

"I believe so easily," I said, rubbing my eyelids mechanically. "And you?" I asked Hopkins.

"Me, I've just bought the evening newspaper, that I read while you were asleep."

"Anything interesting?"

"No, nothing…Ah! oh, yes there is…a crime too complicated not to be too simple."

"Where's that?"

"At Trafalgar City!"

"In Tennessee?"

"The same. Look."

And Hopkins handed me the folded newspaper, underlining with his finger the article pointing out the crime in several lines of capital letters:

THE TRAFALGAR CITY CRIME

A MURDER FOR NOTHING

FRIGHTFUL DEATH OF THE VICTIM

THE MURDERER IS ARRESTED

THE LIME PIT MYSTERY

Following these five lines was an extended story of the crime. After the affair of the Standard Trust, no really interesting event had come to interrupt the monotony of our life at Black Road. That's why I hurried to read the newspaper article, persuaded that if Hopkins had pointed it out to me, it was because he saw in it interest of a hopefully mysterious and complicated affair and, as such, to the taste of his desires as a logician sure to vanquish the shadows and to come, by the force of simple reasoning and deduction, to the manifestation of the truth.

I therefore read this:

—Trafalgar City, 20 juillet—by telegram from the American Messenger special service

"—Yesterday, a crime as barbaric as inexplicable was committed in Trafalgar City in particularly odious circumstances. The gravedigger of that city, a man named Joe Bradford threw a man named Jim Jackson, a gravedigger aide, into an eighty-feet deep lime pit. Before throwing his victim in that well, Joe Bradford had smashed his head that was crushed under the violence of the blows. In the pocket of the victim was found the two dollars of weekly salary in addition to a large gold ring. Theft does not seem to have been the motive for the crime. Joe Bradford has been arrested by the Trafalgar City constable and immediately jailed. Following these events, he seems to have lost his mind. They have been unable to get from him any information susceptible of throwing light on that atrocious drama that has caused a strong feeling of horror in Trafalgar City."

Having read that, I returned the newspaper to Hopkins.

"What do you think about that, Sanfield," he asked me.

"I think that there is a really horrible crime. That Joe Bradford beating the head of his assistant into mush is really a veritable brute. In truth, that's a murder of the most odious kind."

"Did nothing in the crime itself seem particularly strange you?"

"No, nothing, if it was not the incomparable savagery of the murderer.

"So this crime without a motive seems admissible to you? You can conceive that it could have taken place just as the American Messenger related it?"

"Why not? That has been seen to happen."

"That's not a reason."

"What do you mean to say, Hopkins?"

"Why did this Bradford, after having crushed Jackson's head throw him in the lime pit?"

"To hide his crime."

"Then why didn't he go through the things on the cadaver? The newspaper said that they found two dollars and a big gold ring in his pockets."

189

"Perhaps he didn't have enough time."

"That's not probable, because the newspaper said that the constable had proceeded to the arrest. Therefore, it was after the crime that Bradford was arrested; so he certainly had time to empty the pockets of his victim."

"That could be."

"Anger doesn't take the precaution of dissimulating in this way, since throwing the cadaver into the lime pit demonstrated the dissimulation. But how that man who had gone mad had been able to accomplish that act of prudence, understandable in a murderer in command of his faculties, in comprehensible in an individual deprived of his reason. If, after the crime, that man had become suddenly demented, that's because a horrible thing, overwhelming, had struck him. What is that thing? There's the interest. There's the snag. There's the interest, there's for us the classic 'bread and circuses.' I presume, Sanfield, that affair is more interesting than we can suppose."

I saw immediately what Hopkins was coming to. Despite the heat I would have been able to shout, parodying the antique: "Pain, you are not an evil!" "Heat, you are not an impediment!" Silencing the cry of my heatwave dejection and taken up again myself the desire for new adventures from which our life for three months had been a widow, I simply asked the perspicacious and humble rival of Sherlock Holmes:

"Holmes, when do we leave?"

"I think there is a train about eight o'clock," my friend said. "That will give us time to dine comfortably and to buckle our valises in a leisurely fashion. I like to see, Sanfield, that you are beginning to get a taste for the job of observer. It pleases me to have at my side a man for whom the sentence: 'Sirs, shoot first,' would be in vain."

"And insulting," I added. "I'm American, Hopkins."

"I see that," he said, vigorously shaking both my hands.

And we went to dinner. A eight-ten the train left the station quay in the direction of Trenton, Harrisburg, Cincinnati and Nashville. The next day, we arrived at Trafalgar City. It's a humid, sandy region where clay abounds. That was the origin of those lime pits, in one of which, in a dept of eighty feet, the cadaver of the assistant gravedigger Jim Jackson had been found.

Having found a quiet hotel, Hopkins said to me: "Let's rest first. The journey tomorrow may be laborious."

We were up very early the next morning. My friend's first care was to pay a visit to the Constable. Thanks to his name and the reputation he enjoyed in the police administration, Hopkins obtained all the desired information. As he had justly presumed, Joe Bradford's arrest had taken place several hours after the crime. As for the crime itself, it had no witness. The only proof against the gravedigger was his presence at the edge of the lime pit.

To tell the truth, that proof was not the only one. They had found around the pit the imprint of his shoes mingled with that of the steps of Jim Jackson.

"And those imprints," Hopkins asked, "are they still there?"

The judge confirmed that detail.

"I suspect this affair of bringing us some surprises," my friend finished.

"I am of a contrary opinion," the judge countered sharply. "Bradford was arrested at the place of the crime; his participation, his guilt are without doubt. I am convinced of it. Everyone is convinced of it. I would be curious, gentlemen, to see you bring proof of the contrary."

Hopkins stood up. He said simply: "Goodbye."

And accompanied by me, he started toward the tragic lime pit. It was a truly sinister spot some miles distant from the city in the middle of a ravaged countryside with ruins of a former factory. The cemetery was a quarter-hour distant from the spot from the hollowed-out pit of the lime pit. It was not possible to think that Jim Jackson had been killed in the cemetery by his chief and transported as far as the pit where his cadaver had been found. Besides, that opinion would have to be formally contradicted by the imprint of the steps of the assistant gravedigger and of the murderer. These imprints, on his knees, in the clay around the lime pit, William Hopkins lifted with the meticulous and precise care that he always brought to the most minute details of his investigations and of his observations.

That examination finished, he got up and his eyes seemed to express his total satisfaction.

"Let's go back to have lunch at Trafalgar City," he said. "We will come back here before night fall."

Dinner finished; Hopkins returned to see the Constable. When he left his office, he held in his hand, wrapped in a newspaper, an oblong package. This package under his arm, he returned to the lime pit. I went with him. Arrived at the place of the crime, he opened the newspaper and took out a pair of shoes. I immediately noticed that they were not alike and certainly would have belonged to individuals of different ages.

"First of all, the shoe of the living man," Hopkins said.

The shoe in his hand, he went up to the spot where the traces of the steps were still visible. On one of those prints he placed the first shoe and considered it carefully. He shook his head and replaced the shoe on another imprint. I heard him murmur between his teeth:

"That's it."

He placed the successively in the imprints, and that operation led him within some steps of the lime pit. There, the traces of the living stopped.

"That was really what I thought," Hopkins said.

He took out the other shoe rolled up in the newspaper.

"And now the dead man's shoe."

From the place where the trace of the steps could be seen, to the edge of the tragic pit, the same slow and minute work was again begun by my friend. When that was finished, I saw come to his lips the smile of satisfaction.

At this juncture, the evening had slowly fallen, one of those heavy and silent summer evenings contributing to add to the tragic horror of the funereal countryside where our day had been spent. The oblique shadows of the ruined factories spread out in great broken bands over the ground where an unhealthy humidity rose from the ground. In the distance could be seen the somber mass of cypress trees and poplars of the cemetery. That vision made a strong impression on us, because we went back in silence to Trafalgar City where the evening newspapers gave no news of the crime other than what we knew of the Tom Camp lime pit. (That was the name of that funereal place.)

Early the next day Hopkins saw the Constable again. He had gone to see him to ask to see the gold ring found in the cadaver's pocket. That was done. At the same time, my friend solicited authorization to see the autopsy of the assistant gravedigger in the autopsy room of the hospital where he had been transported. That was a spectacle that is far from being erased from my memory. On a low rough and unfinished table, covered with a cloth of dirty white, reposed the body of the murdered man. The head was terribly damaged. It was only a shapeless, bloody heap of crushed bones, of swollen flesh, a thing without a name where to dark blood clots were mixed some shreds torn from the scalp. Coldly, impassive, Hopkins examined that funereal horror, those pitiful remains. I had stayed to one side, terrified, and everyone will understand that feeling in a man whose profession always kept him far from those painful human dramas. So, it wasn't without shivering that I saw Hopkins seize the hand of the cadaver and put on it the gold ring found in its pocket. I saw that ring was too large, the finger too thin and I understood that it must have belonged to a more corpulent and taller man. I didn't understand any more about the investigative procedures of my friend, but accustomed to considering only the solutions without stopping at the means employed, I didn't let any of my surprise appear.

It was with a sigh of satisfaction that I left the autopsy room, following Hopkins, where this sinister cadaver, touched by the hand of the dead, was the realization of the gloomy phrase which sums up our common destiny: "Brother, you must die!" Melancholy clutched my heart in a confused way at that horrible vision. That man had been happy, had perhaps loved, life had been beautiful during his youth, and he was there, the bloody remains from a tragic and mysterious drama of which we were searching for the how and the why at the same time. Vanquished and resigned, my soul recognized the end of that destiny striking that man. In that moment I recognized the Arab fatalism of : "God wills it! It was written!"

From the hospital, we went to the prison. The murderer, Joe Bradford, was in a narrow solitary confinement cell. The jailer, on the presentation of an order from the constable, took us there. Another face of human horror awaited us in that narrow enclosure where a dim light descended from a sort of basement window. In the shadows, crouched like a beast on the watch, the gravedigger was there, his chin on his knees. At our entrance, he jumped up. Without saying a word, Williams Hopkins showed him the ring. The man let out a bellow that resounded loudly in the sonorous echo of the prison, and, foam on his lips, he rushed forward, fists lifted toward Hopkins, who remained calm.

"Strike," he said, "but listen. Where does this ring come from?"

The guards restrained the man, whose rage was inexpressible. His inflamed eyes flashed in the depth of their deep orbits, blood turned his cheeks red, while a hoarse groan whistled through his teeth from the depth of his contracted throat. Little by little, that groan ceased and it was stuttering that made the unfortunate demented man's teeth claque:

"La…la…ring…ring…la…"

"Please hold his hand firmly," William Hopkins ordered the guards.

The prisoner's hand was grabbed tightly at the wrist. When it was immobile, Hopkins slid the gold ring over the rigid finger. This time the ring was again found to be too large for the fingers of the living man as it had been for the fingers of the dead man.

That examination finished, my friend asked the guards to release Bradford and we all left that dark cell profoundly impressed where the mad man was howling, the one described in the newspapers of Trafalgar City as "the monster of Tom Camp."

"That seems like a Divine punishment," I said to Hopkins, when we reached the countryside.

"Not anyone who wishes can be an atheist," he replied in a sententious tone that he willingly affected. And he added almost immediately:

"Let's hurry. Time is short. We need to have the solution this evening. Let's burn our ships. That man must go into an asylum for the insane. It's cruel to let an innocent man stay there."

"Innocent!" I exclaimed. "Then you believe he's innocent, Hopkins?"

"But, of course, dear friend."

"And why?"

"I hope to tell you that this evening. Let's walk faster."

"Where are we going?"

"To the cemetery."

"To the cemetery, Hopkins?"

"Yes, we must."

"Is it really necessary?"

"What's this, Sanfield? Are you afraid?"

"No, Hopkins. Let's keep walking."

"As you wish. I'll keep up with you."

And we walked faster.

I have said it before: The Trafalgar City cemetery was located a few miles from the Tom Camp lime pit, about a quarter of an hour's walk. We soon reached it and Joe Bradford's replacement came to open the iron gate to the funeral field for us.

"Do they bury many people here?" Hopkins asked the man, who looked at us, somewhat surprised.

"Oh! No, sir, This is the old cemetery. They no longer bury anyone here since the new cemetery was finished. That's why only two men are needed here."

"Two men, ah! Really?"

"Yes, several days ago there was Joe Bradford and Jim Jackson, but since the murder, I'm alone here."

While chatting, Hopkins had wandered into the central alley of the cemetery, looking at the ancient tombs ruined by wind, snow, rain. In the high grass there was only some broken crosses, some cracked stones, the field of desolation in this field of the dead. Hopkins stopped abruptly. On the left side of the pathway there was a gapping trench, a black pit in the bottom of which lay scattered bones mixed with the oily earth and the debris from the coffin. The earth seemed to have been freshly removed. A pick still lay at the bottom of the pit,

"What is that?" Hopkins asked, pointing with his finger.

"That," said Joe Bradford's replacement, "is a pit whose concession had expired. They are removing the bones to take them to the bottom of the cemetery. That's what Joe Bradford and Jim Jackson were working on the day the misfortune happened."

A light shone in Hopkins eyes.

"Are you certain of that?"

Oh! Very certain, sir!"

"Who was buried in this site?"

"The clergyman, Price Weston."

"Did you know the dead man?"

"Yes. He died ten years ago. He's the one who married me to Eddy Jackson from Raleigh."

"Good. What sort of man was he?"

"A tall man, very solidly built."

"Big?"

"Really very big."

"Very corpulent?"

"Yes. That's how I knew him."

"Was he married?"

"Yes, a widow."

"Any children?"

"No, his wife died, I believe, after several months of marriage in the wreck of the *Gil-Baltar*, near Trinidad."

"Is there still anyone alive in Trafalgar City who knew him?"

"Oh! Yes, the man named Boss, who was his servant, still lives in the city, and the housekeeper Lia is at the Old Age Home. They knew the Reverend Price Weston very well.

"Marvelous. That's enough. Come, Sanfield."

Hopkins walked away rapidly. We went down the wide alley of that melancholy cemetery, where the dry gravel cracked under our feet. In the distance the burning red sun was going down very slowly behind the walls of the silent enclosure. We soon reached the iron gate that creaked mournfully in its oiled hinges. Without saying a word, Hopkins continued his way toward Trafalgar City. I turned around one last time to contemplate the tragic sight of that cemetery in the middle of that desolate plain, and in the distance, standing beside the open pit, I saw the new gravedigger leaning on his shovel.

Chapter X

"Where William Hopkins reconstitutes the drama below and proves that the real criminal isn't the one thought to be."

"Hopkins," I said to him while I followed him almost out of breathe, "will I soon know the key to that troubling enigma?"

"No man is great for his *valet de chamber*," he answered, "as there are no secrets from a true friend. You're going to see the key to the mystery, Sanfield. What the devil! Be a little patient. We're here now."

We went across several streets in silence, then, abruptly, after having gone across an impasse, through a dark corridor, we reached the Palais de Justice*

---

*   Law courts of France

administration in which the doors of the constable opened.

"What remains for me to do," Hopkins said, "is hardly worth your time, Sanfield. If you would like to, go smoke a cigar and come back here in an hour. There will then certainly be something new."

He disappeared behind a low door.

I went downstairs to take a walk under the elms on a beautiful avenue bordering the Palais, while smoking a dry Havana, mastering my impatience. I watched the minutes, the quarter hours. The half hour sounded. I slowly began my walk again. At the hour itself I found myself in front of the constable's office. A bailiff ushered me in. The judge wasn't alone with Hopkins. An old man and a very old woman were standing in the office. As I entered, they were leaning over an object which their position hid from my view. I heard the voice of the constable ask:

"Then you recognize it, formally?"

"Yes," the old man said.

"I swear to it," said the woman.

"You are sure that you are not mistaken in anyway? Not deceived by a resemblance?"

"No. No," the man protested vehemently.

"I am absolutely certain," the old woman added.

"In that case, you may leave."

The man and the woman bowed and left. Then I saw the object on the judge's desk. It was the ring found in the pocket of the dead man.

"You see, Constable," Hopkins said, "the man named Boss and that woman Lisa, former servants of the Reverend Price Weston have formally recognized the ring as having belonged to their former employer."

"What does that prove?" exclaimed the judge with apparent bad humor. "That doesn't diminish in any way the charges against the murderer of Jim Jackson. Does that explains his presence at the edge of the Tom Camp lime pit beside the cadaver? No, isn't that right? So what is the use of the recognition of Price Weston's ring by his former servants, and what does its presence in the pockets of gravedigger mean to me?"

"Its presence proves Joe Bradford innocent of the crime of which he is accused!" Hopkins said forcefully.

The Constable smiled mockingly.

"Are you joking, Sir! What is the relationship between the ring and the crime?"

"It is this: that Joe Bradford is innocent of the death of Jim Jackson."

"Again!" The judge said, stamping his feet.

However, surprised by my friend's insistence, he added almost immediately:

196

"Please explain yourself. I am ready to consider your reasons, if, however, they seem acceptable to me…and compatible with the respect that you owe, as well as I must, to justice. I'm listening to you, sir."

"Point by point, instant by instant, I'm going to tell you, Constable, what happened between those two men, and what I'm going to tell you is based on more than certainties, on proofs."

"I would be truly curious to know them," said the magistrate phlegmatically, seated behind the desk like a president of the Criminal Court behind his tribunal.

"Last Tuesday…."

"The day of the crime?"

"Exactly. Last Tuesday, the two men, the dead man and the prisoner, were digging in a grave of the old Trafalgar City Cemetery. The Reverend Price Weston, married and widowed after a few months of marriage, had reposed in that grave for ten years."

"How do you know that?" interrupted the judge.

"I know it," Hopkins said, "because I speak only with certainty. The ten-year rental agreement had expired. Price Weston's bones had to be transported to the back of the cemetery. In proceeding with that chore, they unearthed the gold ring, the marriage ring with which Price Weston had been buried. It was a large and heavy ring, since the Reverend was tall and very corpulent. That ring is there in your sight, Constable. The assistant gravedigger, Jim Jackson, picked up that ring, wanting to appropriate that valuable find. At that, Joe Bradford intervened, claiming either to restore the ring to the earth to avoid sacrilege or to take it for himself. In any case, it doesn't matter. An argument broke out between the two men. Feeling himself the weakest or overcome by fear, Jim Jackson ran away, followed at some distance by the gravedigger."

"What facts do you have, Mr. Hopkins, to support that?" questioned the Constable.

"The traces of their steps. The dead man had smaller feet than the prisoner. Those came ahead of the others."

"And the fight took place near the lime pit?"

"Not at all. The younger man was more lively, faster. The desire to escape from Joe Bradford gripped him. He ran with his head lowered. He came near the lime pit…."

"And there?"

"He didn't suspect the danger. He believed he was jumping across a not very deep pit. At no time did Joe Bradford come near his assistant. The steps are there to tell that. Seeing Jim Jackson swallowed up, he must have let out a cry of terror and there, his mind violently struck by that catastrophe, by that death of which he felt guilty, his reason abandoned him. Horrified, demented, he remained near the pit, and it was there that he let himself be arrested. That's the truth. That's also why the ring stolen from the dead was found there in the cadaver's pocket with the two dollars' pay for the week."

At these words, the judge's expression expressed surprise, disbelief, and finally admiration, each in turn. When Hopkins had finished speaking, he abruptly stood up and held out both his hands across his desk to my friend.

"Your logic is admirable, Sir," he said. "I truly give you all my admiration. Please forgive my somewhat disobliging first words. I recognize that I was wrong."

"I have seen everything, understood everything, forgotten everything," said Hopkins with a smile, shaking the hands of the Constable.

Returning to our hotel, my friend took me by the arm and said:

"Sanfield, do you know the French saying?"

"Which, Hopkins?"

"Bow your head, proud Sicambre. Burn what you adored; adore what you have burned."

"Actually, I know it."

"Don't you find that this Constable has a head that would make a proud Sicambre?"

"Hopkins," I said, "you have as much humor as genius."

"No, no, sympathetic friend," was his response. "You exaggerate. I am less than a man of genius."

"You are the best of friends!"

"There's the praise that pleases me the most."

The unfortunate Joe Bradford died several years ago in an asylum for the insane in the outskirts of Atlanta, where he had been placed after the closing of the investigation so ingeniously led by William Hopkins, the worthy rival of Sherlock Holmes.

Chapter XI

"The ten mysterious numbers on the Black Road Door"

A few days after our return to New York, the case of the Trafalgar lime pit cadaver cleared up, another mysterious adventure happened to William Hopkins. One evening, when coming back from the theater, just as he opened his door, my friend noticed the number 10 in crayon on the varnished wooden door. He stopped, surprised.

"Look here, Sanfield," he said to me.

I looked carefully, but the number had no meaning to me. After having reflected, Hopkins himself gave up trying to explain it. He wiped off the number, wished me good evening and went to bed. The next day, Hopkins found his door with another number, the number 9. It was the same size as that of the number 10 of the day before. That time my friend seemed worried. The houseboy wiped off the mark of the crayon, and the next day, which was a Monday, again found on the panel a big number 8.

"Ah! Ah!" said Hopkins, "the jokers are prolonging the joke, I believe."

This time the number was not wiped off. We waited for Tuesday. On the door was the number 7.

Hopkins became silent. He was obviously trying to penetrate the enigma of those mysterious numbers of which the sum went down every day. Wednesday, the door was barred by a new number, the number 6. The mystery grew. Hopkins mounted guard behind the door. Thursday, having abruptly opened the door, he saw, without having heard them being traced, the following numbers thus laid out.

$$5\,X\,.\,.\,X\,1$$

Friday brought a new set of numbers.

$$4\,X...X\,8$$

My friends disposition became gloomy. His beautiful friendly humor had vanished. A deep wrinkle cut across his forehead. Only his eyes, his beautiful, fine perspicacious eyes, under the bushy eyebrows kept their luster. Saturday found this on the door.

$$3\,X\,...X\,9$$

That day Hopkins set up watch in the elevator of the house on Black Road. But the authors of the ciphers must be subtle fellows, because Hopkins' watch did not stop them from writing a new set on the door Sunday.

$$2\,X...X\,3$$

That time Hopkins shut him self in, staying awake the entire night on I don't know what work. The next day I went down to pay him a visit and in arriving in front of the door I found this number on the panel:

$$1$$

And to the handle of the door was attached a green tie. At my doorbell ring, Hopkins himself came to open the door. I pointed out the number and the tie. I saw him become frightfully pale. He leaned against the wall and in a voice that he tried, however, to make steady, he murmured:

"Come in, dear friend."

After me he bolted the door, after having detached the green tie.

"Do you understand something about all that, Hopkins?" I asked him.

"I have just at this instant understood," he said. "I now know why they are after me."

"What do they want from you?"

"They simply want my death."

"Your death!"

"Oh! Those strong fellows are equal to it! But I am also up to answering them. The game will be a rough one."

"But, then, who are they, Hopkins?"

"You don't know, that's true, Sanfield. Have you ever heard of the Green Tie Gang?"

"That one whose Chief was electrocuted in Baltimore?"

"Yes, in 1893. He was a man named Fierling, a great fighter, on my word, and a total villain. When caught, he found out what happens to the vanquished, because the Supreme Court that feared him if he was free, was without pity for him as a prisoner. That man had risen to the supreme rank of Commission Agent. At nineteen years of age, he had become head of the most feared gang in Baltimore. I spent seven years spying on him, following him. Each time, with a devilish audacity, by superhuman luck, that bandit escaped me. But I had sworn to myself to catch him, short of losing my skin at it and as careful of it as that which carried Caesar and his fortune. My fortune! I would have given it joyfully, with pleasure, with good will, to capture that fellow! That capture was my pride; to catch him, that was all I wanted; to catch him was all I desired; just that, and then *après moi le déluge!* Finally, after seven years, the day so long desired came. Fierling stupidly let himself be caught in a very clumsy trap. That criminal of genius lacked talent that day. He foolishly fell into the trap. I was there with my hand opened. That hand closed. Fierling was taken. It has often been said that each soldier has his Marchal's baton in his cartridge pouch: that's true. Fierling's capture was my Marchal's baton. My wishes had been fully granted; my word had been kept. The process was long. Fierling, from the bench of the accused, threw out to the breathless crowd, the sentence summing up the whole program of his criminal and troubled life: 'Let those who wish to live and die with me do the same.' It was not until later that I understood the whole import of those words. In the audience, a young, favorite student of Fierling, in hopes of escaping punishment, had come to testify against him. Fierling heard him in silence, and the policemen guarding him were the only ones to heard him murmur those truly pathetic words in that mouth of the young murderer: 'And you too, my son!'

"After that, picture the criminal. October 3, 1893, Fierling, seated in the electric chair that was going to make a cadaver of him, at the moment of feeling the death mask put on his head, said to me these words that have remained deeply engraved on my memory:

'I would rather be in my place than in yours, because one day you will learn what my friends reserve for you.'

"Well, Sanfield, it's the friends of Fierling that I'm dealing with today."

"Are you really certain of that?" I asked, suddenly feeling a dark presentiment go through me.

"Absolutely. I even know the names of those who are trying to trap me."

"Really?"

"Yes, and here's how. The Green Ties Gang, under Fierling's royalty, counted thirty-two members. Eight have been electrocuted; twenty-two died in prison or at hard labor. Therefore, there are two left. They must have been freed recently. They are: Clarkson, the first one; the second one named Morgan. Last night I thought about the numbers written sequentially on my door, 10, 9, 8, 7, 6, 5, 4, 3, 2, and finally 1, meaning simply 'you have ten more days to live; then 9, then 8, then 7, then 6, then 5, and so on. Until number 6, I could ignore who this sinister warning came from. At number 5 I was put on the path. Each of the following numbers was accompanied by another number which, if subtracted

X..X

gave the following result:

$$5 = 1$$
$$4 = 8$$
$$3 = 9$$
$$2 = 3$$

These four numbers represent a date 1893…"

"The date of Fierling's execution!" I exclaimed, terrified.

"The same," Hopkins calmly said.

Now today is the twentieth of October. The number 1 on my door today tells me I have only one day to live and that I will be killed the 3rd, the anniversary at which, thanks to me, Fierling expiated his crimes in the Baltimore electric chair. Now do you understand, Sanfield?"

"Yes, and the Green Ties…"

"The green tie was there to remind me of Fierling's last words. It means in prison language: 'Let the King's justice be done.' That King is dead and it's his last wish that those who escaped punishment or who were only sentenced to hard labor were waiting for the time of revenge ordered by the chief on the Baltimore death chair. That's the mystery of those numbers on my door for the last ten days. That's what is called, Sanfield, not to dance, but to speak on top of a volcano, because, don't forget, today is the evening before my death!"

"But you're going to defend yourself," I said, "alert the police, ask for help…?"

"What can the police do when I feel myself already hesitating, half disarmed! But be reassured, Sanfield! My life is dear to me! These fellows there were wrong to warn me and I'm not ignorant of the fact that a man who is warned is worth two. Do you see these two toys? With those I'm waiting for my Morgan and my Clarkson on a firm footing and I hope to make holes in their green ties!"

From the inside pocket of his jacket, Hopkins had, while speaking, taken out two pistols of burnished steel, and he handled them with evident satisfaction and a secret pleasure.

"If the Green Ties come, these little birds will sing a little song!" he said calmly, putting them back in his pocket.

"Hopkins, let me come here tomorrow to keep you company. Two men are often worth more than a man alone."

"The solitary man is truly strong," observed my friend. "It was Ibsen who said that. It must be believed. No, Sanfield, I don't at all wish to expose you to the danger of the visit of these fellows. I hope to see you tomorrow evening in perfect health. Until then, promise me to stay in your apartment. The sound of my pistols will tell you what should be done and if intervention is useful. Now take a cigar, Sanfield; pour yourself a glass of pale ale and let's talk about something else."

Chapter XII

"William Hopkins' little birds did not sing their song and the man electrocuted in Baltimore kept his promise."

It is with a broken heart, reproaching myself for my small amount of friendship, that I write this last page in the memory of my friend, William Hopkins, the rival of Sherlock Holmes. The dark presentiment that, the 20th of October, had agitated me was confirmed the next day.

"What happened? What took place?"

"No one knew. No one will ever know. But here are the facts: All day, faithful to the detestable promise made to William Hopkins, I remained in my room, my ear listening for sounds, waiting for the least sounds that could come from my friend's apartment. The morning went by. I heard nothing abnormal. The afternoon passed by. There was still silence. The pistols hadn't spoken. Then, almost reassured, I went down to the floor below to find William Hopkins, whose fearlessness and cold audacity had wanted to confront the last two remaining members of the Green Tie Gang. I rang the bell; I knocked.

What silence! What eerie silence! I knocked again. Again! Again! Then terrified, understanding that the tragedy had taken place in the horrifying silence of the mystery, in a desperate effort, I pushed against the door with my shoulder. The panel cracked. I rolled into the antichamber; I rushed toward the studio, opened the door.

Terror!

William Hopkins was stretched out on the floor, his tie snatched off, his arms in a cross. I fell on my knees beside him and leaned over his face.

"Hopkins! Hopkins!" I cried out; "are you wounded?"

A gasp answered me.

"No, I'm dead."

That was all…yes, all.

My friend's head fell back heavily.

"A doctor! …A doctor!…For the love of God!" I shouted into the elevator.

I went back to the bedroom. Everything was in order. The two bull dogs were on the table, intact.

Alas!…poor William! The little birds had not sung their song…; their great black wings of death had touched that pale forehead.

The doctor came.

The constable came.

For what good?

In the mystery of an unexplained death, without a cry, had gently passed the man of genius who refused the luxury of fame like that of Sherlock Holmes, always equaling him, sometimes surpassing him.

He is the one I weep for, because I was his friend.

END OF THE RIVAL OF SHERLOCK HOLMES